LOVE-IN-A-MIST

GREENWING & DART BOOK 5

VICTORIA GODDARD

UNDERHILL BOOKS

CHAPTER ONE

It is perhaps emblematic of my life that breakfast, the morning after I died and returned to life, was not the most awkward meal I had ever attended; though it was, I admit, within the top five. Possibly even the top three.

There was that supper, the evening my father had returned from the (twice-reported) dead, three years afterwards, to find his wife remarried and his reputation besmirched.

There was that breakfast, the morning after I had successfully argued that my ex-paramour Lark had written a final paper unbecoming of a Morrowlea student (and because of which she should therefore fail her final exams), and Lark had egged all the students (save for Hal alone, who had stood by me) to throw literal stones at me until I fled to the hospital wing in an access of bruised bones and broken heart.

There was that dinner party interrupted by the cult—that meal after I found I had spent years under a curse—that lunch after my father came back *again*—

And then, yes, there was this breakfast. Top five, then.

I was glad withal that my father was safely on the other side of the Linder mountains and did not have to participate.

The conversations to come, when we got home and I had to explain what happened on Mr. Dart's and my excursion to Orio City, would be difficult enough without him actually being present through the aftermath.

It was not an early breakfast, all things considered. I had gone to bed after my midnight resurrection, and fallen asleep with unexpected (but appreciated) ease. I woke again just after dawn, to one of those glorious early-winter mornings where hoarfrost rimed every blade of grass and holly leaf. The window had been left uncurtained, and the thin, golden light poured in, unobscured save by a high, feathery haze of clouds coming in from the west.

The view was southerly. I took in what I could see of my surroundings curiously. I knew that we had managed to escape the prison-palace of Orio City by means of a faery islet outside the world's bounds, and subsequently arrived at the hunting lodge of the King of Lind.

We were therefore now somewhere in the western Linder mountains. I had never been to this part of Lind before. Hal and Marcan and I had come across the southeastern march of the country on our walking tour in the summer, and Mr. Dart and I had crossed to the north of the Crook of Lind as we travelled to Orio City—by the Lady!—less than a week ago.

The Linder mountains, which are usually called the Crosslains on the Fiellanese side, form the border between South Fiellan, Chare, and Lind. On our side they were steep, bald-topped, and with a limited area of wooded foothills. When I was a little boy I always thought they looked like old men getting up and dropping their lap-blankets in folds around their feet.

This side the mountains were much more relaxed in their demeanour, with long sloping flanks thickly forested. The forests seemed different from our side, lighter and yet more luxuriant. I contemplated the interplay of light and frost and

2

shadow. On our side most of the trees had lost their leaves, except for a few lingering oaks and the semi-evergreen Tillarny limes in the Woods Noirell. Here the mountains had stretches of dark green conifers and soft brownish-grey deciduous trees interspersed with great splashes of brilliant yellow larches.

After the gloom and grime of fog-bound Orio City, the sunlight and the bright blue sky overhead was altogether marvellous. I fiddled with the stiff latch of my window until I could open it and breathe in the crisp air. Someone in the distance was making charcoal; I could see the smoke rising in a steady leftward twist from the fold of two hills. Closer-to was sweet-smelling woodsmoke.

Wood doves cooed to each other, drawing my eye down from the white-tipped mountains to the forecourt below me. Three or four birds, soft grey and fawn, moved and murmured in the gravelly space below me, pecking at lumps of horse manure. They moved like the prayer-birds in the dead space between this life and the entry-way to the world to come.

Would I ever be able to look at this world again and not see that other place? I watched the birds, content in the moment, in the thought that surely I could not.

In that place *beyond*, I had met Ariadne nev Lingarel, the disgraced governor and great poet. She had found salvation in the architecture of the prison in which she was incarcerated, and grace (such a great mystery!) in the response of those who read, and loved, her poem in the years since. Even me. *Especially* me, she had said; she had waited to greet me on that side of the passageway.

My thoughts touched on that, then lifted away again, embarrassed in a way I had not been *there*. It was excruciatingly difficult even to imagine meeting soul to soul, here and now on this side. *There* it had been—not easy, precisely, but there had been time and patience enough to wait until the soul was ready and able to face itself, and others, clearly.

3

Those Mountains were the home of the soul, and in the Wood of Spiritual Refreshment between our lives here and the Mountains there lay all that was necessary for us to be able to reach them. For someone who had not felt at home in himself, let alone in any particular place, since childhood, this was truly a grace unfathomable. I wished I knew what I was to do with it.

I glanced around the room, but could not see my copy of *On Being Incarcerated in Orio Prison.* I hoped Violet or Mr. Dart had claimed it, during our tumble-down exit from the fey island linking prison and hunting lodge.

I considered the Linder mountains again. The air was thin and cold and splendid.

It was actually Violet's copy I had been using to decipher our path. Mine would be with my other belongings in our coach, wherever that was at the moment.

Eyes on the wood doves, I prayed to the Lady, Her face unclear in my mind but my heart singing with the memory of Her, that when I forgot, as I inevitably would forget, that I would be reminded of the Mountains and the true home of the soul.

Down below me a thickset middle-aged man dressed in well-worn leathers came around a corner with two shaggy-haired deerhounds beside him. The tall dogs were scenting the air, taking delight in scattering the wood pigeons, one taking a moment to mark his territory. I smiled at them, their unconscious beauty of movement, their elegant lines. One turned its head up to look at me, ears pricked forward in eager interest.

The handler called from the next corner, and the dogs left off their investigations to trot obediently away. I let out a deep breath and realized I was hungry.

❧

My room was not large, nor excessively luxurious, but it was well-appointed in a rusticating-lord sort of way. The bed was a sturdy four-poster with heavy damask curtains in green and brown, a down quilt and a well-sprung mattress underneath. An ewer and washbasin to one side had lukewarm water in it, evidence that a servant had entered and exited my room before I had woken. The fire was newly-lit as well.

I poked around and discovered my clothing on a chair, cleaned and neatly folded. I considered this even as I found the materials for shaving in a drawer on the washbasin stand and meditatively worked to lather the soap. I was wearing a plain linen nightshirt, loose and large on me, undoubtedly borrowed from the household. I felt surprisingly clean given all the dust and grime of our adventure in the palace-prison.

It was only when I was nearly finished shaving, with the assistance of a small and somewhat warped hand-mirror, that I realized that someone must have washed my body as part of the laying-out rites.

It was a ... *disconcerting* thought.

I finished my ablutions and changed into my clothes: dun breeches and white shirt, dark blue waistcoat and medium-blue coat. A cravat, tied in the Mathematical style at my neck and a pair of newly-polished if very well-worn boots on my feet completed the outfit. I gathered my hair back into a queue with a black ribbon I found next to the hairbrush in the drawer, wished for a toothbrush of some form, and folded the borrowed nightshirt over the back of the room's chair.

There was nothing else belonging to me in sight. This included, alas, a distinct lack of my hat, which had probably fallen off at some point in our journey. My boot-knife was in my boot, and everything else had been with the coach we had been preventing from reaching by our capture.

My stomach rumbled, and I tentatively opened the door. The warm water and the lit fire suggested that the servants, at least, anticipated the unexpected guests might arise soon, and that led me to hope for breakfast.

I had never been in this sort of place before. I wandered down the hall, admiring details of the interior architecture and trying to piece together how it fit with the palace-prison. It was not so elaborately decorated, but there were hints, here and there, of repeated motifs in the carved wooden doorways and in the subtle changes of stone walls and floor.

I doubted I would ever have thought to look for such patterns if I had not had Ariadne nev Lingarel's poem to guide me through the ones in the palace-prison, and the new knowledge that the hunting lodge was connected magically as well as architecturally to that building.

The hall took me down two sides of a square gallery to the head of a staircase, whose bannisters were beautifully shaped and had richly carved finials displaying a series of gargoyle and goblin-like forms. I examined them for a few minutes, tracing out the underlying spiral snake, wondering how Irany had persuaded the workmen to build what she needed without revealing what she was doing.

"The breakfast room is downstairs and three doors to the left, sir," a voice said.

I looked up to see a middle-aged woman in an apron. She was regarding me with polite deference, no awe or distrust in sight. She didn't seem surprised to find me there, so presumably she knew of the strange arrival of half-a-dozen mostly-strangers, but perhaps not the odd miracle in the middle of the night.

"Thank you," I said, sketching a bow. "And good morning."

She shook her head and turned away, but she was smiling at my foolishness as she did so, so I counted that a small victory.

I found the breakfast room, which relieved me by being laid out quite similarly to the Darts'. I might of late have become the Viscount St-Noire, and I had *learned* appropriate

6

manners from my mother and at Morrowlea, but I was not yet accustomed to moving in these sorts of circles.

Still, I was glad it was only the hunting lodge of the king of Lind, and that said King of Lind did not appear to be in residence. (I expected our reception the night before would have gone rather differently had he been so.) No one else was there, as it happened, when I entered, but I was quickly followed by a young maid-servant in a starched cap and clean white pinny.

"Good morning, sorr," she said with a rolling burr of an accent. "Coffee?"

"Yes, please."

"There's porridge and toast and kippers and sauces to come," she added, moving around to a sideboard where cups and saucers were laid out. "His highness likes a good breakfast of a morning, he does, when he's hunting."

It took me a moment to remember that Marcan—studious, religious, heartily athletic Marcan—was the second son of the King of Lind, and therefore *his highness*. When he wasn't the Count of Westmoor. I confess I didn't quite understand the titling conventions at work here.

"He does like a good breakfast," I agreed, remembering many such meals at Morrowlea. His sporting demeanour—Marcan was partial to the javelin and other field sports, as well as rowing and rugger—and corresponding appetite were legendary among our cohort. "We were at university together, he and I."

She bobbed an agreeable curtsey. "It was a sore surprise for you to arrive so unexpectedly in the night! And no carriage neither?"

"We did go a little astray of our intended route," I said to this indirect question. "Cream, if you please. Are you from around her, miss?"

She blushed. "Aye, sorr. Born and bred down in the village."

7

"I'm from Ragnor Bella, over the mountains. Are we far from the pass over to the Coombe, do you know?"

She held the cream jug, which was surprisingly enough a whimsical piece in the shape of a sheepish-looking cow, and considered this carefully. "I think the road goes there, aye, sorr. Perhaps fifteen miles? Twenty? I've never been that far, sorry, sorr."

Until I had gone to Morrowlea, I had never been farther than fifteen miles from home, either. Except that one trip across the Leap with my father. I smiled at her. "Thank you. Has there been snow up in the mountains, do you know?"

"Aye sorr, but not so much to bring the game down yet," she said, more confident at this question. "The master huntsman said there's weather coming, but. His highness is most eager for the mountain goats."

It seemed strange to me that Marcan would so relish hunting. But then again he was sporting, in all senses of the word, and the Lady of the Green and White had her Huntsman at her side.

(Though ... not when I saw Her. Which did nothing to put to rest the question of whether the Hunter in Green traipsing around the hills and forests surrounding Ragnor Bella was the divinity, or someone mumming the part. I was inclined to think it wholly a disguise, but I didn't know that for certain and it seemed prudent to behave circumspectly.)

I thanked the maid for the coffee, when she eventually surrendered the cream jug to my use, and asked for toast as a safe thing to start with. I disliked kippers and wasn't at all sure what *sauces* meant when it came to breakfast foods in Lind.

Before I had even begun adding sugar to the tar-thick brew I had been given the rest of my party began to straggle in. First was Mr. Dart, who stopped in the doorway to regard me with a somewhat resigned expression. "I half-hoped, this morning, that the whole sequence of events of the past two days was a dream."

Mr. Dart is not a morning person. He looked so awake that I guessed he hadn't slept at all. I pushed my cup over to him. "You seem as if you might need this more than me."

"You do look disgustingly awake for someone who was dead most of yesterday." But he accepted the cup and took a long draught, shuddering as he did so. "Vile stuff. They should add chocolate and sugar as they did at that coffeeshop in Tara."

"It's a style I'm sure Mrs. Jarnem the Sweet would take much delight in you bringing to fashion."

He sat down opposite me. He was wearing his plum and grey suit, and clearly the hunting lodge servants had been busy through the night with their laundering, for it, too, was freshly clean and pressed. Even the grey sling cradling his petrified arm had neat creases down its centre line.

The pensive look suddenly cleared, and he gave me a pene-trating glance, eyes a sharp, bright, blue. "I *am* glad to see you, Jemis, notwithstanding the spiritual upheaval you have thrown us into."

"The Lady was —" but the door opened on Marcan, and I stood to greet my friend and involuntary host properly. "Good morning, Marcan — your highness, that is."

He scowled at me and flung himself down into the hefty seat at the head of the table. He didn't look like he had slept, either. "None of that nonsense, Jemis. If you *are* Jemis."

"Oh, this is Jemis, all right," Mr. Dart said, grinning at me. "No one else could have *quite* that matter-of-fact air about referencing the sweet-shop seller in Ragnor Bella."

The maid came back with my plate of toast, presented Marcan with another bobbing curtsy, and set down the toast on the counter so she could serve him with coffee. He greeted her politely and said that 'his friend here' would like the Linder sauces for breakfast.

"Very good, sorr," she said, then blushed and curtsied again. "Your highness, sorry, sorr.'"

He waved her off. "No matter that, Clara. Tell Master

9

Swentin that I won't be hunting this morning. I must see to my guests."

"I do thank you for your hospitality," I said on this reminder.

"It's not as if you gave me any choice," he grumbled. "Falling out of nowhere into my bedroom, dying, coming back to life … I've spent the night praying, I'll have you know."

I thought of all those white prayer-birds. "I do know. Thank you."

He shifted uneasily. "Yes. Well. I'll be speaking to the Archbishop of this. What is your direction?"

"We're on our way home to South Fiellan," Mr. Dart said. "Is the pass over to the Coombe still open, do you know? Are we far from it?"

"It's about fifteen miles north from here," Marcan replied, thus proving Clara to be quite correct. "There's been snow on the heights but the passes should still be open, if you hasten. Swentin said there's bad weather coming down. You might want to go all the way north and cross over the Crook."

Mr. Dart glanced at me. I shrugged, as aware as he that it was all too likely that the Indrillines would have sent out their forces to intercept us. We would be coming from an entirely unexpected direction, and might indeed manage to pass *behind* them if we were lucky, but that was not a sort of luck I had ever had much truckle with. Games of chance, yes. Chances with life, no.

"We'll discuss it with the others," Mr. Dart said, and obviously changed the subject. "What sort of hunting do you have here? Bear? Boar? Stags?"

Marcan leaned forward enthusiastically. "All of that and more. Mountain sheep, too, and chamois. There are even a few cougars in the upper ranges. Do you hunt?"

"Fish, rather. We have salmon and trout—"

"Salmon come so far up the Rag? We don't have them this side of the mountains, alas—"

And they were off.

I smirked at Mr. Dart over my now refilled cup of coffee, thinking of all his invitations to go poaching, which was a sport everyone in our barony partook in at some point or another. Well, everyone but the actual owners of the river-rights, which consisted of the baron, Mr. Dart's brother the Squire of Dartington, and my uncle. Everyone else nominally rented certain rights but actually poached from the good pools on the baron's private stretch.

This relentlessly ordinary conversation was interrupted by the arrival of, first, Violet, followed closely by Hal, and thirdly by Jullanar Maebh. The former two came in, greeted Mr. Dart and Marcan with grave (so to speak) courtesy, and smiled uncertainly at me. Neither appeared to have slept well either.

I was about to ask Violet after her brother, whom I had not yet properly met, when Jullanar Maebh, who had moved to curtsy to Marcan, caught sight of me and emitted a short piercing scream. Quite as if she'd seen a ghost.

I startled, half standing to return the salutations, and stared at her. She lifted her hand to her mouth, eyes wide and fearful. "Dear *Lady*. Can—dear goddess—I don't—I can't—"

"Good morning," I tried.

Mr. Dart buffeted me in the arm. "It's all right, cousin. He's alive."

"He isn't," she insisted. "I laid out his body. I've laid out bodies before. He was *dead*."

"It was a miracle," I offered.

"Sit down and be quiet, Mr. Greenwing," Mr. Dart ordered sharply, eyes flashing a colour I could not quite name. The air shivered around him, but I wasn't sure if anyone noticed besides Hal, who raised his eyebrow briefly, and perhaps Violet, who frowned.

Mr. Dart walked around the table and took his cousin's— really his niece's—arm to lead her gently but firmly from the room, talking intently in an undertone the while.

11

I sat down obediently, then smiled apologetically at Violet, who was still just taking her seat. "Mr. Dart is coming to be more decisive of late, or so I've discovered. It must be our Morrowlea influence; Stoneybridge appears to have been much more reserved."

Marcan said, "You're actually Jemis Greenwi—Wait. Do you mean your Mr. *Dart* went to *Stoneybridge*?"

CHAPTER TWO

I have to admit that never in my life before had anyone been more startled by Mr. Dart's name than my own. I was still greatly under the influence of spiritual peace: I found it gratifying.

"Yes. He read History at Stoneybridge."

Marcan gave every evidence of awe. "He wrote the most amazing paper on the campaigns under the Emperor Eritanyr —oh! I had *no idea* he was just our age. My tutor said he'd been offered a fellowship at Tara. She desperately wanted him for our faculty, but didn't expect he'd pass up a full fellowship there. Who would!"

"Mm," I replied, thinking of Mr. Dart's mixed behaviour at Tara, but Marcan wasn't attending.

"I was sure he was already on his second degree at Stoneybridge. Lady, I must have read half of his *term* papers! I can't believe it. There was a truly incredible account of the Orkaty campaign in last spring's *Journal of Astandalan History*. So much has been written on it, of course, what with the extraordinary courage and fortitude shown by Major Jack Greenwing under the command of General Halioren, but Mr. Dart's paper —"

He shook his head in wonder. "And then that essay on the

Gainsgooding Campaign, which he did in conjunction with some colleague studying Classical Shaian poetry supplying the translations."

He frowned suddenly at me. I assumed this was in some reflection on the fact that said Major Jack Greenwing was my father, but no. "*You* spent half of second year on those poems, in correspondence with your friend at Stoneybridge."

I hadn't realized Mr. Dart had actually put our results in for publication. Mind, he might well have told me at some point when I was deep under the influence of the wireweed and consequently unheeding of outside concerns. "Yes? That was this Mr. Dart."

"Those are good translations," he said grudgingly. "Mind you, pretty well all the historians think you went rather too far into the abstruse with your decipherments of their so-called esoteric meanings."

I had forgotten how bull-dogged Marcan could be about the *facts, and only the facts, Jemis*. It always amazed me how devout he was at the same time. I suppose if you accepted the tenets of faith as axioms, then a strict adherence to dogma made sense.

Still, I was mightily pleased that I now actually had proof of my process. "We just escaped Orio Prison by exactly the same method of analysis, though the subject was Ariadne nev Lingarel's *On Being Incarcerated in Orio Prison*, not one of the Gainsgooding poems. Albeit I think she might have been one of the undiscovered conspirators—"

"Dear *Lady*, not that bloody poem again. Hal, how can you stand this? You heard even more about that poem than the rest of us."

Hal sipped from his coffee with ducal equanimity. "I have to admit that Jemis did manage to provide us a means of escaping the reputedly inescapable prison with only the poem and his studies of the architect's works in the Archives."

"Well, there you have it," Marcan said triumphantly.

I stole my cup back from Mr. Dart's place and rallied arguments, unreal as they seemed at the moment, and wholly unnecessary in the event, as the door opened on the maid, bringing a tray of dishes to set on the table.

She set a platter of sausages in front of me, along with a fresh plate of toast. "Here you go, sorr, Linder sauces. M'lady, what would you like? There's toast, and kippers, and sauces, and porridge."

"Porridge, thank you," Violet replied demurely. "I must thank you, Marcan, for your hospitality. I'm afraid I didn't greet you properly last night."

Marcan nodded, a little stiffly. He'd been there, of course, for the disastrous end of our Morrowlea education, when he and Hal had stood by me—and Violet by Lark. "Is your brother feeling better this morning?" he asked carefully. "I hope the physician was able to be of assistance, though we're limited in our resources here."

She glanced at me and Hal. "The physician suggested his ailments would be best served by taking him to the Halls of Healing, on Nên Corovel. I would like that very much." Her voice faltered. I tried to remember what I'd learned about her brother, and by extension herself, back in the prison. It was not that I didn't *recall* it, precisely, but that everything from before my death felt ... remote.

The Halls of Healing on Nên Corovel were the premier school of medicine on Alinor. I wasn't sure if they were simply located near, or actually were a part of, the Lady of Alinor's court there. The Isle had been noted for healing waters for many, many centuries.

Long before the coming of the Empire there had been stories about sacred wells and magic flowers and unicorns and all sorts of similar wonders. The Summer Country, it was named in many stories. The Rainbow-Girt Isle in others. Once, it was said, it had floated around the world on the back of a whale.

15

My father had been healed there, after being rescued in the summer from the pirate ship on which he had been enslaved.

I let the conversation flow around me as I attended to the 'sauces', which were quite delicious, flavoured with a herb I didn't recognize. In a quiet moment I leaned over to Hal, who sat next to me, and asked him if he knew what it was. It was something like thyme, but a little saltier and with a hint of parsley or something like it.

"Summer savoury, I believe," he said after taking a bite. "These are good."

He had gone for the kippers, which looked delicious. They always tempted me, when I saw them, but I always regretted them afterwards.

"I like the gravy, too," I said, wishing I dared use the bread to sop it up.

"That would be most appreciated, Marcan, thank you," Violet said gratefully. Hal and I both turned enquiringly to her.

"Marcan's offered us the use of his carriage," she explained. "We should be able to take a ship safely from one of the free ports along the Arcadian coast. Ru's too unwell to ride, I fear."

Ah yes, her brother's name was Ruaridh … and he was the son and heir of the Lady of Alinor.

The knowledge slid into place easily, then sat there awkwardly.

Violet, whom I had thought an Indrilline spy, was instead a spy for the Lady of Alinor *on* the Indrillines. And the Lady had been keeping herself remote and reluctant to act against the growing might of the Indrillines not only because of her attention being focused on their rival criminal gang, the Knockermen, who had pirate fleets in the Northern Sea, but also because her heir Ruaridh had been held hostage in the prison of Orio City for the past six years.

Mr. Dart and Hal would have a far better sense than I what might change in the world as a result of this rescue. I have to admit that I was more interested by the realization that this meant that Violet was actually someone I could appropriately court. I would have done so regardless, but I couldn't pretend it wouldn't make it easier all round.

The daughter of the Lady of Alinor was more than a tad high for me, in fact—except that I was the Viscount St-Noire, according to Hal second-most-eligible bachelor of Northwest Oriole after himself, and surely that had to be good for *something*.

Hal elbowed me. "Jemis, stop smiling like that."

I blinked at him. "How was I smiling?"

He hesitated, which I took to mean that I was showing too much emotion too nakedly. From his relieved expression when I straightened my expression, it was too close a reminder of last night's miracle. I wanted to sing out to the heavens that I had *seen* the heavens, and how goodly they were indeed; but that was not how well-educated young gentlemen of our day behaved.

"You'll have to leave soon, then, if you want to catch a ship before the season's over," Marcan said. He looked over at Hal and me. "What are your plans? Not to say that you may not stay here a while, if you'd like," he added, less enthusiastically.

I repressed an amused snort. Hal simply nodded and replied at face value. "Thank you, but I do need to return to Fillering Pool as quickly as possible. There have been some strange developments this past week, and I must confer with my advisors." He gave an oblique smile at Violet. "I shall have to make some adjustments to the list of invitations for our Winterturn Ball, at the very least. You're coming, I hope, Marcan?"

"My father won't give me permission to take orders before I come of age," Marcan said glumly, which was evidently the agreement Hal expected, for he simply clouted him on the shoulder.

"Our hunting's not so fine as your mountains, but we do have some excellent deer."

Marcan nodded more happily. "Well, that's all right then! So you're headed north, over the Crook?"

"And my party to the pass to the Coombe," I put in, "if we can make it before the snow closes it in."

"You'll want to get mules at Finoury's Inn, in that case. Let me think."

We all continued with our meals as he pondered. Clara wandered in and refilled everyone's coffee, stating in a desultory sort of way that our other guests were dining in their rooms. I hoped Jullanar Maebh recovered from her fright soon. I didn't think I was at fault, precisely, but obviously it was my doing she was so overtaken.

"I have it," Marcan said after a moment. "Violet, you and your brother will take the carriage south—I'll give you a letter of recommendation in case anyone stops to enquire why you have it. You may meet my father on the way, he's coming up for a week's hunting some time soon. I'm afraid I don't have any riding horses to spare for the rest of you. I know Jemis doesn't mind going longshank, and Hal, of course you walked with us from Morrowlea, but we shouldn't subject Mr. Dart's cousin to the exertion. If you will pardon the indignity, I will direct the carter to take you all in the heavy dray towards Finoury's Inn, where Hal can collect the stagecoach or a hack, and Jemis's party can hire mules to take them over the pass."

We all agreed to this reasonable suggestion, and shortly after broke up our grouping to tell the rest of our party the plan and collect our few belongings together. I had nothing at all, and after informing Mr. Dart that we would be leaving in an hour or so, I wandered along the upper hallway examining the carvings.

I encountered Violet at the far end of the gallery. She had just come out of a door as I turned the corner, and startled badly.

"Violet," I said, sweeping her one of my foolish becurlicued bows and giving her what I hoped was an engaging smile.

"Jemis," she replied severely, though there was a hint of a dimple at the corner of her mouth.

I wasn't sure what to say. I had given last night the messages I had been entrusted with, from various late relations, but once spoken the news had faded out of my mind; they were not my secrets to know, or to keep, only to pass on. Violet's had been from a grandmother, I remembered vaguely, but nothing else.

"It was a beautiful place, where you were?" Violet asked suddenly. "On the other side."

I leaned up against the gallery balustrade. The upper floor of the lodge was arranged in a square around a central two-storey space. It was all very solid and material. "It was," I agreed. "There was a forest, and a stream, and flowers. The Mountains in the distance."

"And Ariadne nev Lingarel waiting for you."

I smiled at her, the delight thrilling through me again, the mystery and the grace of that encounter. "Yes. I don't understand it, you know. I've never read much theology. I met her, and we talked, then she went on to the Mountains and I went to a kind of glade where I saw my mother and stepfather and the others and talked with them."

She was silent for a few minutes, looking down. I waited patiently. Finally she said, "And was that Heaven, do you think?"

"The Mountains are our true home," I said with the certainty I had felt on seeing them. "The forest there ... Ariadne called it the Wood of Spiritual Refreshment. She said it takes everyone different lengths of time to be ready to go on. I know I would have been there a while ... She said she hadn't been a good person, in this life, and it was only through her poetry that she learned her way to the Mountains. The Lady

19

said that no one who desired the Mountains would be left behind."

Violet looked up at me, and I recalled the deep secret she had given as coin for her passage through the Labyrinth of Ihuranuë, that her brother's long imprisonment and consequent broken health were the result of an ill-judged and ill-spirited prank of hers.

I judged it best to change the subject.

"I think you'd look very well in the dress Ariadne was wearing," I blurted out without thinking further. "It was very simple—a columnar skirt, gathered under the bodice, with a sort of square neck—"

She burst out laughing. "Are you truly giving me fashion advice from the afterlife? Oh, Jemis!"

I blushed, but laughed along with her. "It was a lovely dress. I remember wishing it had been in fashion."

"I've seen pictures of that period. They can be most flattering garments."

"And not current style anywhere at the moment."

"A point to be considered, certainly," she replied, eyes dancing.

"Violet," I said impulsively, "may I write to you?"

Her face went still and sober immediately. "Jemis ..."

"Violet," I said again, "you told me I shouldn't trust you, that things were not as they seem. But now I know that you're on the Lady's side—"

"It remains to be seen whether she will let me *stay* at her side."

We were speaking of two different Ladies, one the Lady of the Green and White, the goddess, the other the human great mage who was Lady of Alinor. I changed tack to that thought. "She's your mother."

"She's the Lady of Alinor first," Violet replied shortly.

I remembered the dark-skinned woman Mr. Dart and I had encountered in the Lady's Pools in the Coombe, my first weekend back in Ragnor Bella, when Violet had been haunting the barony (so to speak) with a red herring pie. That woman had laughed merrily on seeing us nearly fall into the Lady's Pool before her; and who was she meeting there, if not her daughter the spy?

"Still," I said. "Will you tell me, please, if your heart cannot incline in my direction? I will not belabour it if it belongs to another—or to none at all, of course."

Violet sighed. "Oh, Jemis, you know it doesn't."

We looked at each other. I smiled at her resigned declaration, hardly the stuff of romantic legend but still—but still!—

"For yourself, Violet, disregarding all the rest, may I write to you?"

"I can hardly disregard all the rest, and neither can you, my lord viscount! But—" She reached out her hand to me, and I took it as gently as I could with both of mine. Her Crimson Lake ring and mine flashed in the sunlight coming in some high window behind us. "Oh, Jemis, yes, you may write to me."

And she smiled, so my heart turned quite over.

Never letting my eyes stray from hers, I lifted her hand to my lips and kissed it.

"And here I had thought that only the mountains and Ariadne nev Lingarel's poem would show me the way back to that other country of our souls," I said.

"Oh, Jemis," said Violet, laughing. "You are *such* a romantic."

CHAPTER THREE

I
t was a gorgeously beautiful day, golden sunlight illuminating the yellow larches and striking the grey-brown bark of winter-bare trees into tender magnificence. Over the mountains white clouds were starting to pile up, but they were nothing like the dreary close fog of Orio City.

I would have dearly liked to go for a long run through the countryside, exploring the wooded slopes, but alas, that was not to be. Instead Jullanar Maebh, Hal, Mr. Dart, Violet, and I gathered in the stone-paved court in front of the hunting lodge to say our farewells.

The invalid Ruaridh had already been settled into the carriage. He was so swaddled with blankets and hot bricks that I could see nothing much of him but a dim blur of sallow features. He did not look well, as might be expected of someone recently rescued from six years a prisoner in an oubliette, abused for his magic as well as his political capital.

Violet stood with her hand on the door of the carriage. "Thank you, Marcan," she said gravely, curtseying politely to him. She nodded to Hal and Mr. Dart, smiled at Jullanar Maebh, and gave me a long look. "Safe travels, everyone. Thank you for your assistance."

I bowed, unable to stop the smile from creeping onto my face. She shook her head, sighing, and said, "Oh, Jemis," but before she turned to enter the carriage I saw the dimple at the corner of her mouth make its appearance, and did not mind in the least.

~

Our cart was nothing like the smart gig Violet and Ruaridh had borrowed from Marcan. It was a hefty beer wagon, in fact, drawn by four heavy horses with blue roan colouring and dramatic white feathers. The carter was an older man, careworn and careless in his clothing, who held the reins with a negligent hand and disdained more than the most basic of greetings.

"In t'back w'ye," he slurred, though that might have been his accent.

We clambered in, Jullanar Maebh with some visible discomfort, and settled our best on lumpy piles of dusty sacks sandwiched between barrels. Marcan had said something vague about replenishing supplies from down the valley before his father the king arrived. I was glad, withal, that there was a purpose in the carter's journey besides simply depositing us at Finoury's Inn. He did not seem the type to relish pointless journeys on behalf of the gentry. Not that I could blame him for that in the least.

The carter clucked to the horses, which set off at a steady plod. The first part of our route took us through a heavy forest, mostly evergreens mixed with the yellow larches. The air was crisp, promising the coming season, but still just barely autumnal rather than wintry. It was hard to believe it was barely three weeks until Winterturn began with the solstice.

I settled back on my sacks and tried to think about all the things that might come about as a result of our adventures in Orio City, but they were on the other side of last night's miracle, and remote as a book I had read some time ago. Violet's smile when she said I might write to her was much more present, and I could not help but fall into daydreams of what I would say to her on our next meeting.

Hal and Mr. Dart and Jullanar Maebh started talking about their various areas of study—Mr. Dart was embarrassed at the report of Marcan's enthusiasm for his scholarly prowess —which was a conversation I did not feel a strong need to participate in. They already all knew what I had studied, and though I didn't know Jullanar Maebh well as of yet, I was sure there would be plenty of opportunities to hear more about the scientific properties of water at some point.

We descended steeply through the trees. The spruces and larch gave way to holly and oak and bare-branched ash, and the air, still crisp, grew richer with the scent of decaying leaves. I watched various small birds flit across our path, not able to identify more than the most obvious sparrows and robins, enjoying the songs filling the air.

As the track levelled out and joined another, wider one, the horses picked up their pace and began a steady smooth trot. I eyed the speed with which various elements of the landscape passed us and decided they were now going faster than my walking pace, but still slower than my running speed.

Would it be tremendously rude of me to leave them to the ride and run ahead on foot?

Hal caught my eye and shook his head silently, but with amusement on his features. I sighed, then grinned at him—I probably *was* that obvious—and entered into the conversation, which was now on the subject of Winterturn holiday traditions.

Jullanar Maebh's account of Outer Reaches traditions was somewhat wistful. Mr. Dart was very attentive, asking questions about specificities, but it did not seem to occur to his newly-discovered relative that he might wish to ensure that her first holiday with her father's family was not entirely alien.

I thought her account of a candle-lit carolling ceremony one that sounded splendid and well worth adopting in our region. It did not seem unlikely that my father could be persuaded to participate in it. As a child we had gone to Arguty Manor for the feast-day meal itself, and otherwise decorated our cottage with greenery and candles in honour of the Lady of Winter according to my mother's Woods-Noirell customs.

Mr. Buchance, my stepfather, was from Chare, and had brought mostly food-related traditions. Not that I could say anything against the spiced cookies and festival pies he had introduced to our family (and by way of his second wife's brother, the town baker, to the town at large).

"My Winterturn this year will be focused on the coming-of-age ball," Hal said, almost glumly, but he brightened when he went on. "We have a family meal in the morning of the solstice, and there's always a great feast in the evening for all the surrounding gentry, with carolling and bonfires outside for the tenantry, and usually several roast deer. Before the Fall we used to have a full winter fair, with entertainment and booths and people coming from all around. I decided to start that again—we're going to have so many guests for the ball, I thought we might as well give them something to do besides send their sisters and daughters to woo me."

Jullanar Maebh gave him a doubtful glance. "Are you so very eligible, then?"

Hal grinned at her, realizing a moment before I did that she evidently had not yet discovered his rank. "I am, alas! I see I have somehow managed not to introduce myself properly—Halioren Leaveringham," (pronounced *Lingham*), "Duke Imperial of Fillering Pool, at your service, Miss Dart."

She stared at him, nonplussed. "You're the Duke of Fillering Pool?"

"In the flesh," Hal replied.

"I've read about you in the *New Salon*. I had no—we're sitting in a *cart!*"

I glanced up at the carter, who did not appear to be paying the slightest bit of attention to us and our conversation. He was slouching with a distinct sideways tilt on his bench, and at some point while I'd been daydreaming had pulled out a large flask. The horses, thankfully, seemed to know where they were going, and went along smartly with little direction from their driver.

At least I hoped they knew where they were going. The road was fairly well-travelled, at any rate, if the increasing number of ruts were anything to go by.

Hal laughed. "I did go to Morrowlea, you know. And Jemis is not the only one who finds his name in the *New Salon* with regularity."

"Alas," I muttered.

Jullanar Maebh shook her head in amazement. "And they didn't *know?*"

Hal gave me a speculative glance. "Jemis, did you? Tell us honestly, now! I know Marcan didn't—I knew of his name, and he mine, of course, but we'd never met, and neither *Marcan* nor *Hal* are such odd names as to make us think immediately of each other."

Jemis, on the other hand, was very unusual in our part of the world, although until recently only my father was famous.

I thought back to my first encounter with my new room-mate. I had been so grateful for his friendliness, barely regarding how his accent and colouring and general demeanour all betokened 'good breeding'. Albeit I had noticed how he had treated the simple act of picking up a tray with his meal on it, in the college refectory, as an adventure of the highest order.

"I knew he was well-bred," I replied. "Obviously of good wealth and standing—but did I ever for a moment think to myself, 'Ah yes, this must be the Duke of Fillering Pool'?—no!

It never crossed my mind. After about the first week I honestly didn't think about what his people might be. I didn't want to talk about mine, not if I didn't have to, and it was against the rules besides."

Hal gave me a brilliant flashing smile, relief and pleasure evident in it.

He had told me at some point that he had chosen Morrowlea because he wanted to know who he was without all the trappings of rank. He had been seven when he became the duke, surrounded his whole life by privilege and wealth.

(I had chosen Morrowlea to get out from the shadow of my father's name, whom I loved and mourned and respected, and who was considered once one of the greatest heroes, and then one of the greatest traitors, in late Astandalan history.)

"Morrowlea sounds much more interesting than Tara," Jullanar Maebh said.

I agreed, but it was hardly polite to say so, so I offered, "I don't think we had anyone teaching about water. It's land-locked, of course."

"The department of Natural Philosophy is excellent," Hal opined. "Of course, I'm biased as Botany falls into its demesne, but I *am* considered a reasonable judge, I'll have you—oh!"

The right front wheel of the cart crashed suddenly down into a hole, jolting us all out of our seats and knocking half the barrels out of the wagon. The carter swore and dropped the reins. One of the barrels bounced forward and knocked against the rearward horse. It squealed and lunged forward, scaring the others into bolting.

We lurched. The carter swore. I grabbed the side of the wagon and nearly swallowed my tongue when with a loud tortured whine the harness snapped and the whole front of the wagon dropped.

The carter swore some more. More barrels fell out. Jullanar Maebh had to scramble not to be tumbled out with them. I grabbed at her even as Hal fell towards Mr. Dart, whose stone arm seemed to be caught between the side and another barrel, but this movement unbalanced everything and with another crack the whole wagon tilted up and over and tumbled us unceremoniously out onto the ground.

Something clouted me on the elbow, and I swore breathlessly before remembering the presence of Jullanar Maebh. She herself was uttering a series of words in what I took to be Outer Reaches slang, and did not appear to notice my transgression.

"Well," I said, catching my breath and sitting cautiously upright. "Is everyone in one piece?"

"More or less," Mr. Dart said. "Cousin, are you sound?"

There was a pause as Jullanar Maebh seemed to realize she had been voicing her thoughts in a less than ladylike manner. She flushed and accepted Mr. Dart's outstretched arm to stand up and brush herself off. "I confess this is not at all how I had expected my journey to my father's home to go."

Mr. Dart nodded in sympathy. "I should probably not have embroiled Mr. Greenwing in my affairs."

I brushed fruitlessly at my mud-spattered coattails. "I would hardly have let you go on your own."

He sighed gustily and began searching around for his hat, which was underneath a distant barrel. "I feared what would happen if I left *you* alone."

Hal uttered his surprising whoop of a laugh. "The mind boggles! We're only missing the Fair Folk now."

I raised my eyebrows at him even as I clambered to my feet. "I would not speak so loud, even this side of the mountains. Also, I suppose you have forgotten my grandmother's coachman and his six Ghiandor horses, which made the run from Ragnor Bella to Orio City without a change and barely a rest."

"I stand corrected. No harm done?"

My elbow seemed likely to bruise, but otherwise was sound. "Only to my clothes."

"They can be mended later. I am less certain about our conveyance."

It was not so long ago that I had had precisely one set of good clothes, and feared they would be the last. I *still* actually only had one good winter-weight suit, the much-abused items of clothing I was currently wearing, but at least I had more on order from the haberdashers of Ragnor Bella, and money to come from my stepfather's bequest to pay for them.

The wagon was decisively overturned, the front wheels worryingly aslant from each other and their common axle. The load of barrels and sacks were scattered widely around and down the trail, and the horses were nowhere in sight.

I was closest to the carter, who was sitting akimbo on the ground. "Are you all right, sir?" I asked him, offering him my hand. He brushed it aside with a muttered oath, groping for his flask instead. Once that was in his grip he took a long swig, belched, and lumbered upright without affording us the least bit of attention.

"Excuse me," I tried, touching his shoulder, but he shook my hand off.

"Bloody horses," he said, staggering off into the woods.

This left the four of us and the wrecked cart. We waited a few minutes, but neither the horses nor the carter came back.

Hal shook his head and bent to examine the axle. "It's snapped," he announced after a few minutes. "We could right the wagon but even with the horses we wouldn't be going anywhere fast."

Jullanar Maebh set one of the barrels upright and sat down on it, wrapping her arms about herself. Mr. Dart had retrieved his hat and set another barrel next to her. "Any bright ideas?" he asked the air.

I rose up on my toes and down again. "Marcan said it was about fifteen miles to the inn at the crossroads. I reckon we've come seven or eight."

"Is that all?" Jullanar Maebh asked in dismay.

"Those horses were going a steady three and a half miles an hour on the flat," I informed her. "Less on the uphills. I judged against my pace running."

I peered up at the sky through the trees. The clouds were getting larger and darker and with strange shapes and protuberances to them, evidence of crosswinds at high altitudes, I guessed. Not enough to be an immediate cause of concern, I didn't think, but a little ominous. "We don't have any baggage here, and the carter didn't seem the most trustworthy. What do you think? Shall we start walking towards the crossroads inn? We should get there before dark easily enough, even at an easy pace. We're about the same distance from the hunting lodge, and there's not much point in returning there if we don't have to."

Hal, I knew, walked a goodly rate when not distracted by interesting plants, and Mr. Dart was well accustomed to wandering about on excursions picking mushrooms and other intriguing nighttime activities afforded by our barony. Jullanar Maebh seemed fit enough to ramble at least an hour or two.

"You might run ahead and bespeak us rooms at the inn," Mr. Dart suggested. "And supper. Perhaps a bath."

"If they've got a carriage or even a better-sprung cart to send back to us, that would be useful as well," Hal put in. "You can ask them to send a messenger back to Marcan at the lodge so they know what happened to the carter."

"If there's more than just the inn there, you could see if there's a cartwright, too," Jullanar Maebh added.

"Or send for our own Cartwright," Mr. Dart said wistfully, straightening his sling.

"Cartwright's your man, isn't he?" Hal asked. "Do you think he will have left Orio City, or stayed in the hopes of your escaping or being released?"

Mr. Dart pondered a few minutes. "The duplicitous Violet was of the opinion that while the Indrillines would hardly want our escape noised abroad, the necessary efforts at finding us are sure to have been noticed. So ... we can hope they left. Next time I will know to provide a rendezvous for unexpected adventures."

"We could send a message on to his mother outside Yrchester," I said.

That met with approval. Hal had a notebook and a new-style fountain pen in his waistcoat pocket (for taking notes on the interesting botanical specimens he encountered, he claimed), so Mr. Dart wrote a note for his valet, and Hal, after a bit of thought, one for his mother at home in Fillering Pool, as well as one back to the hunting lodge for Marcan. "She'll be worried at the news," he said laconically. "We need to start gathering our allies again now that Ruaridh is no longer a hostage."

"He didn't seem ... well," Jullanar Maebh said.

"Well or not, he's the Lady's heir until she announces otherwise, and as she hasn't through all his absence, it may be because there isn't anyone else of proper stature or skill."

Magistra Aurelia Anyra, the professor of magic I had met at Tara, had proclaimed herself a great mage. She had also said she had met the Lady Jessamine (whom she rather resembled) in the course of trying to find out more of her birth family, she having been abandoned as an infant, so it was not as if the Lady of Alinor didn't know of her existence.

Well, there would be politics at work.

It was none of my business, anyway, except at the most tangential. Thank the Lady.

"Here you are, then," Hal said at last, folding the paper cleverly into a semblance of an envelope. "Shall I use a glob of mud to seal it, do you think?"

"Did you sign it with all your titles?" I asked.

"Of course not," he replied. "It's with a family nickname, to my sister's."

"And will your sister appreciate the mud?"

"Probably not. She's quite finicky, Elianne. Probably why

she's all for marrying her mathematics tutor. —Oh, that's not common knowledge yet, Miss Dart, so I would appreciate it if it didn't turn up in the *New Salon*'s gossip pages until *after* our announcement at the ball."

"I shall keep it as close as the trees."

"Do. And do go on, Jemis, we'll keep bantering with or without you."

I hastily aborted the rude gesture I began in his direction, tipped my nonexistent hat to Jullanar Maebh, and after tucking the notes into my waistcoat gladly lifted my feet into a proper distance-eating pace.

Oh, how *good* it was to be moving again!

CHAPTER FOUR

We were farther from Finoury's Inn than I had estimated, or else the distance was longer than Marcan had thought, for it took me a good hour and a half to reach it. The run would have been exceptionally pleasant had I not come out of the trees onto a ridge, half an hour or so along, and seen ahead of me the mountains reaching up until their peaks disappeared into quickly-developing dark clouds.

I paused at the ridge to examine the terrain. The road slanted back down a steep hillside, through another conifer-thick forest, towards what seemed a more open and cultivated valley bottom some miles away. To my left was one more range of wooded foothills and then the mountains proper. Ahead and to my right the hills fell into the wooded rolling western marches of Lind, with smoke rising here and there from various habitations. It was not a thickly populated part of the country by any means.

I could see, down in the middle of the valley below, something like a minor mansion or small stately home. It was built of a pale stone that caught the eye, set as it was into wide gold-green lawns cut out of the surrounding woods. It looked as if it were set well back from the road, assuming that followed the central line of the valley as was logical, and I guessed it had been built for a reclusive lord of one sort or another.

Further to the north a cross valley met the one I was looking into. I reckoned this might be at the right distance for the expected road up to the passes into Chare and the Coombe, and the bigger road leading down into central Lind. There was a worryingly thick column of black smoke rising from somewhere near the intersection.

In the hopes that it was not my destination, I set off carefully down the hill—no sense spraining an ankle if I could avoid it—and picked up speed once the road levelled out again on the relatively flat valley floor.

This road was hardly better travelled, and even muddier than the portion closer to the hunting lodge had been. I had to edge my way alongside great ruts, calf-deep and full of yellow mud at the bottom. They meandered across the road in slow curves, evidence of another drunken carter or perhaps some oddity of the road, which did seem to have a leftward slant about it.

What could have caused them was something of a mystery; even our wagon, pulled by heavy horses as it was, had nothing like this wheel span or depth. I ran alongside the tracks at an easy, mile-eating lope, rejoicing in clear lungs and clear, crisp air, resolutely ignoring those blue-black clouds boiling up over the mountains, and pondered.

Where was this heavily-laden wagon coming from, and whither was it going, and for what purpose—and to whose profit?

When Mr. Dart and I had left Ragnor Bella in my grandmother's falarode (drawn by six possibly-fairy Ghiandor horses, but of narrower wheel-rim, I thought, than these tracks), we had left at dusk according to the coachman's strict insistence. We had not made it out of the Arguty Forest bordering Ragnor barony to the north without being accosted by three different sets of highwaymen.

The first (the Hunter in Green) had requested our conveyance of himself to Yrchester, the second (Myrta the Hand) that we convey a load of barrels of illegal whiskey, and the third (Moo of Nibbler's gang) that we take possession of five kittens.

I had forgotten about the kittens. I hoped Cartwright was taking care of them for us.

The road took a bend and a stone wall emerged out of the woods to run alongside it. It was built of a dark grey stone, much encrusted with lichens and patches of ferns, thick festoons of ivy making mock of the vertical slate coping at its crown. I could without any trouble have contrived a crossing, even with the eight-foot height to climb before the loose slates. Though of course I would have followed the wall away from the corner at the road until I was out-of-sight of any passersby before I hazarded the trespass.

That first night, Mr. Fancy, the coachman, had taken the falarode and the barrels after leaving us in the care of Mrs. Cartwright, who had been shocked at the request but valiantly rose to the challenge of accommodating two gentlemen and her son for the night. She made perhaps the best Linder rarebit I'd ever had the joy of tasting, along with a jug of fine home-brewed ale that I hoped she was able to sell to supplement her widow's portion.

Both falarode and coachman, not to mention the six Ghiandor horses, were ready and eager to continue on the next morning, so I had not enquired any further into their dealings. Mr. Fancy was a strange and uncanny person, and I much preferred to keep on his good side. Not to mention I was already in unfortunately deep with various nefarious goings-on in Ragnor Bella without actively searching out trouble.

That was a lesson I should take good heed of, I suspected. I

turned my thoughts back to Violet and began composing a
letter in my mind.

After a time I ran past the entrance to the great house I'd
seen from the ridge. A pair of ivy-encrusted stone pillars with
stone pineapples as their finials bracketed a high, ornately
worked iron gate. There was no gate-house, and the gate stood
open, which I found curious for such a remote place.

The heavy, wide, cart-tracks turned into the gate. I
paused a moment and considered what the track told me. I
was no great woodsman or tracker, but Mr. Dart was no
slouch at the art, and possessed of a deep investigative
curiosity to boot, and moreover took delight in informing me
of his ways.

So: on the turn, the rear wheels had crossed to the inside
left of the outer, which indicated that the cart had gone in, not
out. Which I could see anyway by virtue of the direction of the
hoof prints, but it was good to have confirmation. There was
some confusion amongst them, as if a rider or several had
crossed the wagon-tracks after they'd been laid.

I had no idea what the weather hereabouts had been the
past few days, so couldn't guess at age, but they looked fairly
fresh. Several small piles of horse droppings seemed to confirm
this.

A few steps onward, and I discovered that the wagon, now
even heavier if the ruts were anything to go by, had turned out
again and was continuing along the road in the direction I was
heading. This time the wheel tracks distinctly went *over* the
incoming hoof-prints.

This was perhaps even more curious. A heavily-laden
wagon turning into a country manor: well, some sort of
delivery was obvious, even if the origin of it was not. (It could
easily enough be a back-country distiller or brewer or indeed
even something so mundane as a load of firewood.) For the
same cart to re-emerge, equally heavily laden, and continue on
away from either its origin or the house, was more puzzling.

Country houses did not, in my limited experience, tend to send *out* heavy loads.

Unless of course they were like the Talgarth's, and occupied in growing drugs under the pretence of studying the inheritance characteristics of sweet peas.

Whatever riding party had entered between the cart's arrival and its departure could have had something to do with it.

What the people at this country house were doing was absolutely none of my business but occupied my thoughts pleasantly for the next mile and a half, at which point I reached the crossroads and the still-burning Finoury's Inn.

A dozen men stood around with buckets of water, but the building was far too well gone to do anything but keep the fire from spreading. It was obvious they'd been hard at work for hours already, so sweaty and grimy were they. I slowed down to a more ordinary walk as I came out of the woods and into the cleared area around the inn.

It reminded me quite a bit of Grightmire's Cross, up in the Crook of Lind fifty or sixty miles north of here. Like that inn, it was built right at the crossroads, something that was simply not done in South Fiellan on the other side of the mountains. We buried suicides, traitors, and murderers under crossroads, and considered it very unlucky indeed to build within a furlong of one.

Also like Grightmire's Cross, there was no community to speak of around the inn. Even the Green Dragon, the most isolated of the public houses in Ragnor barony, had a handful of houses trailing off down the road from it. Approaching Finoury's Inn I had crossed a couple of fields after leaving the woods, both fallow stubble after the autumn harvest, but seen no houses.

From what I could see, the inn had been built out of elaborately carved wood, with a wood-shingled roof. Another building a few dozen yards away must have been the stable, with a corral of spooked and restless equines next to it. It was strange that the stable was so far from the inn building, but presumably there was a good reason. Perhaps there was a spring over there for watering the horses and mules? The placement had saved animals and building today, at any rate.

I hovered at the back of the group even as a brick chimney in the middle of the inn suddenly gave way and collapsed in a huge fountain of sparks. The gathered men let out a shout and hastened to put out the flakes of burning tinder before anything else could catch. I stamped on a few glowing strands that floated in my direction, but most were soon extinguished.

"It's fortunate that the wind is calm," I said to no on in particular.

A rotund older man next to me startled, jerking back with an oath and then apologizing in almost the same breath. "Sorry, lad, I didn't see anyone behind me there, like. What was that you said?"

"Nothing of consequence," I hastened to assure him. "Merely that it was fortunate that the day is calm."

He scowled up at the column of thick black smoke, which rose straight for perhaps a hundred feet before angling sharply sideways. I felt foolish, but it had not looked like that half an hour earlier.

"There's a storm coming," he said bleakly.

"Surely the rain will help put it out?"

"It'll be snow," he said flatly. "Coming over from the Coombe, this time of year? First of the Lady's Snows. It's never good when it comes before Winterturn Eve."

"We say the opposite," I murmured. *First Snow in November makes for a fair Spring in February.* But that's the other side of the mountains."

"Were you hoping to cross, then? Your accent says you're an educated man. Going down to Chare are you? Or over into the Coombe?"

I looked resignedly at the burning inn. "I was hoping to

hire mules and make the pass to Fiellan before the snows closed it, yes. My party's back along the road yonder—our, er, cart caught a rut and overturned."

"I'd hire you the mules but you'd not make it over. That's a treacherous height to the fork down to Chare, lad, and worse along the Fiellanese side. Takes lives every year. You'd be best going back up north and down again. A longer journey but a safer one, I tell you."

I eyed that dark cloud. "How long do you reckon before that storm hits?"

He shrugged, attention on the burning building. "An hour, two at the most. The wind's already started, as you can see. At least it'll put out the flames."

A shout went up from the other direction, and we both turned with alacrity to see a lone rider come cantering down the road I had just arrived from. "That's the Post come along from Hillend," the man said. "I must go meet him."

I let him go, then remembered my letters and and followed despite feeling like an utter imbecile for wanting more when the destruction of the inn was clearly the deserving focus of everyone's attention. By the time I arrived the Post-rider was being regaled with the story.

"It began around dawn," the man I'd been talking to was saying. "One of the grooms woke me to say he could see smoke coming out of the roof. I thought he meant the chimney, but then when I saw what he meant it was unmistakable. We couldn't figure out what was causing it ... there aren't any rooms up there, just old lumber and broken furniture and the like. Well, we got everyone out and sent a boy down to the village for help, then started with the water buckets, but ..." He shrugged helplessly. "So you see."

"I do," said the Post-rider. "Do you have any messages you want me to take back up the line? I'll come to Orwells within the hour."

The innkeeper, as he must be, shook his head. "I can't think straight," he said. "Tell them—by the Lady, what am I going to do?"

I recalled that I, as the (very newly discovered) local lord of St-Noire, had an obligation to assist my (hah!) villagers, including the innkeeper, in their need. "Who lives in the great house down the valley?" I asked. "Would they be able to send assistance?"

There was a silence. It was patently obvious no one expected help from that corner. "Welladay," the innkeeper said at last, "they *might* send us some food and supplies."

"Emperor knows they've got enough of it," someone else muttered.

"The Master there is—eccentric," the innkeeper said. "You're from the Coombe, you said? So you've probably heard tell of the Witch of the Woods Noirell. Well, she's got nothing on our Master Boring."

"Except for the even more eccentric young heir," the Postrider put in. "Slaying dragons he is, I hear tell. You wouldn't catch anyone at Master Boring's house doing *that*!"

Everyone guffawed at this tall tale. I decided not to mention that I was the eccentric young heir in question. Or that I was quite proud to have slain a dragon, thank you very much, all things considered. I smiled politely instead. "Oh?"

"A party of bright young things came through here a few days back," the innkeeper said. "Gone to visit the Master. My guess is that he's getting old and wants a look-see at his heir before he offs it and leaves him all his money. They're there for all Winterturn, and much joy may they all have of it!"

Whatever had happened as they passed by Finoury's Inn had not endeared them to the locals, it was clear.

"They won't take in my guests, that's for sure," he said. "Not high enough for the likes of their company, no sirrah! I've had to ask for spare beds all through the village, and that's for just my regulars. The missus and I will be in the stable with the grooms. No one else will get a look-in before the next village up."

That was, alas, clear enough. I scratched my head, wishing for my hat, and turned hopefully to the Post-rider. "Will you take a few letters north for me, sir? I was sent ahead after our cart tipped."

"Is that the slang nowadays?" the Post-rider asked genially. "Certainly. Where are they going?"

I pulled out the letters, exceedingly grateful that Hal had thought to be discreet in the address of the one to his sister. "Fillering Pool in Ronderell, and Little Finchely, east of Yrch-ester in Fiellan. Oh, and one to go back to the king's hunting lodge in the other direction—they'll need to know about the cart."

The Post-rider's eyebrows went up at this indication we'd been on a literal cart, not a carriage, but he accepted the letters from me.

"They'll not be surprised," the innkeeper said dourly. "Their carter's a drunkard in half this county's inns, I tell you."

Right. That would have been helpful to know earlier. Though likely Marcan didn't know. And anyway we were dependent on Marcan's generosity, and it would have ill behoved us to ask Jullanar Maebh to walk, after all the hard-ships we'd already put her through when she'd asked for refuge.

"A wheatear will see them on their way," the Post-rider said.

I fished in my waistcoat pocket for the change, long prac-tice at Mrs. Etaris' bookstore and at the Morrowlea student-run store letting me distinguish coins by feel. I presented him with the wheatear and a second one for his trouble.

The innkeeper had gone back to the bucket brigade. They seemed to have things well in hand, and I did not like the look of the clouds now descending from the pass. The column of smoke from the inn was drifting sideways at a sharper angle, too.

I touched my hand to an imaginary hat to the Post-rider and set off at a quicker run to return to my friends. The wind was cold on my back, and smelled of the cool, dusty, effervescent odour of coming snow. It looked like we were going to have to throw ourselves on the dubious hospitality of "Master Boring" of notable eccentricity.

CHAPTER FIVE

I found my friends sitting glumly on some rocks at the ridge overlooking the valley. I hadn't been able to see them on my return up, but evidently they had seen me.

"Tell us that isn't the inn burning like that," Mr. Dart pleaded.

I could only grimace apologetically.

"At least that those clouds betoken a storm over Ragnor Bella?"

"It could be," I replied judiciously. "I was informed it would likely hit Finoury's Inn within the next hour."

"The hour!"

"It was two hours, an hour ago," I said.

Mr. Dart looked hard at me. "You're rather complacent, Mr. Greenwing!"

"He's been running," Hal said, "and that's after his religious experience. Come now, have you come up with a cunning plan?"

I sat down on a rock beside them and stretched out my legs. "I don't know about *cunning*, but yes, I have a prospect. I was informed at the inn that all the regulars were billeted at the village there, and no room for anyone else, and that there

43

was no way we'd get safely over the pass now. The innkeeper recommended we go north and across the Crook again. You still might be able to hire a hack, Hal, as their stable was spared."

"I do thank you for the thought!"

I ignored this sally. "The Post-rider arrived shortly after I did, so I gave him our letters. We talked about the house down there, which I think is our best option for the night, as I don't fancy roughing it through a snowstorm, personally."

"Does it have a reputation for hospitality?"

"A snob's one. They call the owner Master Boring. Apparently his heir and some friends are staying for Winterturn."

"That'll be you, then," Hal said in a voice that brooked no argument. "I'm not announcing myself down here to a party of backwoods toffs if I can avoid it! You're local enough, at least, for it to make sense you're here. You can say we were visiting the Count of Westmoor at the hunting lodge and journeyed so far just as we have done. That won't be the nine-days wonder I would be."

"I am apparently already reckoned an eccentric in local gossip," I said, mostly resigned. "Very well. We should head on down, if we're all ready? It's a mile to the gates and the house, you can see, is set back."

"And that storm isn't retreating," Mr. Dart added gloomily.

We set off again. I found myself walking beside Jullanar Maebh. "I always liked the idea of a walking tour," she said, taking my arm to negotiate a steep part of the descent. "I'm not sure about the reality."

"Did Hal speak of our tour this summer?"

"A little. You came up from Morrowlea, he said?"

"Yes, up the length of West Erlingale, through northern Chare, and up Lind to Fillering Pool, though we kept to the central plains rather than these hills."

I kept talking, as she seemed to appreciate the distraction. My stories were a bit scattered, it was true, as I had been

recovering from the illness brought on by an overabundance of
wireweed and subsequent withdrawal from the drug. I could
still regale her with Hal's determination to look into every
interesting garden we passed, and Marcan's insistence that we
take in all possible tombs, chapels, and historical sites, but only
so long as they were no more than a mile's detour from the
nearest pub.

Marcan was going to be the kind of abbot or archbishop —
the second son of the king of Lind was hardly going to remain
some country vicar — of which legends were told. Hard-hunt-
ing, hard-drinking, and devout as the knight and the unicorn.

"And you?"

"I was heartbroken from the duplicitous Lark," I admitted.
"I would walk with them through the day, then when we'd
found an inn for the night, often go for a run about the countryside."

"No wonder you are so thin!"

"I prefer *lean*."

"It's true, you are too short to be a beanpole."

"I do thank you, Miss Dart!"

She laughed, then sobered. "It's so strange, being called
that. I always was Miss Ingridsdottir at Tara, and Jullanar
Maebh to my friends. We don't always take the father's name,
at home, so no one thought it odd I went by my matronymic
once they heard I was from the Outer Reaches. I never knew
anything about my father except that he was from Fiellan
somewhere and that I was something of a mistake."

"An accident, perhaps, but no mistake," I replied.

"You're most gallant, sir."

"I was there when your mother's letter came by special
messenger. There can be no doubt Master Dart was surprised,
but also that he was pleased that you thought of him in your
need."

She blushed a little and ducked her head. "Thank you."

I doffed my imaginary hat to her, and she giggled, which

suited her, and at my wistful comment that I missed the fine tricorner I'd acquired in Fillering Pool, continued all the way to the iron gates with a discussion of the haberdasheries and other amenities of her soon-to-be new home in Ragnor Bella.

～

It was a full half-mile from the gate to the house, and by the time the building finally hove into sight, it was starting to snow. They were big, wet flakes, whirling in slow spirals back up towards the clouds. I looked up at said clouds warily. They did not betoken a quick snowfall in the least. Even as I watched, the clouds entirely obscured the mountains. A flash of lighting in their depths was echoed by a double retort from the surrounding hills.

Jullanar Maebh cringed against me. I grasped at her arm again in astonishment, for she was no fainting maiden. She blushed, but clung close. "I abhor thunder," she said in a low, embarrassed voice. "I do apologize, sir."

I myself had contracted a stubborn fear of small enclosed spaces only a month ago. I hoped very much her dislike of lightning came from a more ordinary source than my amnesiac escapade, which—since it had been some form of a mystical and magical preparation for a perverse rite to do with the Dark Kings, preventing the fulfilment of which was most of the reason I had been returned to life—I was just as glad not to recall in the slightest.

We were all quickly soaked by the wet snow, and no doubt equally quickly chilled. We three gentlemen endeavoured not to show any discomfort before the lady, and the lady was so fearfully attentive to the horizontal crackles of lighting and ever-encroaching thunder that she made no mention of anything else, merely bent her head so the ostrich plumes of her hat draggled down over her copper hair.

We were sheltered from the worst of the wind by the overgrown woodland of the entrance park. Large trees, oaks with rattling dry leaves, stood at gracious spacing, their venerable lines blurred by choking brushy undergrowth as much as the snow. It couldn't have been much past noon, but as the clouds advanced overhead the temperature dropped precipitously and the light dimmed to a strange pale grey, shadowless except when the lightning flickered.

A russet flash caught my attention, and I turned my head just in time to see a fine fox go trotting past us. It turned its head as it passed and met my eyes with what seemed an uncannily *knowing* expression before leaping gracefully out of sight.

I bit my lip and turned back to the weedy gravel drive, just then noticing that at some point in the past few hundred yards one set of the ruts had disappeared. The outgoing set, from the direction of the hoof prints, had come straight down the drive, but not the incoming.

The curiosity was blown from my thoughts as we exited the woods to cross the lawns before the house. From the ridge, in the sunlight, it had seemed a pleasant, grassy mead, a fine setting for a jewel of a house. With the wind now bearing much smaller and harder snow-pellets before it at a stiff horizontal angle, I was much less enamoured of the open space. The house itself was a dim blur ahead; but it had a light burning in a window near the front door.

Hal reached it first, alongside a great crack of thunder that seemed to come from directly atop us. Jullanar Maebh sagged against me, and Mr. Dart hastened up to support her with his good arm. We got to the door just as Hal had made a fist to bang on the heavy timbers.

"No surety they'll hear the bell," he said, indicating a long pull that was swaying against the house. We huddled under the portico, which was in a classic style I didn't feel up to determining just that second, the wind howling meaningfully at our backs. There was certainly no way we would have survived a mountain crossing in this. I wasn't too sanguine of our chances, wet and unprepared as we were, in the woods. Even Hal's magic—or Mr. Dart's—would be hard pressed to keep a fire going in this wind.

Thankfully, the door opened, and we all stumbled through it before the door-keeper could make a noise of question or protest.

"I thank you, sir," I said, only to be elbowed by Mr. Dart. I caught my breath and refrained from glaring at him, then brushed off the wet flakes of snow from my shoulders as best I could. The man in front of us regarded us with a wary, jaundiced eye. Hal slammed the door shut behind us, cutting off most of the wind.

The building rang with unquiet silence. Jullanar Maebh turned her head into Mr. Dart's shoulder, and Hal stood a half-step behind me, face calm. I took another breath. We had decided I would do the talking.

The butler, or so I presumed he was—from his garb and demeanour he was clearly an ancient retainer of the tyrannical kind—stared at me with a curiously speculative expression I did not quite like.

Not that there was much choice of refuge, alas.

"We were travelling from the hunting lodge of the King of Lind to Finoury's Inn," I said by way of establishing our credentials. "Our vehicle caught a pothole and broke an axle. We left the driver to round up the horses and continued on afoot. I went ahead to see if I could bespeak a carriage at the inn, but when I arrived discovered the building was on fire."

I paused there, as the butler stirred. "Aye," he said at last. "We've had the Post-rider here and back again already."

The butler was a tall man, cadaverously thin, with striking deep-set dark eyes. His hair was all white, though his protuberant eyebrows were black, and his skin was paler than mine, yellowed like old parchment. He seemed as if he should have retired long since; his breath rattled in his lungs.

"I went back to my friends," I went on nervously, "and we

continued along, hoping that we might prevail upon your hospitality, until we were caught by the storm just by your gates."

I gestured vaguely at the rest of my party, but they were silent, half-dazed with the relative quiet after the howling gale outside, I suspected. My own extremities were tingling as they warmed up, and I dearly wished to find a fire.

"Aye," the butler said again, in a slow, ponderous manner. His eyes measured every inch of my Fiellanese winter-weight suit and the garments worn by the others. They were muddied and torn and wet, but all, I hoped, of sufficient quality to show that *we* were Quality, so to speak. It irked me that we should have had little hospitality otherwise, but now was not the moment for a democratic revolution.

Alas.

"And what names shall I give to the Master?" he enquired.

I tried not to sigh in relief. We might yet be relegated to the kitchens, or the stable-loft, but we were not being summarily ejected into the first winter storm of the season. Another crack of thunder made Jullanar cry out and cringe back to the door. Hal and Mr. Dart were attending her assiduously so I kept my focus on the butler.

"I am Jemis Greenwing of St-Noire," I said, bowing slightly. "My friends here are Mr. Dart of Dartington, also in South Fiellan, his cousin Miss Dart, and Mr. Leaveringham of Ronderell, whom I met at Morrowlea."

My friends ignored my introductions, which was odd, even with Jullanar Maebh visibly wilting as the excitement from the rush to reach the door faded, but when I looked back to the butler after gesturing at them his deep-set eyes were fixed on me.

"St-Noire, eh," the butler said slowly, with a strange expression. I watched him nervously, ready, as always, to defend my father's honour if he latched onto the far more famous *Greenwing*. After my sojourn in the Far Country it was a

49

much less painful matter than it had been before, but I couldn't say I wasn't yet wearied of the need to keep defending what had been a terrible mistake.

"It's not far over the mountains to the Coombe here," he said after another pause. He was fingering a handsome green-stone brooch he wore on his breast. It was an excellent piece for even a superior servant. "The old Marchioness is not unknown in this house. She lives yet?"

"She did a week ago," I replied. Jullanar Maebh took that moment to sneeze, which seemed to shake the butler out of his stupor even as Hal took her arm in support and Mr. Dart fished in his pocket for a dry handkerchief.

"Come, come," the butler said to me. "I'll call the maid to show you to rooms. The Master's nephew and niece are visiting with some friends, and there's plenty in storage from earlier days, so I daresay we can find you some dry clothes."

His gaze wandered up and down me again, taking in the rents and tears and numerous stains., new and old. I was sure some were of the faery islet beyond the world. "If you have none coming along behind you?"

"I've left word of our proposed direction, but the falarode couldn't take the road we'd determined to follow," I replied, I hoped suavely.

"Got your grandmother's flair, have you?" he said, with a hacking cough that put me disquietingly in mind of the former physicker of Ragnor Bella, Dominus Gleason. Or rather, the priest of the Dark Kings who had been pretending to be Dominus Gleason for seven years. I shivered, grateful that I was still near-dripping wet and therefore of ready excuse for any apparent vapours.

I realized I should have taken offence at his familiarity, but was too late to do so with any poise. "Miss Dart is in sore need of dry clothes," I said instead, meaningfully.

"Aye," he said, and rang a handbell that stood on a table beside the door with sudden vigour. Hal jumped and stared at me; I looked back on him in confusion. He shook his head and smiled crookedly, then turned back to Mr. Dart, who said something to him in a low voice I couldn't hear over the butler's croak. "Bessie! Guests!"

While we waited for Bessie to appear, and the butler stared at me with what I was determined not to read as a predatory light in his eyes (at least not until I had further acquaintance), I looked around the entry hall. It was all apiece with the butler: dusty, old, a little odd.

More than a *little* odd, to be honest.

The butler said, in a slow, drawn-out sentence, that the hall was reckoned a fine example of High Court Linder architecture, and we should take particular note of the carved panelling as we were escorted upstairs.

There was no possible way for us to see the carved panelling. Everything but the narrowest possible track was full of *stuff*.

Perhaps five feet in from the front door was a wall of papers and boxes and chests and objects, all covered in dust. A narrow track led into the dim depths between the piles, which reached above our heads. The only illumination came from glazed lights set into the ceiling, which must have been an impressive effect during ordinary daylight, when the glass was clean, and when the hall below was not so comprehensively filled. At the moment it merely emitted flashes of lightning that came through a coating of snow.

A musty, unpleasant smell filled the space, like an unaired cellar. My mind supplied unwelcome thoughts of rats and mice and other vermin. I felt yet another pang of sympathy for Jullanar Maebh. At least the thunder was not so loud indoors.

A thin middle-aged woman of faded prettiness emerged out of the gloom. "Oh!" she said on seeing us, and curtsied in confusion to me. I eyed the butler sidelong but he was merely observing us without expression. Bessie—oddly informal for someone who was surely the housekeeper, given her age, the quality of her garments, and the chatelaine of keys at her waist—went on, "I thought you meant our other guests, sorr."

She had the same burr of an accent as Clara over at the Hunting Lodge. No doubt locals could distinguish them—probably the ridge demarcated two ancient parishes, though I hadn't seen a church this direction (hidden, no doubt, with the rest of the village near Finoury's Inn)—but my ear was not so fine.

"We have new guests, Bessie," the butler said, with a surprising air of amused condescension. "The new Viscount St-Noire and his friends."

His accent, I noticed in comparison to hers, was much more refined and well-educated, hardly dissimilar from our Circle Schools-shaped ones. He sounded most like Marcan, naturally, being from Lind.

Well, it was not so long ago I would have looked on becoming a rural lord's butler as being higher than my likely fate, Morrowlea education or no.

"I see, sorr," Bessie said, looking askance at the water dripping off me. Hal and Mr. Dart were still crowded by the door, apparently trying to soothe Jullanar Maebh out of her unwanted panic. "Are they staying with us?"

"Through this storm, certainly. See to their rooms, give them baths and fires and clothes, borrowed if you must, out of storage if you can," the butler said. "I will see if the Master will receive them. He's a great eccentric," he added to me, with evident pride. "He may choose to stay secluded and rest."

With that he left us, edging sideways into the wall of *stuff* without any apparent embarrassment.

"I wish he *would* rest," Bessie muttered, almost inaudibly. She picked up a candle-lantern on the table next to the hand-bell, and stepped forward to attract my friends' attention. "Welcome to the house, sorrs, m'lady. You met with an accident, it seems?"

Mr. Dart and Hal perked up as the light fell on them. Mr. Dart said, "Yes, and lost all our belongings, I'm afraid."

"We'll see you to rights," she said comfortingly, and indicated we should follow her into the maze.

We edged along behind her. Bessie gave no indication that anything was amiss or unusual about the place. She looked back to see that we were following from time to time, smiling with an indulgent air at us.

"It is so good to see young people about the place," she said as we turned a corner and discovered a pile of tarnished brass and silver candelabras, many of them still with globs of melted wax on them. "You will enjoy meeting our other guests, I am sure. The Master's heirs and their companions. They have recently arrived for the Winterturn holidays."

"How pleasant that must be for you," Mr. Dart said weakly. He was closest to the housekeeper, myself next in line. I was watching how he kept his face resolutely forward. Mr. Dart heard the voices of the inanimate at times, and there were many, many objects.

We wound our way through the canyons of things. Papers gave way to trunks, and trunks to furniture, and furniture back to papers and books. "The Master is a great collector," Bessie said at one point, proudly, as we had turn sideways to get past a particularly bowed stack. "Why, he has entire estates sent to him to go through."

"It is remarkable," I said, nudging Mr. Dart gently. He swayed a little; even in the dim light he seemed very pale.

"The stairs are here, sorr," Bessie said at last, turning around a stack of what seemed to be years' worth of *New Salons* and revealing a beautiful wooden staircase all the more resplendent for having nothing on it whatsoever, not even a carpet runner. I took a deep, relieved breath and immediately started coughing from the dust.

"I'll show you to rooms and call on Walter. He's got a deft hand with clothes, he does. We've not many servants in the house, not like in the old days, but you'll not find our hospitality lacking."

"I shouldn't imagine so," I replied politely, wondering mightily. The *old days* were probably the glorious final years of Astandalas, when money and magic had both been abundant. At least for the upper classes.

We reached an upper hall, wooden-panelled with woven tapestries adorning the walls, parqueted wood flooring partially covered by a long deep-red carpet that ran the length of the hall.

The stair arrived near one end without any form of a landing, simply an arched opening leading to the hall. A suit of armour of a particularly impractical style, all spikes and golden inlay, stood just to one side of the arch. As I glanced around, noting that doors stood at regular intervals all down each side, I saw another suit of armour, even more extravagantly bedecked with protuberances and spikes, standing at the far end in an embrasure matching our own.

Bessie led us to the left. "The guest rooms are all along the southern wing, to catch the sun. Here we are, miss, let me just ring the bell so Hettie—she's the upstairs maid—can come assist you."

We waited awkwardly in the hall while Bessie escorted Jullanar Maebh inside. There was no opportunity to talk, and nothing much to say besides comments on the peculiarities of the house, which was hardly polite or politic when we didn't know who might be in earshot. Thankfully we were not left long before Bessie reappeared and directed us down the hall to a series of three rooms in a row.

"The Master's nephew is in here," she said, pointing to one on the right, "and his friend on that side. The Master's niece and her friend are back up by your cousin, sorr, and Mr. and Madam Veitch are in their room in the south wing. Here you are. I'll ring for Walter to come with the clean clothes while you're having your baths. We have the new copper boilers, so there's a plenty of hot water, never you fear, and well stoked they are with the Master's relations in residence."

Sweeter words have rarely been spoken! It wasn't until I was standing beside a fire—lit, and wasn't that an impressive efficiency?—untying my cravat and trying to peel off my coat, that I realized I had yet to find out the Master's real name or standing.

CHAPTER SIX

There are few things in this life quite so wonderful as sinking into a deep, old-fashioned bath, the water steaming hot, with all the soaps and unguents one could wish for, and warmed towels and clean clothes awaiting. I bathed with these delicious amenities, determined that I did not need to avail myself of the shaving equipment helpfully laid out on the table next to the mirror in the room (I may have dark hair and fair skin, but a beard does not give me shadow until the second day), and enveloped myself in a quilted dressing-gown I discovered next to the towels.

The clothes laid out for me in the dressing-room next to the bath were all clean and strongly scented of lavender. Bessie — for all that I had spent barely ten minutes with the woman — had clearly sized me up and determined the clothes I needed could come out of storage.

I sneezed a few times as I shook them out, admiring the quality of the silk-wool blend of the upper garments, the silk stockings, and the supple linen of the shirt and drawers. The undergarments were ivory, with foamy lace at the cuffs, while the coat and knee-breeches alike were of the deep, rich blue-green I suspected was called teal, after the duck, and extravagantly embroidered with what seemed to be Voonran-style floral designs in silver and silk threads. The waistcoat, in a lighter shade of teal, was even more thickly encrusted with threads and what seemed to be sequins and glass gems to catch the light.

The style was something from well before the Fall. I was grateful for a term's acting in a play set at the Astandalan court in the earliest days of the Emperor Artorin, when this was fashionable among the Alinorel nobility, as it meant I knew how to put it on. Though this was the real thing, not the facsimiles we had struggled to create as our costumes in the Sartorial Arts classes. The complexity and fineness of the embroidery said as much.

First the linen shirt and drawers. Then the breeches, which had silver buttons at the knee. The buttons were carved with what looked like thistles as the crest. Then the waistcoat, which was longer than the current style, coming down below my waist. It had a long line of buttons along the front matching the ones on the knee-breeches. I did them up carefully, noting how well they were polished. There was a faint thrum of energy around them which I took to be a spell, perhaps, keeping away the tarnish. I'd have to ask Hal to check there wasn't any sort of adverse enchantment on them.

Over the waistcoat went the long fitted coat, which flared out below my waist so the hem went to my knee. It was not meant to be worn closed, as were the coats I was used to, but instead had wide embroidered panels at the cuffs and along the full length of the lapels, with more embroidery swirling up the back from the bottom hem.

It also had a long range of fine silver buttons, larger and more dramatic than the ones on the waistcoat, the central thistles this time set with what looked like carved amethysts and peridots. The sleeves were close-cut until the wide cuffs, which were worn folded back, so the lace at the wrists fell half over the backs of my hands. There was a jabot of yet more lace to fall halfway down the waistcoat, *and* a cravat, which I tied in a complex Waterfall in honour of the great Beau of the Kingsbury Court in those days, whom the Emperor had once complimented on the nicety of his dress.

I should have been wearing buckled shoes, but it was indoors—and with the wind still rattling the windowpanes, I was hardly intending to go back outside—so the embroidered silk slippers were not entirely impractical. These matched the outfit, in the same dark teal of the coat and breeches, with silver buttons and even more complex silver-thread embroidery. As a sop to practicality they had leather soles, a little stiff with disuse but by no means uncomfortable.

Thus garbed, I brushed out my hair and plaited it back, tying it with the black ribbon I'd put on this morning, and regarded myself in the oval dressing-room mirror. It, too, was old, with wavering glass and a bronze frame, but showed me well enough.

I needed only a horsehair periwig to be a perfect example of a country gentleman of my father's generation, come to court to make my leg to the Emperor; the clothes were not of sufficient quality to suggest the Emperor would do more than nod at me from his throne. Court costume for an Imperial title would be another order above this again, and in a style utterly dissimilar, drawn from Zuni formal garb and not Alinorel styles. From all accounts the Astandalan court had relished its distinctions. The only time I had seen high court finery outside of a painting was in the vision of Hal's double on the faery islet.

I was hardly going to meet the Last Emperor, and it seemed more than a little overdressed for a country house, not to mention twenty-odd years (and the Interim) out of date, but it was what my accidental host had decided on, and I would wear it as best I could. I straightened the jabot to fall more centrally and looked around the rooms given to me.

Apart from the bath and alcove acting as a dressing room, I had been allocated a small but generously furnished bedchamber. A fourposter bed—presumably a fashion in this part of Lind—hung with soft red curtains took up an alcove between two windows, tightly closed against the wind still shrieking past them though a few draughts made the curtains inside the room sway.

A fire burned in the grate opposite the bed, with a chaise longue and a comfortable-looking wingback chair, both upholstered in crimson brocade, set beside it, each with an accompanying side table in polished walnut. A wooden desk and chair sat below one window, with a brace of lit beeswax candles on it. The desk had no drawers, but a quick investigation of a small wooden box next to the candlesticks determined it held blank paper, a quill and ink pot, and some red sealing wax. A small bookcase beside the bed was half-filled with tomes mostly running towards scandalous Ystharian novels of Imperial days and a handful of tracts on agriculture, along with one on *Legends of the Linder Mountains*, which looked intriguing.

All in all, it was a very pleasing room, and clearly denoted that the butler had agreed to my identity and status. The clothes I had been wearing were nowhere to be seen, which hopefully meant they were off being cleaned. I had nothing else, and though I was certainly more inclined to ringing for a cup of hot chocolate and sitting by the fire with the book of legends, I knew I should go down and greet my host and the other guests properly.

Before I got drawn into an account of gryphons (gryphons! But we had encountered one, on that fairy islet between the palace-prison and the hunting lodge ...), I set the book down next to the wingback chair and forced myself out the door with the plan of knocking on Mr. Dart's door, or Hal's, and inveigle them downstairs with me.

Before I got two steps out, I saw another figure down the hall. She turned at the sound of my door closing, and took a few faltering steps towards me.

"Jemis?"

I blinked, and blinked again, but it was still a young woman I knew from Morrowlea. "Hope!" I said, and then bowed. "I bid you good afternoon."

"It *is* you," she said, marvelling, and closed the distance between us. "Whatever are you doing here? And dressed in — what *is* that?"

"Taking refuge from the storm without. This is what I was given to wear while my own clothes are cleaned, my baggage being nowhere nearby. And you?"

She bit her lip and turned her head aside. "It was … difficult … at home. Anna—you remember Anna?—invited me to spend Winterturn with her, and then she and her brother were invited to her uncle's and she wanted someone here besides her maid, as his friend is a bit of a warm one …" She blushed at the slang, which was decidedly moderate—but then Hope had always been rather prim.

"I'm sure she'll be glad for your company," I said.

"Are you here by yourself?"

"No—my friend Mr. Dart, who was at Stoneybridge, and his cousin Miss Dart are with me, and Hal, too."

"*Our* Hal?" Hope said wonderingly, lifting her head then ducking it again, a blush darkening her cheeks.

I considered her for a moment. Hope was darker-skinned than Violet, though not as dark as Hal (but no one was as dark as Hal), heavy-framed and partial to fluttering pastel-coloured clothes. She was currently wearing a pale pink round gown, in the Charese fashion. She would, I thought, like the style I had seen Ariadne nev Lingarel wearing, which would accentuate her generous curves. Her eyes were a beautiful dark brown, and I always thought of her as *soft*—soft-voiced, doe-eyed, gentle of temper, kind—which made her chosen field of study, geology, all the more interesting.

Hal had always said that the natural philosophers needed to stick together against the students of literature and languages, to ground us. Since Marcan was a theologian and

Hope's roommate and friend Anna was doing something with the history of fashion, this left Hal and Hope together more often than not, laughing at our philosophical arguments and resolutely talking of practical science and pragmatic inventions.

They had always gotten on very well, and I'd thought perhaps the feelings were developing into something warmer over the last year at Morrowlea. But they'd never publicly announced anything, and Hal—

And Hal was looking for a bride who might love him and not just his title ... but of course he *was* an Imperial Duke, and therefore had a List, supplied by his Aunt Honoria, of eligible ladies. He had shown me it, a month ago in the course of our lessons in *noblesse oblige* and etiquette, and I knew there were no *Hopes* on it.

Two *Prudences*, one *Grace*, and one *Charity*, yes—we had marked them particularly, curious as to which might be the mysterious and only recently acknowledged Ironwood heiress, whose given name was a virtue, and who was, according to Hals' Aunt Honoria, a *most promising match*—but no *Hope*.

Hal had, I thought, been perhaps a little disappointed.

Hope had gone to Morrowlea and was therefore of perfectly well-educated charm and deportment, and no one could criticize her alma mater.

"Jemis?" Hope said, gently breaking into my thoughts.

"Oh! I am woolgathering. My apologies. Yes, our Hal! Mr. Dart and I—he's a friend of mine from childhood, from Ragnor Bella—were travelling back from meeting his cousin at Tara, and encountered Hal along the way. He came with us to see Marcan, and then we were going to part ways at the cross-roads just above here, him to continue north into Ronderell and the rest of us across the pass into Fiellan, when our cart overturned and we were forced to seek shelter from the storm."

There. The truth ... if decidedly not *all* the truth.

Hope gave me a puzzled look. "Cart?"

61

It was my turn to flush. Damn my too-honest tongue. "It's a rather complicated story ..."

She laughed. She had a nice laugh, too, like a cheerfully burbling stream. It countered Hal's great whoops most nicely. "It always is, with you, Jemis! I'm so glad to see you much more the thing than this spring."

"You can imagine how happy I am to *be* much more the thing! Hope—ah—we are out of Morrowlea now—"

"More's the pity," said she.

I acknowledged this with a wry nod. I, too, had loved those halcyon days away from our surnames and all their baggage and requirements.

Some of the poison of Lark's actions had been drawn out of me by my sojourn in the Wood of Spiritual Refreshment. I no longer felt quite the bitter pang, recollecting Morrowlea, as had before been the case, when knowledge of what exactly Lark had been doing to me had cast a pall over all that had gone before.

"And so?" Hope asked.

I collected myself. "Ah yes—I was wondering about your surname?"

Strangely, she blushed again and looked down. "It's Stornaway."

"Miss Stornaway? A lovely name."

She curtsied promptly, the way we had been taught by the Etiquette Master. "And may I know yours, sir?"

I bowed, with curlicues and heel-click, wishing again for my hat, and braced myself. "Jemis Greenwing, at your service."

Her reaction did not disappoint. Her large, expressive eyes went huge, and she uttered a soft gasp. "Greenwing? Truly? Oh, you poor thing!"

"My father was no traitor," I said stiffly. "And indeed, the reports of his death were a piece of the slander."

"Is—is the play true, then?"

Having visited the edges of the Lady's country, I could not now damn Jack Lindsary to hell, even rhetorically, though I *could* wish him to learn what grief he had given me and mine. I forced a smile. Hope was a close enough friend that I wanted to tell her more than the barest facts; though indeed, even the barest facts were complicated, too much so for an encounter in a hallway.

"It has truth in it, I admit. My father did return home three years after Loe to find my mother remarried and his reputation in tatters. He then disappeared, we thought dead, but it turned out only last month that he had been captured by brigands and sold into the pirate galleys a slave. He was on the ship that was captured this summer."

"So he's alive, then?"

Hope and I had spoken more than once of our shared status of orphans. She would understand what it meant to have a parent thought dead return to life. I nodded, unable to say anything, though I was sure my crooked smile spoke volumes.

Her eyes were huge with astonishment. "Oh, Jemis!" she said. "And that after this spring! What a year you've had!"

And that wasn't even the *half* of it.

~

Hope went into her room on whatever errand had brought her up in the first place, and I knocked on the door next to mine, which turned out to be Mr. Dart's.

He burst out laughing when he saw me. "You're the very model of an Artorian gentleman!" he cried. "Come in, come in, sir, and tell me all the news of the Astandalan court! What intrigues are afoot?"

I followed him into a chamber not dissimilar from mine, albeit the colour scheme was blue instead of red, and he had two wingback chairs and no chaise longue. I sat down in one and flicked my vast lacy cuffs back. "While you, sir, are a very Tulip of the Hunt!"

It was true: Jack Lindsary could hardly dress so ill, with all the fortune come from his famous play behind him. Mr. Dart wore breeches and a striped waistcoat in the Linder fashion, along with a swallow-tailed coat. So far, hardly to be accorded a second glance—until one noticed, as one could hardly avoid doing, the cut and the colours.

The breeches were dark grey and the waistcoat lemon striped with white, and the coat a severe black that called attention to the extreme tightness of the cut and the padding in the shoulders, which would be unfortunate enough except that it was entirely unnecessary for Mr. Dart's figure and thus looked even more bizarre. His white shirt had an extremely high starched collar, very much to the point; the corners were near to poking his eye out if he turned his head too quickly. His stone arm was held in a sling fashioned out of a lemon-yellow kerchief that matched the one in his breast pocket.

"You look very smart," I congratulated him.

"Go away with you, now!" he cried, his cheeks pinker than their wont. "The Master must be a scrawny sort of man, that you fit into his old clothes."

I ignored this sally, which was probably true; my borrowed clothes fit remarkably well, being only a little tight about the shoulders. "Would you like my assistance with the cravat?"

"If you would," he said, blush subsiding. "Walter, the manservant, has just gone to assist the Master's nephew. I understand it is nearly time for tea."

"How civilized of them."

"Indeed."

I had assisted any number of friends at Morrowlea with their cravats, this being the one area of fashion in which I was indisputably in the forefront, so it took little time to tie Mr. Dart's into a simple but elegant Torian Knot, which did not counteract the effect of the waistcoat nearly so much as I had hoped.

"Well, it will have to do," he said resignedly, picking at a piece of fluff on his sling. "I look the fool, Mr. Greenwing."

"We all know you not to be," I murmured soothingly. "Perhaps this is a costume borrowed from one of the other guests — imagine what *he* might be wearing to impress the Master tonight!"

"Harumph," said Mr. Dart. "I wonder who else is here."

"Two women Hal and I know from Morrowlea," I said. "Hope Stornaway and her friend Anna, who is one of the eager relations. I don't know the rest." I reflected a moment. "Nor did I ask the Master's name."

"It's boring," Mr. Dart said.

I looked askance at him. He busied himself with adjusting the sling again. "Come again? That's what the folk at Finoury's Inn *called* him."

"Boring is the name of the Master — Master Boring, to be exact. I asked Walter. The relations are his sister's, so their surname isn't that — it's Garsom, I believe, Walter said."

Garsom was the surname of our village simpleton, who with his friend Mr. Pinker was hired by the town council to pick up the litter and generally keep the place relatively tidy. "Indeed," I said, trying not to smile.

"Best to get it out of your system now," Mr. Dart advised sagely.

This was good advice, though I was interrupted in my chortling by a sharp knock on the door. Mr. Dart called out an invitation, and Hal opened the door to come in, a half-amused, half-outraged expression on his face.

"You will never guess whom I have just encountered — Jemis! How did *you* warrant that outfit?"

Hal, taller and broader than both Mr. Dart and me, wore the garb of a courtier whose heyday had been a generation again before mine. His coat, breeches, *and* waistcoat were cut from the same mustard-yellow cloth, figured all over with a scalloped or scale pattern of embroidered red thread, each scale centred with a red sequin to catch the light. His jabot was not quite so full as mine, nor was the lace at his cuffs as deep, and below his stockings (a dull red silk) he had court slippers of plain yellow.

"I look like a fool next to the two of you," Mr. Dart complained.

"*I* look like some flunky of my grandmother's," Hal retorted.

"Not many could suit that yellow," I said soothingly.

"Not many would try!"

I grinned at this sally. "Well, we can but do our best with what we are allotted. Hal, you said you encountered someone? Was it Hope?"

"Enough of your allegories, sir! I grant that you have ample reason to be spiritually moved, but this is a matter of concern."

I looked at him in disappointed confusion. "I meant that quite literally. You recall Hope, do you not, from our year at Morrowlea?"

His face flickered with a sudden pang of quickly-hidden emotion. "Oh—*Hope*! I mistook your meaning."

Perhaps I would not need to do much at all to foster this connection. I smiled at him. "Miss Stornaway, I gather, is here with her friend Anna—whose surname I neglected to determine, but may be Garsom."

He made a dismissive gesture. "No matter that. No, I encountered—" He took a deep breath and turned to face Mr. Dart squarely, to my greater confusion. "You recall a conversation we had, Mr. Dart, regarding an unpleasant experience of yours at Stoneybridge? I am distressed to say I was just now introduced to a servile excuse of a fribble by the name of Henry Coates."

Mr. Dart, never a poltroon, paled. "Hell."

CHAPTER SEVEN

"And who," I asked, carefully, "is Henry Coates?"

The fire, burning nicely in its grate, flared with a purple tinge to its flames. I tried not to let my eyes rest on it too obviously. Mr. Dart's magic was growing ever more noticeable, and while in Ragnor Bella that was a bit of a social *faux pas*, in Lind I feared it would be a more dangerous revelation than that.

Still, Hal was a trained wizard, and I felt more secure with him standing beside us. I did not think Mr. Dart would ever intentionally hurt anyone, but there were far too many stories about uncontrolled wild magic for comfort.

Angry untrained mages had been known to destroy large swathes of real estate, very often unintentionally.

Avoiding that was the whole *point* of the development of Astandalan Schooled magic.

Mr. Dart was clearly not afraid of Mr. Coates. He was, I feared, angry.

The fire spat a handful of silver sparks into the room. "He is a *crook*," Mr. Dart said in disgust. "A hanger-on and toad-eater of the filthiest kind. The sort of man you warn your daughters or sisters about, and take care never to leave alone

67

in a room together. The sort of man you warn your friends about, and take care never to leave any valuables in a room he will be in. I know all I need to know about our host's nephew's character to know that *he* is here as his guest!"

"Hope—Miss Stornaway, that is—did mention that Anna didn't like her brother's friend, and asked her here as company. She described him as a *warm one*."

"Hope did?" Hal asked in astonishment that she had used any slang at all, however mild. Then his face clouded. "The devil Anna did! Putting Hope in harm's way, all to protect herself …"

This was an intriguing line of thinking. I had very little opinion about Anna, one way or another—which was perhaps a little strange, as we'd been more or less part of the same group of friends for three years—Anna and Lark had had some sort of détente going on—but Hal, it appeared, was of a more negative opinion.

"It seems sensible of her to bring a chaperone," Mr. Dart said. "Even at her uncle's house, with her brother here, if that creature is with him."

Another flare of silver sparks. These ones hung in the air, twinkling, like the magical Winterturn decorations of our childhoods. Hal wasn't attending, but was still frowning over the idea of Hope being considered *merely* a chaperone. "Jemis, you understand," he said in appeal to me. "It's inconceivable that Hope should be so abused. Anna has her brother and uncle here as support—to bring Hope, with no one for her!"

I thought the allegorical implications quite sound, but decided neither of my friends was of a mood to discuss the theological role of the graces. "We cannot avoid this Mr. Coates," I pointed out. "And it behoves us to warn and watch over Miss Dart, who is already overset by the storm. We must not let her think we are entirely unable to provide her with appropriate assistance."

That made both of them stop their own thoughts to stare

at me. Mr. Dart uttered an incredulous laugh. "Mr. Green-wing, we have already seen her captured, kidnapped, impris-oned, escaped, witness to a death, witness to a resurrection, and overturned in a cart! She can hardly be surprised when our refuge turns out to have mysteries and strange occur-rences in it. She has made your acquaintance and knows your name."

"It's not *only* the Greenwings who have adventures," I protested.

Hal had finally noticed the sparks. He made an imperious gesture at Mr. Dart. "Look to your temper, sir. I do not fault you, not with what you have told me about your dealings with that fribble in the past, but even so. Like calls to like, when it comes to magic."

I felt a brief pang of loss. What sort of magic had I had, that I called a dragon out of the Wide Dreaming?—but it was gone, stolen and corrupted by Lark, then abnegated by myself as sacrifice to permit us to escape the Oubliette of the palace-prison of Orio City. I could feel the faint thrum of magic in enchanted objects, and no more.

That reminded me. "Hal," I said, even as Mr. Dart stared at his sparks with a combination of trepidation and wonder.

(And yet, in the dreamscape between this life and the next, when he had guarded my body through the night, he had been equally adept at wand and sword.)

"Yes?"

"Can you tell me if there's anything to be worried about with these waistcoat buttons? They struck me as having some magic about them. I think it's just to stay untarnished, but in case ..."

"In case indeed! I had not thought of such things—it used to be a matter of concern at the Astandalan court, I've been told. Enchantments, poisons, potions, seductions, all sorts of crimes and corruption." He brushed his fingers down the buttons, whispering a few words in Old Shaian I didn't quite catch. A faint white light gathered around his hands before fading again to a meaningful sparkle.

"It's an enhancement of the silver," he announced, "to sparkle and stay polished. It should also warn you of any attempted ensorcellments, by growing warm. It all seems to be well in order. Well spotted, Jemis."

"I am told that a passive sensitivity is all the magic left to me," I explained.

"Lark?" Hal asked sympathetically.

"And then I sacrificed the rest." I turned to Mr. Dart, who had managed to shoo the sparks back into the fireplace, where they foamed around the flames without dissipating. "Are you done?"

He stared at the grate. "I'm not sure I know how to do any more than that. Do you think the servants will be too frightened?"

"If you find the fire out when you return, you will know."

"I am not sure I can entirely countenance your newfound serenity, Mr. Greenwing."

"It will probably pass with time," I replied a little wistfully.

I knew better than to press him about this Mr. Coates, since he had yet to tell me about the man. I did wonder how he had come up in conversation with Hal, when the duke stayed with me in Ragnor Bella, but perhaps that would be revealed later as well.

I said, "Shall we go down to see who else is here? So far we have two women known to us from Morrowlea, and a man known to you from Stoneybridge. We just need an acquaintance of Miss Dart's from Tara to have the Three Sisters *and* the Three Rivals in one room together."

Those were two names given to our universities, rivals for the title of most prestigious university on Alinor and therefore the Nine Worlds. Tara was the oldest and usually took the claim on that point, but Morrowlea and Stoneybridge (second and third of foundation) were both arguably better in terms of academics. Certainly both were superior in terms of architecture.

"Let us see if Miss Dart is inclined to go down," said Hal, and accordingly we proceeded along to the door two of the three of us agreed was the one allotted to her. (I had not been paying much attention on the way up, having been distracted by the suits of armour, and did not gainsay them.) Mr. Dart knocked, and after a moment Jullanar Maebh answered.

She was pale and drawn, and was wearing a brown velvet housecoat. The sight of our respective outfits did put a small smile onto her face.

"I see you rejected your offering," Mr. Dart said. "Do you have the headache, cousin? We are going down, but we can certainly make your apologies if you would prefer to stay up here."

Jullanar Maebh sagged a little with relief. "Thank you," she said. "I do feel rather overcome."

"It has been a trying few days for everyone," Hal said sympathetically. "Has the maid brought you refreshments?"

"Yes, yes, I am well taken care of," she replied vaguely. "Thank you, sir. Cousin." She gave me a still-wary look. "Mr. Greenwing."

I bowed. "Miss Dart."

She shut the door, and we retraced our steps to the staircase descending into the gloomy maze filling the ground floor. "I had half-forgotten all this already," Mr. Dart said, frowning at it as we paused a few steps above the floor, trying to make sense of the narrow paths weaving through the dusty stacks.

"We came past the *New Salons* and that pile of candelabras," I said, pointing towards one path.

Hal nodded. "If that leads to the outside door, it would be logical from the architecture that the parlours would be to one side ... Which, of course, is the question."

"We should perhaps have rung for a maid to show us our way," I murmured.

Mr. Dart had tilted his head, eyes half-closed. "That way," he said, "to the left." And without further explanation set off into the maze, threading his way with certainty.

I was reminded of his ability to guide us through the streets of Tara. This made rather more sense to me, strange indeed as the idea was that the inanimate objects around us could speak to one who could hear them.

It was hard to see our way, as the lightning seemed to have passed off and the skylights in the ceiling were now fully opaque with snow and more blue than white in colour. Mr. Dart seemed to be leading us indirectly to the centre. The dust rose thickly around us but did not settle or mar our clothes. I sneezed nevertheless.

"That a clever enchantment," Hal whispered to me as we edged our way past a complicated arrangement of mahogany furniture that looked rather like an upper-class revolutionary barricade. "It's on your clothes primarily, to keep them clean. It must have been a frightfully expensive outfit."

This from an Imperial Duke, largest single landowner in the continent? I brushed my hand across the embroidered waistcoat, Crimson Lake ring tapping softly across some of the sequins. "And yours?"

"The enchantment is faltering a little on mine but I can strengthen it."

"It's such a waste for magic to be out of fashion, when all that means is the unscrupulous are using it and none of the law-abiding. I don't disregard what happened with the Fall and in the Interim, but it seems to have settled down properly now."

"Hush," said Mr. Dart from ahead of us, stopping with his good hand on the lip of a crate.

I looked at the tall pile of identical wooden crates stacked beside him. "This is all boxes of tea. There must be a serious fortune of it here, if it's still good."

"I don't think leaf tea goes off," Hal said, "not of it's been properly stored. It's like spices … in a well-sealed container they can last for years."

There must have been twelve of the three-foot-cubed crates. If they all held tea, this was a fortune indeed. One or two crates, judiciously sold, would pay to rebuild Finoury's Inn.

I looked around the large entry hall, full with teetering stacks of *things*. "There must be several fortunes over in here. And none of it being used."

Hal glanced at me as if to say, And you think it a waste that magic is out of *fashion*? But he said nothing, as Mr. Dart took a tentative step sideways, angling towards the crates of tea but focusing on something beyond them. His voice was low and a bit abstracted. "Can you see what's behind there, either of you?"

I leaned around the side of the crates, peering at the dusty shadows, but had to admit defeat. "It's too dim. I think it might be a chest? There's something glinting—perhaps the hinges."

Hal very softly said a few words in Old Shaian, conjuring a soft golden werelight. With a murmur and a flick of his hand he sent it worming behind the wooden crates. The topmost button of my waistcoat grew warm—Hal's spell, presumably.

I stepped to the side, trying to line up the gaps between the crates, and crouched down. The werelight made gentle lavender-grey shadows that moved as Hal directed the light here and there.

Behind the crates was another wooden box, this one with holes pierced around its brim. It was perhaps four feet square. The glints I had seen before were from the metal buckles on leather straps holding the lid in place. I stared at those air holes with a sinking feeling.

"There's something alive in there," Mr. Dart said, with authority.

"It's as dusty as the rest," I objected, if reluctantly. It was true: the dust was feathery and two inches thick on the box and all around it.

"It needs us," Mr. Dart said.

I looked at him thoughtfully. His voice was strained, his eyes frantic, and the air was starting to shift around us, lifting the dust in spirals like the dust we'd disturbed, and which had *fallen down undisturbed again*, in the governor's palace-prison. Hal said, "Jemis ..."

"Hold my coat," I said, shrugging off the beautiful garment and handing it to him.

"You don't *always* have to listen to him," he muttered.

I gave him a bright smile and a quirk of my eyebrows, and he subsided with a reluctant smile. "Very well. I'll hold the light for you."

"I do thank you, your —"

"Sir!"

"Mr. Leaveringham," I corrected, fairly smoothly, and was grateful for how small I was compared to either of them. It was not so difficult to climb up the stack of tea crates and down their other side, but the space between them and the box was narrow and cramped. As I descended each crate one button after another on the waistcoat started to warm.

I paused. The air was tingling. The ring on my finger was also warm, pleasantly so. I waited for a moment, closing my eyes in an attempt to feel the shape of the magic around me.

If I had not known I was in the middle of a strange country house replete with a hoard of dusty treasure, I would have thought I stood in the midst of a cool woodland, spring in every scent and touch of air. I breathed deeply. It was not yet the Lady's Wood, nor the faery magic of the islet between Orio City and Lind, but it was very certainly not Astandalan Schooled magic, nor that of the Dark Kings.

"Jemis?" Hal called softly.

"There is magic here," I said, but stepped down into the tiny piece of unoccupied floor below me. It was reassuring that the way up was unblocked and open, that a skylight, however snow-muffled, was above me. I took another breath, tasting woodland and not dust. "I don't think it is evil, though I'm not sure if it is safe."

"Wild magic," said Hal.

Which by definition was never *safe*.

Though not evil, either, for all the disquiet those accustomed to Schooled magic felt about it.

"Please, Jemis," said Mr. Dart.

I bent down and picked up the box, which was surprisingly lightweight. Something inside shifted and made a strange noise, almost like a nicker. I flinched a little, having expected— if anything could be *expected*—something like a cat. But the noise inside was not of claws or padded feet, more like scrabbling hooves.

Hooves? Had someone put a *fawn* in a box?

I lifted the box as carefully as I could, and set it on top of the crates so I could climb up after it. This accomplished, I swung my leg over the topmost crate and sat there for a moment, looking down on my friends. The werelight had come up to hover over my shoulder, illuminating them both clearly.

Mr. Dart was nearly dancing with eager impatience, like a child waiting for Winterturn morning. Hal's expression was more calculating. With my teal coat slung over his arm he looked like a very superior attendant, perhaps the high priest of some ancient Astandalan ritual.

I climbed down the stack, four crates to the ground, the box with its distressed occupant lowered down from crate to crate as I dropped down each. At the bottom I hesitated. Hal nodded at me gravely when I caught his eye.

Something was going on here at a deeper level than I had any ability to understand. My passive sensitivity to magic caught the edge of great power moving, but to what end and with what purpose I didn't know. It seemed utterly absurd that we had fallen into significance here; but it was obvious that we had.

"Open it," Mr. Dart said, his voice a bare whisper.

I set the box down on the ground and knelt by it so I could work the straps out of their buckles. Whatever was inside had stopped scrabbling, but I could hear panting coming from it. The air coming from the holes smelled sweet, like the best hay mixed with ripe strawberries. I took another deep breath and felt unaccountably relieved, as if I stood once more in the Wood of Spiritual Refreshment.

There was such eagerness to the air. It was filling with a resonance, so I could only think once more of that time Hal and I had spent the night on the roof of the campanile, woken by the morning bells shaking the world around us.

The leather was stiff, but I worked it out of the buckles eventually. One strap, two. The silver sparkles were in the air again, silver and green and gold, as if all the dust had turned to jewels. The Magarran Strid had thundered around me at the Turning of the Waters, when a gorge emptied of its water and refilled again in a torrent, and I had not been so breathless as this.

The last strap came free and flopped down. I licked dry lips, my heart thundering. The lid was snugly fitted, almost stuck. I worked at it with shaking hands. All I could think was, *This is not for me*.

Not for me, but yet I was midwife to its happening. Inexplicably, tears were forming in my eyes, and my breath was catching, and the air was full of sparkles, like fireworks caught in the moment of expansion.

With a last sharp tug, the lid finally came off. I rocked backwards, then set the lid down gently beside me as we all stared down into the box.

Inside on a bed of thistledown was a unicorn foal.

CHAPTER EIGHT

The unicorn foal was tiny and perfect. It was perhaps the size of a cat, with a pearly white coat that had lavender tinting and a tiny nub of a horn the colour of the golden pearl I had been given in strange fashion by the cook of the Faculty of Magic at Tara. Its hooves were golden, too, and were, I noted somewhere in the distant back of my mind, single like a horse's, not cloven like a deer's.

It was not otherwise that much like a horse, but clearly more like a horse than anything else. Its bones were delicate, its muzzle very slightly dished, and its mane and tail a shining silky white. But its eyes, oh, its eyes were a deep limpid black, like the Lady's Pools over the mountains in the Coombe. It was looking up at Mr. Dart, who stared down at it with his lips parted and his own eyes blue as the sky.

"That is not here for you," Hal murmured.

"No," I replied, regretfully.

The dragon had come for me, with riddles and violence and a strange treasure of honey and jade for my inheritance. I had answered its riddle, and slain it when it brought violence against my kin, and the world had closed back over its disruption like water over a falling stone. People were *astonished* by the dragon, by its existence and its slaying, but my reaction had been to offer the carcass to Morrowlea for the Scholars to study, and to learn what place in my community it had given me.

This unicorn foal, unfolding delicate legs to stand unsteadily on those golden hooves, eyes still fixed on Mr. Dart's face, was not for either Hal or I. Hal's magic was part of Schooled wizardry, tamed and orderly. Mine was gone, but it had responded well enough to Hal's teachings. Mr. Dart's, however, was a wild magic in every sense of the word.

"He will be the Lady's heir," Hal murmured very softly.

That made me snap my head away from the unicorn. "What?"

He started and lifted his hand to his mouth. "Don't repeat that!"

"*Hal,*" I whispered, more urgently.

"We will talk of it later," he said firmly. "Listen, we need to get him upstairs and away from here—who knows who will show up next? Think!"

I resented that, rather, but I obeyed. Mr. Dart had reached out his good hand for the unicorn to sniff; it responded by licking his palm with a pink tongue. He smiled at it foolishly. "Is it that way, then?" he asked out loud, and reached down to lift it out of the box that had held it. It squirmed in his grasp until it was resting its chin on his breast, its nubbin of a horn angled towards his chin. He rubbed his thumb down its nose.

"Oh, Jemis," he said, looking up at me, eyes brilliant.

"Come, Mr. Dart," I said quietly, taking him by the elbow and turning him back into the maze.

It struck me as peculiarly apposite that his given name should be Peregrine, after the Lady's knight who had saved the unicorn that was ever after the symbol of Alinor.

~

We tucked Mr. Dart back into his room, where the fireplace still overflowed with burning silver sparks, and left him to bond with the unicorn foal while Hal and I retreated into the hall to look at each other.

"So," I said.

"So," replied Hal.

We stared at each other. Our court costumes of earlier generations added to the surreality of the experience. Was it only the day before yesterday we had been captured in Orio City's notorious palace-prison? Was it only yesterday I had died of wireweed overdose and the abnegation of my magic? Was it only this morning that I had woken after being returned to life by miracle?

"Do you think," I said slowly, "that it's too early for a drink?"

Hal let out an explosive breath. "By the Emperor, *no.*"

"I can help you there," a bright, mocking voice said, and we turned to find Anna coming out of a room further down the hall. "You gentlemen seem to have turned a corner out of the past—you aren't ghosts haunting this house, are you?"

"No, thanks to the Lady," I said, sweeping her a bow of the kind we'd learned for the theatricals the term we'd worn such outfits. "Good afternoon, Anna!"

She paused doubtfully, a few yards away. "Do I know you, sir?"

I straightened, surprised, and made eye contact with Hope, who had just come out of the room behind her friend. She laughed, her cheeks flushed and her eyes sparkling with merriment. "Look again, Anna!"

We closed the few yards remaining between us, and I had the dubious gratification of seeing Anna respond to me with a shock and horror hardly less than that of Jullanar Maebh this morning, and *she* had seen me dead the night before.

I decided to ignore her reaction. It was probably due to the contretemps with Lark this spring, which had ended up with the stoning and my subsequent departure from Morrowlea convinced I had failed out at the end and lost all my friends except for Hal to boot.

"Miss Stornaway," I said, drawing Hal up beside me. "You recall Mr. Leaveringham, I imagine?"

"It is a pleasure to see you again, Mr. Lingham," Hope replied, curtseying properly. "Mr. Greenwing, Mr. Lingham, may I present Miss Garsom?"

Hal and I both bowed, even as Anna—Miss Garsom— responded with an automatic curtsey. Her colour remained high, though I really wasn't sure with what emotion.

Anna was Charese, with dark curly hair and olive-toned skin. She wore a Charese-style day dress of a soft aquamarine colour that matched my dark teal all too well. It was a pity, I thought, glancing at Hal and Hope, who were regarding each other with shy sideways glances, that their outfits clashed so terribly. Mind you, Hal's mustard-yellow-and-red would clash with almost everything.

"I think," said Anna, putting her hand on my arm, "that it is entirely time for a drink. Shall we go down?"

"Please," I said, though I wondered what reason she could have for it. "Would you guide us? We came unexpectedly on the house and are unfamiliar with its ways."

"My uncle *is* old-fashioned, albeit not perhaps to the extent of your clothing," Anna agreed.

"Our baggage is behind us,"—somewhere, anyway— "and our host kindly offered us the loan while ours was cleaned. We had an upset with our, er, carriage, and then were caught in the storm."

"It is a fearsome one," Anna said, shuddering. She led me past the staircase we had taken earlier and around the corner of the building. "No, not down there. You may have noted that my uncle is a great collector."

"It is hard to miss."

She giggled and patted me on the arm. "You are a card, Jemis! Mr. Greenwing, that is. Now, we go through here and down this stair—yes, that's so."

She led us to the stair guarded by the fantastic suit of armour. It was not so beautiful as the one we'd come upstairs by, but not a servant's back stair, either. At the bottom was a blessedly uncluttered short hallway with several doors along each side. The one at the end looked as if it might lead outside, given the heavy bar across it, and I made note of its location. Who knew what further trouble might arrive unexpectedly!

"Hope and I are here with my brother and his friend." Her voice soured at this reference to Henry Coates, whom she apparently liked as little as Mr. Dart did. "My cousin and his wife are here also. My uncle invited us for Winterturn."

"That will be nice—to have your family together," I suggested, thinking of how much I was looking forward to the time spent with my father, and with the Darts—all the Darts—too.

Anna, like Mr. Dart, was an orphan of the Fall, her parents lost travelling on their way to or from Astandalas the Golden. She frowned. "My uncle is devoted to the idea of family, more perhaps than the reality. He has retreated in confusion to the solitude of his chambers."

"Ah," I said, adding this to the reputations for snobbishness and eccentricity I'd already been given.

"We all gather in this wing—the dining room is to the left, there, and there is a billiards table in the library, there, and and a front parlour, here, which connects to the dining room as well. I'm afraid the back parlour isn't usable at the moment—a problem with the chimney, I believe—but I hope you will not be offended with just the one."

"I'm sure we can make do," I replied, not mentioning that I was currently residing in a flat above the bookstore where I worked. Although I suspected Hope would find it intriguing, Anna would not find that either amusing or appropriate.

She opened the door onto a pleasantly appointed room. It was more cluttered than was to my taste, but with a relatively ordinary quantity of furnishings, nothing like the maze of objects in the main hall. The only concession to that desire to accumulate showed in layers of carpets on the floor and some coy stacks of books and boxes in the corners, which had been disguised as end tables by means of setting oil lanterns on trays atop them, and the prodigious quantity of paintings and other items hung on the walls.

I surveyed the room cautiously. The air was heavy and warm, with a fire blazing hot in two fireplaces, one on each side wall. This seemed a very strange architectural feature when I realized there was a pass-through on each, and that there was a shared chimney and grate with the rooms next over. Wood was stacked in elaborately carved wooden holders next to each andiron, which were themselves in the shape of elongated gryphons.

There were half a dozen seats of varying shapes, sizes, and periods, most from well before the Fall; Hal and my outfits matched tolerably well. They were mostly upholstered in dull gold and crimson velvets, faded but still elegant.

The floor was soft underfoot due to layers of multicoloured carpets piled in rich profusion. I didn't recognize any of their styles, which suggested they had been imported from somewhere from far away during Imperial times. They could have come from the non-Astandalan parts of Alinor or Zunidh or Voonra or even farther away for all I knew, even half-legendary Kaphyrn or Daun.

The walls were covered in an old, faded damask fabric, wide stripes of a blurry floral pattern in two shades of pink, or at least what you could see of it between all the many, many paintings, etchings, and odd artefacts and weapons from a wide variety of cultures. Most of the portraits were not particularly good, but there was enough common features to suggest that the family had been much more extensive in the past.

I eyed a collection of daggers—long, short, pointed, wavy-edged, with handles of wood or ivory or steel or leather—that went up between two very ancient and lovely tapestries depicting incidents in the tale of the Knight and the Unicorn. That ... was a strange coincidence, if coincidence it was. It was hard to believe in coincidences after my sojourn in the afterlife, even if it had been clear, then, that our choices were free and consequential.

The ceilings were high and plastered, and there were only two windows, on the far wall opposite the entry. These were hung with heavy curtains, already drawn against the storm, but the sleet or snow pellets rattling against the outside was quite audible. The curtains were a deep crimson, almost new, and by far the brightest colour in the room, drawing the eye like a splash of blood.

There were three gentlemen in the room, if one could judge by their dress (and one *usually* can, of course). Two were about our age, the third at least a decade and a half older. They were all large men, bigger in every dimension than either Hal or Mr. Dart; our borrowed clothes had not come from any of them.

This was additionally curious given the fact that both the young men wore coats of exaggerated tailoring, bright of waistcoat and black of coat and collars of the highest points. Mr. Dart would visually fit right in with their company. I would be willing to bet they also possessed driving coats of an excessive number of shoulder capes and horses that were flashier than their substance.

No, that was unfair. It was quite possible they were better judges of horseflesh than haberdashery.

All three had stood when we entered, no doubt expecting the ladies. On seeing Hal and me, the eldest set down a broadsheet, the second a book. The third and apparently youngest seemed to have been staring into a cup, for he set something down on a side table with a click, and all I could see before he shifted to look at us was a porcelain demitasse and saucer.

"Good afternoon," said the older man. He had a deep voice, rather attractive in its way, as was his person, which was comfortably ruddy and full-fleshed with excessive love of food and drink if I did not mistake my mark. He had a genial expression and a pleasant smile that did not quite reach his eyes.

"Good afternoon," I replied, inclining my head. A heavy gust of wind rattled the windowpanes behind him, but never mind that. We were warm and indoors, and despite the niggling disquiet I felt knowing the fate of Finoury's Inn, all any of us could do was our best with what lot we were given.

"My uncle was not expecting other visitors, I had thought," the man said, with a faint frown. His eyes were on our fantastically inappropriate garments, though, so his confusion was not untoward.

"We were caught out by the storm," I explained yet again, "and our host in his kindness loaned us these garments while ours are being seen to. Our luggage was behind us."

"I see," he replied, his expression lightening.

"May we know your names?" the younger of the other two men asked. His voice was medium-toned in all respects, neither pleasant nor unpleasant, educated without being mellifluous.

I looked at them. Unlike the brown-haired and pale (albeit rubicund) older man, these were both olive-skinned and dark-haired. The speaker looked enough like Anna to be her brother, with the same aquiline nose, thick dark brows, and slight pinch to the lips. He had wide shoulders and a thick neck, and legs like tree trunks; though he was only a few inches taller than I he probably weighed nearly twice as much. A pugilist, I guessed, from the musculature.

His friend, presumably Henry Coates of ill repute, was more massive yet. He was not quite so big as the Honourable Rag back home in Ragnor Bella, who was six feet tall and nearly as wide, but Mr. Coates could hardly be lacking more than six inches in either direction.

I eyed the distribution of his muscles the way Dominus Lukel, the fencing master at Morrowlea, had taught me. Pugilism again, and my guess was that he'd consider himself a crack hand with the whip as well. A high-perch phaeton would be his vehicle of choice, I reckoned, and paid out of someone else's money if Mr. Dart's dislike was well-founded.

(It struck me as quite likely that someone whose magic called forth a unicorn foal, of all things, was probably to be trusted when it came to judgments of character. Not that I hadn't long since thought highly of Mr. Dart's judgment in any case.)

"Jemis Greenwing," I said, bowing with a few extravagances. "This is my friend Hal Leaveringham. We were fellow students of Miss Stornaway and Miss Garsom at Morrowlea."

"Were you now?" Mr. Garsom said, apparently ignorant of my name. His eyes were on his sister, who was still holding my arm in a hot grip.

The older gentleman looked down at the broadsheet he had set aside with a strangulated oath of astonishment. Mr. Coates also obviously knew all the rumours, for he appraised me with a calculating air.

The older gentleman cried out, "Jemis Greenwing? The new Viscount St-Noire! Come here, come here, sir,—my lord, that is—and tell me all about this dragon you're said to have slain! I can hardly express my astonishment."

Anna—Miss Garsom—dragged me across the room. "Cousin Veitch," said she, with a titter, "surely we had agreed that the dragon was only a story?"

"It says right here in the *New Salon* that the carcass has been donated to Morrowlea."

"Ah, yes, the Chancellor came and took possession of it," I said weakly, with a plaintive glance back at Hal, who had settled himself on the settee a proper distance from Hope, in the chair next over, and was regarding the proceedings with amusement.

Mr. Veitch, as appeared to be older man's name, gleefully interrogated me on all the points in the paper, which were far more effusive and speculative than I really could like, given the fact that I knew that Jack Lindsay was writing a sequel to his hit play *Three Years Gone* (about the ill-fated return of my father after Loe) that largely featured these escapades.

Lindsary was, alas, a very talented playwright, and morally unscrupulous to boot. He had boasted that what his audience wanted was salacious gossip done up in pretty words, needing only just enough truth to justifiably leaven the lot; and since *Three Years Gone* had been a hit across half the continent, he was probably right.

Given the sensationalism of the account in *The New Salon*, I could hardly bear to imagine what would come of *The Runner Run*. If Mr. Veitch and Anna and her brother were any example of the audience, it was likely to be even more successful.

"So is it *true*," simpered Anna, "that you killed the dragon with a teaspoon?"

CHAPTER NINE

There are worse places to be storm-stayed than an eccentric country gentleman's even more eccentric country house; even with other guests.

Even these.

By the time we had been served with coffee, I was fully in agreement with everyone's dislike of Mr. Coates.

It did not take more than a few minutes of questioning on the part of Mr. Veitch to elicit the particulars of the Viscountcy, namely that it was an Imperial title, that it meant I was heir to the Marquisate of the Woods Noirell, and that it was the next-most prestigious title remaining to Northwest Oriole after the Imperial Dukedom of Fillering Pool.

It did not take much longer than that for both Coates and Garsom to decide that I was therefore to be buttered-up. Miss Garsom, who had known me for three years, egged them on. I had never experienced such blatant obsequiousness before, and did not much like it.

They asked if I were warm enough, and rang for a servant to build up the fire when I did not disclaim a desire for this quickly enough. They decided that the chair I had initially taken was insufficiently grand, and insisted I remove myself to one that was (I can admit it) more aesthetically pleasing, the dull gold velvet brocade a better match in colour and style to my antiquated garments; if decidedly less comfortable than the later and less stylish furniture I had chosen. They enquired after my horses, and did not believe me when I said I kept no stable. They asked after my carriage, and sniggered gleefully when I described my grandmother's falarode.

Suffice it to say, if there had been any sign of an ally but for the sulky-looking Bessie, who brought in coffee and mended both fires without meeting anyone's eye (and why was the housekeeper herself doing so?) I would have begun canvassing for a democratic revolution then and there. Western Lind seemed ripe for it.

Though both Coates and Garsom were from Chare, as they made haste to tell me.

I wished Anna had made good of her promise to find us a drink, but the coffee tray was all we were offered.

"And wh—*achoo*, excuse me," I said, sneezing at a gust of smoke from one of the fireplaces—"did you attend university, Coates?" I realized a moment later this was an unwarrantedly severe insult due to the sneeze that had covered the *where*. Hal covered a snicker with a hastily-raised hand.

Coates flushed, eyes flashing with anger, though he didn't rise to the inadvertent bait. "Certainly. I went to Tormont."

I managed to *not* ask where Tormont was located, and thus imply it was too inconsequential to be known. I knew that he had some connection with Stoneybridge, and that the town of Stoneybridge was centre of a network of small universities that played many sports and held other competitions with each other.

The University of Stoneybridge itself was the most prestigious, of course, but it hardly the only school of repute, even if I couldn't recall the names of any besides Birckhall and

Carran. It wasn't as if I had any memorized below the Circle Sisters and the first few of the Golden List.

I was saved from giving further insult by Garsom saying proudly, "I went to Stoneybridge, myself. Coates and I met at Gentleman Sam's. Boxing, you know. It's all the rage in Chare."

"Lord St-Noire was always partial to fencing," Anna put in, with another simper. "Quite the favourite of the fencing master at Morrowlea."

"Fencing is a bit out of the way," Garsom said doubtfully, then hastened to add, "but of course, perhaps your influence will bring it back into fashion. Dragon-slaying, what!"

"What, indeed," I murmured dryly, wishing Mr. Dart would finish communing with the unicorn and come down to help deflect conversation. Then I recalled that he was no friend of Coates' and didn't know whether to hope for his appearance or not. But at least any insults would be on-purpose if he came down.

Hal and Hope, who neither of them had been particularly keen on the art of defence (although Hal was good at polo, and Hope a surprisingly excellent archer, almost as good as Red Myrta who was, I had learned last month, the daughter of a bandit chieftainess), were both trying hard not to laugh outright now, and were of no assistance whatsoever. The fact that Hal undoubtedly had all the experience possible with this sort of thing, and was even more undoubtedly enjoying not being the focus of it, was—well, it was irksome, but I really couldn't blame him.

I smiled as winningly as I could at the two pugilists and tried to change the subject. "What did you study, Garsom? Coates?"

"Mathematics," the latter said laconically. That was interesting. He did not look the kind of man to be at all interested in such an abstract subject. I considered boxing, that he was a *warm one*, and reflected that Mathematics covered Statistics, which would probably be of great use to someone who made his way by calculating odds.

"I'm in second year, reading Economics," Garsom put in.

Perhaps I could get them talking about themselves. "Indeed? How did that spring your interest? Do you have a family connection in trade?"

Garsom reared back in affront. "Certainly not, sir! Our family goes back before the land-grants when the Empire came to Chare. We need not sully ourselves with *trade*. The thought, indeed, that we need to make use of those who are desecrating our ancient assemblies with their so-called modern ideas about the distribution of wealth—"

He continued on in this vein for some time. Coates's eyes were flashing again, but he put a smirk on his face to disguise his anger. Hope shrank into herself, dark cheeks flushed with embarrassed outrage, from which I deduced both of their families came from a mercantile background.

Hal smiled gently at her, as if to say *he* didn't mind if she came from that background. I wondered if the Duke Imperial part of him was a bit chagrinned at the thought.

Mr. Veitch was nodding in agreement with his cousin's words, though his eyes kept straying back to the *New Salon*, and he made no attempt to interrupt either to add or deny any points. Anna simpered as if she didn't have a thought in her head, which—as I knew perfectly well she was sharp as a tack, and having gone to Morrowlea, not entirely without a social conscience—was deeply irritating.

Finally Garsom came towards the end of his little speech. I might have ignored it, since we were imposing on the hospitality that was only offered us because of our rank, but it went against all of my personal and political opinions. And at the end, Garsom said, "Surely you understand, sir! We must stand our guard against the encroachments of these—these—these *interlopers*. They think themselves our equals, and what are they? What are their people? No one of repute! I don't think they should be permitted to go to the Circle Schools."

I regarded him with dislike. "I believe that goes against the ancient Charter of the Universities, which was always intended to give places to the deserving from all walks of life. That is the whole point behind the scholarships granted to the top placements in the Entrance Examinations."

Garsom spluttered. "Well, perhaps it isn't so bad for them to learn proper manners, so they don't embarrass themselves in society, but for them to feel as if they *belong —*"

I was not far from my sojourn in the afterlife, and I had loved my stepfather, and was still grateful to the merchants of Ragnor Bella—who were several steps down the hierarchy from the great merchant princes Garsom was so concerned about—for their welcome, when all the gentry save Mr. Dart were uncomfortably but resolutely setting me into my new place outside their ranks.

To *hell* with this snobbery. It did no one any good at all.

"I must disagree with you, sir. My stepfather was a merchant of Chare—Benneret Buchance his name, and I am sure you have been recipient of the benefit of his inventions, though you may not know it—and he was a very good man."

Garsom tried to recoup. "There may be worthy *individuals*, I grant you —"

"As indeed there *may be* in every class and every society," I replied, with what was probably a sharp grimace rather than a smile. "My accession to the viscountcy is very recent, and the estate of my stepfather, who died this summer, was in probate until the Assizes began a week ago. I spent the autumn working as a clerk in a bookstore, and let me tell you, *Mr.* Garsom, I was grateful for the work and for those few who looked at my character and not the fact of my employment."

It was on that note that the dressing gong rang, which I'm sure we were all grateful put a halt to the conversation; but I did see that Hope had a fiercely gratified light in her eyes and Henry Coates was looking worryingly thoughtful.

~

Neither Hal nor I had any other clean clothes to change into, so we stayed in the parlour reading the *New Salon* (Hal, stating that it would be for the best if I let him read it first) and Henry Coates' book (*The Peerage of Lind*, interestingly enough, with a smudged fingerprint on page before *Boring of Hillend Towers*, which unmellifluous name was presumably that of our host). I wanted to talk about Mr. Dart and the unicorn and what Hal thought this meant, but he refused to do so downstairs, where anyone might hear us.

Instead, Hal learned that I was, apparently, not merely eccentric; that I was, in fact, "more than somewhat erratic, albeit deeply interesting."

"I shouldn't worry too much," he said soothingly. "You've inherited both your father's *and* your maternal grandmother's reputations, after all."

"Thank you!"

I, on the other hand, learned from *The Peerage of Lind* that Master Boring's given name was Richard, and that he had been predeceased by his wife and all four sons: one in an mountain-climbing accident, one in a naval battle past the Outer Reaches, one to a mysterious illness, and one as a soldier at Loe, which meant he was one of the many comrades of my father to suffer from the betrayal there.

Master Boring had three sisters, all also deceased, whose surviving descendants were the two Garsom children (Anna's full name was Anna-Marigold, apparently; her brother's was Edmund) and Violetta Zavour Veitch, who was married to the Mr. Veitch I had met. It seemed a terrible run of ill-luck to lose so many of the family in the space of three generations. I could well believe Anna's claim that her uncle was fiercely devoted to the idea of family.

About the only other point of interest was that despite the great antiquity of the family (which indeed did go back to pre-Astandalan days, and might even have been as ancient as the Darts on our side of the mountains), the estate was not entailed. No wonder, Hal and I agreed, that the three prospective heirs had all made haste to join their uncle for the holiday.

Hal disappeared to make use of the facilities. I gave up on the peerage and poked around the room for a few minutes, admiring the weaponry displayed on the wall. An array of knives caught my attention, particularly a stiletto dagger with a narrow half-inch blade and a needle-like point. It was from the disputed baronies south of Chare, unless I missed my guess, and looked designed for wicked deeds done in the dark of night.

I tried to lift it off the wall, but my waistcoat buttons warmed abruptly, and I halted with my hand an inch from the hilt.

"Only family or those the Master permits can lift the weapons," the butler said, startling me.

"Oh, indeed?" I managed weakly.

"Aye," he said, extending the word with a kind of aesthetic appreciation in the sound. "There was a death that could have been avoided …"

"Oh?"

"Aye. The Master asked your grandmother for an enchantment to forestall any more mischief."

We pondered this for a moment. Then the butler, with a bizarrely impish look in his eyes, added, "Pity the enchantment doesn't work on family. Always a weakness of hers, I fear."

That seemed pointed. I decided to change the subject, and thanked him for the loan of the clothing and the general hospitality.

"After the sudden snowstorm, it was a great relief to be inside," I went on. "I particularly appreciated the bath."

"You are welcome," he said. He eyed me with a certain dignified favour, the impish glint extinguished from sight. "You carry your clothes well, young sir."

"They are beautiful," I replied honestly, running a hand down the embroidered waistcoat. My ring caught against one of the silver buttons; both warmed slightly as they touched.

The butler gave me an austere smile. "I have a Inarkios red from the last year of Artorin Damara's reign—one of the classic years, if you are a connoisseur?"

"I have only begun my education," I said regretfully. "I shouldn't wish you to waste it—though I believe Mr. Leaveringham has a well-educated palate."

"To know your limits is a rare thing," the butler intoned, and wafted off without further comment.

The wine he brought us was superb. On his return, Hal said it was almost certainly the Inarkios, despite or perhaps because of my comments; even to Hal, who obviously was indeed well-educated in all the delicacies of the continent, it was a rare vintage. I could hardly feel anything but pleased with myself for having somehow made a friend of the butler rather than the heir.

Heirs, rather. And wasn't *that* a recipe for mischief!

Jullanar Maebh and Mr. Dart appeared for supper, though Master Boring sent his regrets for his indisposition by way of Bessie.

"He's been *indisposed* all week," Anna explained, pouting even while trying to smile saccharinely up at me. Her dramatic skills were not quite up to this challenge. "We had an audience when we first arrived, Ned and I did, and Cousin Violetta too. He was all wrapped up in blankets and scarves and a cap, and that before this storm! Uncle hasn't been well at all, I'm afraid."

"Why we're here," her brother said, then hastily added, "to keep him company over Winterturn, I mean! Not—nothing to worry about. He's not so ill as that, Cousin Veritus says."

Garsom's tone was perhaps a trifle disappointed.

"Don't be ghoulish," Anna said sharply, then giggled as if to say she hadn't meant it, really, though her hands—she was using both—clenched on my arm. She was even shorter than me, so I looked down at her somewhat excessively elaborate coiffure and wondered how she could possibly think this the way to my heart. Lark's dupe I might have been, but did she think me so undiscerning and unreceptive to feminine intellect?

Mr. Veitch—Veritus Veitch, really? And his wife was Violetta? And here I'd thought being named for a racehorse occasionally difficult to bear!—said easily, "Now, now, dear cousin, there's no need for harsh words. I'm sure Ned didn't mean anything by it."

"Of course not, he never does," Coates said in a low voice, coming up to stand on my other side as we waited for the rest to arrive. Jullanar Maebh appeared first, in a blue-grey gown that accentuated her northern fairness and her copper hair. I thought she seemed even paler than her wont, but she was composed as she entered the room and greeted me.

"Now there's a fine piece," Coates said, *sotto voce*, as Jullanar Maebh curtsied to the room in general. I disdained a reply, as it was rude but not quite something to quarrel over. If he repeated anything similar more loudly I would say something, I decided, and stepped forward away from him to make the introductions instead.

"Miss Dart, lately of Tara," I said. "May I present Mr. Veitch; Mr. Garsom of Stoneybridge and his sister Miss Garsom, lately of Morrowlea; Miss Stornaway, likewise; and Mr. Coates, who attended Tormont."

And I'd just insulted him again, with the implication that he had attended, but not *graduated*, the university. It wasn't intentional; but Hope was looking up at Hal with such a shy smile my thoughts went straight out of my head.

Coates gave me a narrow-eyed, unpleasant glare, but said nothing audible across the room. Jullanar Maebh curtsied again politely, smiling with an unexceptional manner at everyone. "I apologize for my absence this afternoon," she said quietly. "I had the headache."

"No need to apologize, miss!" Mr. Veitch said jovially. "What a storm to be caught in! Give anyone the headache! Ah! There's my good mistress now. And who's this behind her? A likely-looking lad, isn't he! Entirely to the point!" He laughed roundly, patting his belly with mirth, even as his wife shook her head with a fond smile and came over to him, leaving Mr. Dart to enter in his too-tight and trying-too-hard garments.

I was on the other side of the room, and despite the two fireplaces and the candle-lanterns the subtler details of his expression were not clear. Mr. Dart was as reserved as Jullanar Maebh, and quite nearly as pale, but his shoulders were back and his posture confident, even easy. I wished I were close enough to see his eyes, and what expression there might be after an hour or two spent with a unicorn foal.

Ned Garsom said, "I say! It's the glory of Stoneybridge! Henry, do you recall Mr. Dart from History—what an *honour*, sir, an honour! You were all the talk of the university. What brings you here?"

"I was travelling with, er, Lord St-Noire, there," Mr. Dart said, giving me a sharp glance. He sounded entirely as usual, which was almost disconcerting. "We're friends from childhood, and went to Orio City together to meet my cousin and convey her home. I hope you are well, cousin?" he added to Jullanar Maebh, who murmured a polite nothing in response. I was sorry to see her so withdrawn and reserved, when she had been the queenly centre of her own group of friends at Tara.

Garsom made the introductions this time round, with a puppy-dog enthusiasm and an apparent total lack of awareness that Henry Coates, next to me, was seething with quiet, inexplicable fury. Before we could have any further conversation, the dinner-gong rang, and we filed through into the dining room behind Mr. Veitch and his wife.

(*Madam* Veitch, apparently, though we weren't informed what the title was supposed to signify. Surely it wasn't being used in the most common, if euphemistic, sense?)

The dining room shared one of the pass-through fireplaces with the parlour. It was similarly furnished to that room, though here the colours ran to a gloomy bottle-green. The walls were almost entirely covered in paintings and etchings, most of which were boring—or I should say, dull—on first sight. The persons depicted might have been Borings of one sort of another.

The portraits were interspersed not with weapons but with strange wooden masks and glass display boxes containing enormous insects, mostly butterflies and dragonflies, all of them bigger than my outstretched hand. Directly across from my seat was a monstrous ten-inch butterfly the iridescent blue of a kingfisher.

Mr. Veitch, as the oldest present, took the head of the table, with Ned Garsom at the foot. There weren't quite enough ladies to permit a strict alternation, but Bessie, who seemed to have taken over for the butler for reasons I didn't know enough about Linder customs to be sure of, directed us to our seats with a firm air. Jullanar Maebh was on Mr. Veitch's right hand, with myself next to her and Anna Garsom on my right, with Coates between her and her brother. Opposite him was Mr. Dart, which at least gave him elbow room to use his left hand; Madam Veitch was next, and then Hal opposite me with Hope beside him and next to Mr. Veitch.

The table itself was a large mahogany oval, gleamingly polished and set with silver epergnes full of fruit, silver candelabras with blazing wax candles, and elaborately sculpted silver, glass, and enamel salt cellars. The collecting habit came out in the salt cellars; there must have been one for each of us, each in a different style. I recalled from some reading for the course covering "Etiquette at all Levels" that salt corroded silver, which was the reason for the enamel or glass dishes.

Mine was in the shape of a sinuous dragon coiled about a jade basin. It did not look anything like the dragon I had faced at the Dartington Harvest Fair; it didn't even have wings, just elaborate finlike protuberances and long whiskers. I glanced down the table, but made nothing out of the fact that Jullanar Maebh's was in the shape of a mermaid, and Anna's to my right in the form of a sea-god holding a triton. I couldn't see anyone else's for the bowls of quinces and apples and pears running down the middle of the table.

We settled ourselves and waited. Madam Veitch made meaningful gestures with her head at her husband, who stared at her in bafflement an amusing length of time before grunting in sudden realization. He then spoke the traditional short grace before a meal, calling on the Lady's protection through this storm and into her season as Lady of Winter.

We all murmured the appropriate responses. A male servant appeared and served us all wine. I watched him moving around the table, his motions a little unpracticed. I hadn't seen him before and wondered if this were the Walter who had assisted with clothing or if the household staff was larger than the state of the rooms indicated.

A butler, a housekeeper, a maid and a man of all work … that was little enough for a small house, though nearly all that would have been needed in Astandalan days when magic made up the slack. This was not a small house, even if the majority of the ground floor was unusable because of the collections stacked there. Presumably there was someone in the kitchen, a cook and a scullery maid at the least. And probably the indisposed Master Boring had a servant to take care of his needs, especially if he were infirm.

The manservant wore neat but not fine clothes. He and a younger maidservant served the dishes in what I assumed was the Linder manner, as it was not quite what we did in Fiellan, nor what was done in the old Astandalan style (with half a dozen liveried footmen and maids for each course; there had been that ill-fated dinner party in September which I had attended in disguise as one such footman). The dishes were neither served from the table nor each course as its own remove. Instead we were all given our meals already plated, each under a domed silver lid. It was like being at a rather odd hotel.

The food was good but more towards the peasant end of the culinary spectrum than the house suggested: venison steaks in a port and redcurrant sauce and delicate herb-flecked dumplings, along with some form of boiled green florets I didn't recognize but quite liked. The wine was not as good as what Hal and I had been served beforehand, but generously poured and not undrinkable.

Conversation was desultory, at least until Madam Veitch said to Mr. Dart, in an unfortunately strident voice, "Did you need some assistance there, dear? I hadn't realized you had a broken arm!"

We all focused on Mr. Dart, who was regarding his venison steak with a thoughtful air. He looked up and saw us watching, particularly Coates who had barely schooled his face from a twisted delight in his infirmity. He turned to Madam Veitch and smiled at her with a disarmingly winsome expression.

"I do thank you for the thought, ma'am! You do not need to trouble yourself, however."

And with that he tapped his fork on the rim of the plate. The porcelain rang with a tuneful chime that seemed impossible to have been elicited even by a silver fork. I couldn't see over the quinces and whatnot to know what had happened, but Madam Veitch and Ned Garsom both exclaimed in shock.

Mr. Dart smiled guilelessly at them. "Do I surprise you? You know, I trust, that there is no need to fear magic any longer."

"It—it is hardly in fashion," Madam Veitch managed, in a shaky voice.

"It will be," Mr. Dart replied imperturbably, and lifted a neatly sized forkful of venison to his mouth.

CHAPTER TEN

"Are you mad?" Hal hissed with an overwrought emotion that was for once not directed at me. "You saw Marcan's reaction yesterday—you could hardly expect better here!"

We had retreated as soon as was at all polite to our own rooms, only to reconvene as soon as no one seemed about in Mr. Dart's room. None of the others staying in the house seemed at all put out by our extremely early retirement. Jullanar Maebh and Madam Veitch had both claimed the headache, and Anna and Hope had disappeared upstairs together as well, leaving the jovial Mr. Veitch, the already half-drunk Ned Garsom, and the odious Henry Coates to take themselves and a large flagon of port to the billiards room.

Mr. Dart's room was warmer than the rest of the house. The fire was still going strong, albeit not, it appeared, with any fresh wood to assist in the burning. The silver sparks had increased in number, and now frothed out onto the hearth.

They didn't seem inclined to burn anything. Indeed, the unicorn was laying fast asleep in the midst of the outpouring. It lay on its side, legs stretched out straight, mane and tail and sparks fluttering a little in the occasional draft making it through the curtains.

"Ballory told me not to be a fool," Mr. Dart said, beaming down at the unicorn foal and then sitting down next to it on the hearth.

"Ballory did," Hal said flatly. I poured him a glass of wine, which he took with an absent air and a frowning countenance.

I had encountered the butler on my way down the hall from my own room, whither I had returned to use the facilities and hide the *New Salon* I had managed to abstract from the parlour on my exit from the dining room, as they shared a door as well as a fireplace. He had given me a sly, knowing look, a basket of fragrant quinces, and three bottles of wine.

I didn't know what to make of the butler, but I wasn't about to say no to the wine. The corks were sealed in wax and the buttons on my waistcoat did not warm until I entered Mr. Dart's room, and that was good enough for me. I had no idea what the quinces were for, but they did have a lovely scent. I set them on the side table along with the spare wine.

"Ballory's the name of the unicorn, then?" I asked, pouring Mr. Dart and myself a full goblet. The goblets had come from an antique cupboard ("Pre-Astandalan Linder work," the butler had informed me; "the goblets are early Dangora XIV from Ysthar, do note the swirls of white bubbles in the glass") and were, according to Hal, priceless.

"Yes, that's what she said."

"What she—no. Just, no," said Hal, sitting down on one wingback chair. "Jemis, please, surely you can speak some sense into your friend? It's one thing to *find* a unicorn, it's quite another to ..."

I regarded him with amusement as he trailed off.

"Oh, for the Emperor's sake give me the wine," Hal said petulantly. "How is your life always like this?"

"It's not *my* unicorn," I replied, passing him the bottle and sitting down in the other chair.

"Dear Lady, you're enjoying this."

I didn't deny this. "One, it's magnificently strange and

wonderful, and two, for once it's not happening to me. Mr. Dart—"

"Mr. Greenwing! You may call me Peregrine, you know, Jemis."

I was astonished. "But you hate that name."

Mr. Dart stared at me. "You gave me a message from my deceased parents and the *Lady Herself* about it."

"Did I? Er, I don't recall. I know I joked with your mother about it, because I was laughing with *my* mother about my name, but after that ... I know I had messages but I don't remember them. They're hardly *mine* to know."

This distracted both of my friends for a moment. "You mean you don't recall what you told me from my father?" Hal demanded, even as Mr. Dart leaned back against the fireplace surround with a stunned look. "You don't recall *any* of that conversation?"

"Er, no," I replied. "Sorry?"

"I was sure ..." Hal looked down. "I think we shall have to ensure Miss Dart knows this as well. She was shaken by your message. Did you tell Violet so?"

"Possibly? I was more concerned about whether she would let me write to her."

Mr. Dart leaned forward again. "Did she say yes?" At my blushing nod he crowed with laughter. "That is splendid! If you insist on falling in love with a virago, at least she has turned out to be on our side."

"Regarding that point," I said, and glanced meaningfully at Hal, who was still frowning. I didn't want to know what message I had given him from his father, who had (I recalled, with that strange unobtrusive sliding-in of memory again) fallen to his death on a staircase on account of the seven-year-old Hal's action. I turned back to Mr. Dart.

"This is better wine than we had at supper," he said, admiring the colour.

"I think it might be more of the Inarkios the butler gave us before," I agreed. "Hal—what did you mean about the unicorn?"

"Ballory," said Mr. Dart again, setting his glass down on the floor beside him so he could lay his hand on the unicorn's flank.

"Yes, Ballory. What significance—"

Hal finally lifted his thoughts out of wherever they'd gone to focus on this (I thought significant) question. "Mr. *Peregrine* Dart, a budding wild mage of considerable power and conduit for a literal miracle of resurrection, found a live and apparently healthy unicorn foal in a disregarded box, and you have to ask *what it means*?"

Peregrine was the name of the second son of that Tarazel who had founded the university of Tara, son also of the Bard Lauchlan Dart and ancestor of my Mr. Dart of Dartington. It was also the name of the—probably unrelated—knight who had rescued a unicorn from a hunter's trap and become thereby first Champion of the Lady of the Green and White, and subsequently consort of the first (human) lady mage of Alinor.

Very few people had encountered unicorns since, but always at moments of great change in the history of Alinor, particularly our continent of Northwest Oriole, once one province among many of the Empire, now the centre of the world.

(And what, I wondered with my too-easily-distracted mind, did the people of Alinor who lived outside the former borders of the Empire think of those of us within?—But I knew the answer to that: they followed the Dark Kings, many of them, or were thralls to fairy princes, according to other stories, or were barbarians without universities to commend them to our notice. Yet there were still centres of learning mentioned in the ancient texts that had never come under the sway of the Empire, and surely Astandalas had not held a monopoly on civilization.)

A little flustered, I said to Mr. Dart, "It seems to mean that you've decided not to deny your magic any longer."

He took up his glass again and regarded me over the rim. I stared back, caught by a deep upwelling of emotion. The fire crackled behind him, and the unicorn snorted softly in its sleep. Mr. Dart was smiling, his eyes blue as a clear sky with a limpid golden clarity to them, like sunlight.

Hal had said something about Mr. Dart being the Lady's heir.

"You are not the only one to have had a life-altering experience last night," Mr. Dart said quietly.

The wind howled outside the windows, shaking the glass and sending a few cool drafts swirling through the room. I could feel no magic, nothing but the pleasant warmth of my waistcoat buttons, the knowledge pressing in on me that this was the Mr. Dart who had defended my dead body against the Dark Kings all through the witching hour, until dawn came in the land between life and the life beyond.

"Do you remember the dream we shared?" I asked him, not dropping my eyes. "At the Grim Crossroads?"

He took a sharp breath. "Yes."

"At the end I swore you fealty."

"Jemis—"

I smiled. "Peregrine."

I set my glass down and stood up. Hal swivelled in his seat and plucked Mr. Dart's goblet out of his hand so that I could reach down and pull my friend gently to his feet. And then, as I had in that in-between place, I kissed Mr. Dart's hand, and his brow, and, kneeling awkwardly, his feet.

"Peregrine Dart," I said, the words coming out of so many stories my mother and father had told me as a boy, "to you I swear my fealty. Loyalty for loyalty, and trust for trust, and faith for faith will I give you. As you have guarded me, so shall I guard you. As you have guided me, so shall I guide you. As you have served me, so shall I serve you. You are my lord, and

I am your vassal. My life have you given me, and I return it to your keeping."

"Do you accept this?" Hal asked in a formal voice.

Mr. Dart's eyes were even brighter than before, and the silver sparks gathered in the air around us. The unicorn whuffed softly. "Oh—oh yes," he said. "Lady help me, I do." And he reached out with his good hand to lay it on the crown of my bent head in benediction.

"So do I witness," said Hal.

We sat down again in our various seats and took up our wineglasses and tried not to make eye contact. We were excellently educated modern young gentlemen, and therefore tremendously embarrassed by the whole thing. Mr. Dart himself was nearly carnation-pink, which clashed rather with his auburn hair. I didn't like to think what colour my face was.

"So," Mr. Dart said, then cleared his throat and took a large gulp of wine for good measure. After he had coughed himself to composure, and crossed the room to collect his smoking kit from the dressing table, he returned to his seat by the hearth and, in the face of our continued silence, went on. "What, er, what prompted that? I'm not sure that I want to set myself up as a petty emperor any more than Hal here!"

"Of course not," I agreed.

"Then so?"

"It seemed appropriate," was about the best I could do, as I wasn't entirely sure myself what had prompted the declaration of fealty, only that I meant it from the bottom of my heart. "My lord duke here has mentioned that I follow where you lead, and I suppose I wanted to formalize it."

"You do recall that you outrank me by a considerable margin, my lord viscount?"

Hal shifted, catching our attention. He looked meaningfully at the unicorn foal asleep in its nest of silver sparks. "Great magi are outside of the formal hierarchies."

Mr. Dart drew his knees up to support his stone arm, then

rested his chin on top in a student's position. The sparks gathered in his hair, like snowflakes. "It really started last year," he said. "The magic. Looking back on it I can see incidents that must have been caused by me but which I thought at the time were coincidence or accident or some left-over residue from the Interim."

"No one in Stoneybridge made mention of it?" Hal asked, frowning. "Even if they're being quiet about it, surely there are wizards and other practitioners around. And without Jemis around shedding magic like his sneezes it should have been fairly obvious it was *you* at the centre."

That put an intriguing complexion on the numerous odd happenings in and around Ragnor Bella since the summer. I had only come back in September, but people had gleefully attached my name to all sorts of summertime rumours. Mr. Dart himself had returned in the spring, in time for the planting season.

Mr. Dart shrugged. "It's like Ragnor Bella. A couple of elderly witches living at the edge of town, an apothecary or a Scholar or two known to have esoteric books in their back rooms, but everyone claims to have put all that nonsense away for a modern, scientific, rational, industrious age. The focus is on trade and taxes."

Hal made a face. "How vulgar. Trade and taxes are to be disguised with pomp and circumstance, everybody knows that."

Mr. Dart chuckled and started to fuss with his pipe, bracing the stem on his knees as he pinched out the leaf to fill the bowl. I refilled our glasses and sipped mine, quietly content.

"My tutor, Domina Black, said a few things that in retrospect were clearly warnings about this, but nothing outright." Mr. Dart sighed. "I shall have to write to her. She kept setting me papers on incipient great magi and the revolutions they tend to start."

That surprised me. "Is Chare so close to one?"

They both looked at me, then Hal murmured, "The wire-weed," and Mr. Dart nodded in confirmation that my state of mind had not been such to attend to these submerged political tensions over the course of the past year or so. Not that I've ever been particularly good at noticing such things.

Hal said, "Jemis, the whole continent is about to go up in flames. The only question is what sparks it."

Mr. Dark shook his head. "And to what end it burns."

Hal toasted him with his glass. "That's where you come in, then. And us, apparently, as I made formal alliance with Jemis —oh, last Sunday, a lifetime ago—and he's now sworn fealty to you." He sighed ostentatiously. "I really thought his democratic revolution would come *after* sorting out this matter of the Indrillines."

The unicorn made a soft nickering sound in its throat and its legs twitched, like a dreaming puppy. Mr. Dart stroked its flank with his hand, his face softening. The air spun around us in a warm wind that did not come from the draughty window. The sparks flared up and hovered in the air, enhaloing Mr. Dart and disguising the ill fit of his borrowed clothes.

I looked down at the mythical scene in front of me. "I'm guessing the unicorn—"

"Ballory."

"—Ballory means that magic is coming first."

Hal snapped his fingers and a spark jumped out of nowhere to ignite Mr. Dart's pipe. "About time, I say."

CHAPTER ELEVEN

W e made simpler conversation as we finished the bottle of wine, at which point Mr. Dart indicated unsubtly that he wanted to retire. Hal and I repaired with the remaining two bottles to my room, as it was not particularly late. In sharp contrast to Mr. Dart's warm and cozy space, my room was chilled and draughty. The snow rattled loudly on the windows, and the wind had increased to a keening roar. I listened to it, marvelling.

"This is quite the storm."

"So early in the season, too," Hal replied, moving the side table over to sit between the two seats by the fire. "We get horrendous storms coming in off the North Sea, but usually later in the winter. All our houses are supposed to have working shutters to protect against it. I always have to fine someone for neglecting to keep theirs in repair ... You don't get this sort of thing on your side of the mountains?"

"No, snow comes at Winterturn, and while we do some-times have storms, they're rarely this violent."

Hal laid himself along the chaise longue. Given his outfit and posture, he looked like a sybarite of the Empress Anyoë's court. "I had forgotten what you told me about the regularity of your seasons. I wonder, now that our friend is coming into his power, whether the surprisingly good weather since the Interim in your barony has to do with him."

I sat down in the wingback chair and then shoved it around so I could warm my toes at the fire. "Could his gift be that strong?"

"Wild magic," Hal reminded me. "No one understands it, but it's obviously far more than hedge-craft magic. There's the unicorn to consider."

I grinned at him. "Ballory."

"Indeed. Ballory the unicorn. Where did *it* come from, I should like to know. Unless ... do you have an idea?"

I spluttered through my wine. "I beg your pardon? Why would I know anything about it?"

Hal rolled his eyes and held out his glass for a refill, which I managed without spilling despite the angle. I set the bottle back on the table a little closer to his side, so he could reach it for himself. He grinned at me. "I assure you that it hasn't slipped my mind that you returned from the dead last night. I thought perhaps the Lady might have said something."

"She called Mr. Dart her Champion."

Hal uttered an oath. "And you didn't think to mention that before?"

"I haven't had much opportunity, and you were somewhat distracted," I pointed out. "That's why he could be the conduit for the miracle."

"I thought—" He shook his head sharply. "I need to think about this. Jemis, I know you wanted to spend Winterturn with your father, but I really think we need to discuss all the things we've learned this week with our allies. If you and your father could come, and Mr. Dart too, that would help immensely."

"I don't have much knowledge of high-level politics, Hal. You know that."

"I know that you're usually very good at understanding how people relate to each other, and your father is brilliant."

I laughed at the infelicity of this phrasing. "I'll ask him," I promised. "Do you think there will be a revolution?"

"What *did* you learn in school?"

"I wasn't taught by a revolutionary from Galderon, recall."

"You work for one."

"True."

"I would like to ask her opinion as well," Hal said. "I doubted your admiration at first, I am ashamed to admit, but my acquaintance with your Madam Etaris has made me most appreciative of her knowledge and wit. You can learn a lot from her."

I gave him a sardonic glance. "I suppose you don't want to invite *her* to your coming-of-age ball?"

Hal sighed explosively. "If only she were a Scholar ..."

I gave him a moment, then something he'd mentioned on the cart-ride this morning came to mind. "You said you were having a winter fair. Perhaps we can ask if she'll come up as part of that. Either to sell or to buy, if you're going to have a bookseller there?"

He brightened. "That is a good idea. I shall write her a letter but you will have to do the explaining, Jemis."

"I would, if I fully understood the situation."

He opened his mouth, either to do so or to chide me for my ignorance, but was forestalled by a tentative knock on the door. I gave him a glance, then answered it.

Jullanar Maebh stood there, still in her grey dinner dress and looking even more pale. "I'm sorry to disturb you," she began in a low voice.

"Come in, come in," I said, ushering her in. "Hal and I were just talking."

"Thank you," she said, and sank heavily into my chair. I found a bench at the foot of the bed and dragged it over to give a third seat.

"Can I offer you any wine?" I said, frowning at her. In the firelight she looked even worse. "You look unwell, Miss Dart. Is it the storm, or is something else wrong?"

She was shivering, but refused the wine. "No, thank you, I find ... I dislike the drink."

In my investigation of the room earlier I had found a stack of woollen blankets in a wardrobe beside the bed. I collected them and shook one out to determine it wasn't too musty or moth-eaten. It had a pleasant scent of lavender, fortunately, so I brought it over to tuck around her shoulders, setting the others on the end of my bench in case she needed another. "I must apologize for the draught," I said. "What a wind to get through shutters, windowpanes, and heavy curtains!"

"Does this house have shutters?" Hal asked.

"I'm not familiar with the architecture," I retorted, though I realized I hadn't noticed either and just presumed from his earlier comment.

Jullanar Maebh accepted the blanket with a twist of a smile. "Thank you, Lord St-Noire."

"Shall I ever become used to that?" I asked Hal, retaking my seat on the bench. "I much prefer Mr. Greenwing."

"As I shall have to become accustomed to Miss Dart," said she in a low voice. Then she shook herself and looked plaintively at me. "I apologize for disturbing your evening, sir, but I had a question ..."

"It is hardly a disturbance, Miss Dart! Unburden yourself, if you would."

She sighed, staring meditatively into the fire, which was burning high what with the draught going up the chimney, but not throwing much heat into the room. The ironwork stove in Mrs. Etaris' bookshop was much more efficient at heating the space. It was one of the new inventions since the Fall.

"You mentioned, when we first met, a man by the name of Roald Ragnor ... I was wondering what—what acquaintance you had with him?"

I tried not to blink too obviously. The mention of Roald Ragnor, to our new acquaintances in a student pub at Tara, had occasioned a strong adverse reaction. Jullanar Maebh's voice now was faltering and low, but it did not seem with hatred or dislike. Curious, I thought, and smiled mildly at her.

"The Honourable Roald Ragnor is the only son of the Baron of Ragnor, and thus one of the leading citizens of Ragnor Bella and our surrounding barony. I know him fairly well, though we fell out of friendship before university, I'm afraid."

"Really?" Hal said. "He spends a surprising deal of time in your company, then."

"We're making up," I replied shortly. I found the Honourable Rag's behaviour more than a little confusing, to be honest. Our quarrel had been on the subject of addictive tendencies, to which my family was unfortunately prone, myself not excluded, and to which I believed him coming dangerously close. He had not been happy with my warning to take care while at Tara, and we had not corresponded while I was at Morrowlea.

Since my return home in the autumn he'd been *around*, blithe and bluff and to all appearances a wastrel hell-bent on losing even his father's large fortune, and behaving quite as if we were still friends—or so at least he had once my place in society was understood to once again be acceptable to the Quality.

That initial dismissal due to my apparent fall out of the gentry still rankled. I would have to work on that, I reflected, or else I would have to spend a long time in the Wood of Spiritual Refreshment doing so. It was a peculiar pain, the thought of having to wait even longer for the Mountains for something I could work on here.

Perhaps that was what the priests meant about goodness being its own reward.

"And ... my father? I ... I know so little," Jullanar Maebh

said, and I drew my attention hastily back to her. "My mother rarely spoke of him, just that he was a good man."

"He is," I said firmly.

"Please, Mr. Greenwing."

It suddenly occurred to me that she must be tremendously nervous, throwing herself on the mercy of a family she had never met. Our inadvertent adventures escorting her on what should have been a simple journey home could not be helping, either.

I cast about for what I could say. "He's the Acting Magistrate for the Winterturn Assizes. I believe it's a position he has long wished to hold, and I expect that he will be permanently appointed in the new year, since I cannot imagine he would be anything but a credit to the position."

Unlike my uncle, the former incumbent, who had resigned after a gibbering confession that he had connived at my father's disgrace and seeming murder in order to steal the family estate for his own. But that didn't seem likely to soothe Jullanar Maebh's nerves. I coughed awkwardly.

"He's the Squire of Dartington, Master Torquin is. That's a very old position, older than the Empire by far. If you go back in the parish records to the coming of Astandalas, the prominent names are the Darts, the Greenwings, the Woodhills, and the Becksides. I don't believe there are any Becksides left in Ragnor barony, but you will meet the Woodhills, and you've met me, of course. If you go back another thousand years, to the time of Tarazel, you will find that a Dart of Dartington was one of her companions."

Both Hal and Jullanar Maebh expressed astonishment. I grinned at them. "Yes, the Bard—Lauchlan Dart was his name, and he is your direct ancestor, Miss Dart. He was the father of the second son of Tarazel, in fact, Peregrine for whom our Mr. Dart was named."

"I'm a descendant of *Tarazel*?" Jullanar Maebh said, as wonderingly as if I'd declared her a distant relation of the

Emperor of Astandalas. Of course, she'd attended the university founded by Tarazel.

I doubted I would be quite so excited to find some distant connection to the founders of Morrowlea, but then again, they were not so exciting (a group of disaffected Scholars who had broken off from Tara, if I recalled correctly, and set up a fiefdom in a corner of what was then the Princedom of Morrowlea). And I had been quite astonished to discover I had fairy blood through my mother's line. Whatever exactly that meant.

"What else can I say? Master Dart collects Collian scrolls, and has a small but prestigious collection of them. His lover, Sir Hamish Lorquin, is my cousin once removed on my father's side. He is a noted portraitist, specifically of miniatures; he was knighted by the King of Rondé for his work. He's also quite a successful farmer. The estates are in good heart ... They produce wool for export, and, er, mangels. But perhaps that will better wait for your arrival. I don't know that much of their affairs, naturally. But they are excellent men, both of them. Mr. Dart will be able to tell you more of his brother, of course. He will not lead you astray."

"Of course," she said faintly, clutching at the blanket. She stood up, with a distracted air. "Thank you," she said, turning to the door, then back to me. "I am grateful for your assistance."

I stood up to escort her back to the door. "I am glad to be of some small service," I assured her. "Master Dart is an honourable man and a good one. He will be very glad to know you."

She smiled wanly at me. I opened the door and peered out to be sure no one was watching before escorting her out and down the hall to her own door.

"Thank you," she said, and went in without further ado.

I returned to find Hal finishing off the bottle by pouring the remainder into his rather-full glass. "Well, that was interesting," he said, but when I asked him why he waved off the question. "I think I'm to bed," he announced. "I have much to think on. We'll talk further before we part ways, I assure you. I haven't forgotten your question about what you're to explain to your Mrs. Etaris."

His tone was perhaps a little snide, but I disregarded that in favour of his own approach, and took the words at face value. "Thank you, and good night!"

"Good night," he returned cheerfully, as we had many evenings at Morrowlea, and wandered off with his glass held at a careful angle.

I saw him to his door, which was two over from mine, decided against opening the third bottle, and sat down with the *New Salon*, which was a mistake.

~

An hour later I had opened the third bottle, which I no longer cared I would likely regret in the morning, and was wondering to whom I might write at the offices of the *New Salon* in complaint.

The slander against my father's reputation was, alas, ongoing. My character was generally portrayed in a more positive light, but it was in constant contrast to the high regard my father had originally had—the hero of Orkaty, recipient of the Heart of Glory, etc.—and the eccentricities of my maternal grandmother, the Marchioness of the Woods Noirell, who had significantly more scandal attached to her younger days than I hitherto imagined.

The Marchioness had apparently been well known for small enchantments and cunning bewitchments. Mostly these were of objects, and mostly they were in relation (I was horrified to read) to the execution of a multitude of inappropriate assignations, not all of them her own.

The implications were strong that I was probably on the

cusp of satyric madness due to my maternal lineage, and that the splendid prowess apparent in my dragon-slaying would no doubt prove to be as ephemeral as my father's heroism, and probably end worse. Although what they thought might be *worse* than being (incorrectly) arraigned as the worst traitor in Astandalan history I did not wish to contemplate.

I closed the paper before reading to the end — I didn't think I could handle either the *Etiquette Questions Answered* column nor the usually pleasant distraction of the crossword puzzle tonight — and slouched in the chair, staring into the fire. It all seemed so far away, and yet still stung. What was I to do?

Yet another knock interrupted my thoughts. I got up, had to pause while adjusting my balance — I *had* drunk too much wine — and managed not to make a complete shambles of getting to the door. I had barely opened it when whoever was outside pushed hastily past me in a blur of pale cloth.

I stumbled aside and was startled when the person shut the door with a near-slam. "I say," I said ineffectually, and then recognized my visitor. "Hope? Whatever is the matter?"

"Jemis," said she firmly, and then peered at me with a pursed-lips frown. "Are you foxed?"

"Maybe?"

"I knew this was a bad idea," she muttered to herself, then pushed me over to the chaise longue and sat me down on it. I swayed a little, hand on the scrolled armrest. The velvet had a lovely texture.

Hope busied herself with the carafe of water and presented me with a glass. (It was lacking in white bubbles and therefore not, I presumed, a priceless Dangora XIV piece. Though of course it might still be priceless.) She took another for herself and poured a healthy slug of wine into it. Her face was reso-lute, which was not an expression I associated with her.

"Not that I am unhappy at your presence," I began care-fully, "but I do wonder what might have occasioned it tonight? Hal's already left for the evening. And I'm by myself."

She burst out laughing, then hastily smothered her face with both hands. We both looked at the door, but a rattling gust of wind against the window seemed to have covered this unfortunately indiscreet noise.

"Oh, Jemis, I know I can trust you to behave as a gentleman ought. Even at your most manic you never offered any insult." She peered at me, her soft eyes expressive with a pleasing concern. "*Are* you well? You are better, I know, but that doesn't mean you are necessarily *well*."

I gave her a wry salute with my glass. "I died of wireweed overdose the day before yesterday, but was resurrected courtesy of the Lady's grace. I find myself much ... renewed."

Hope gazed up at me, nonplussed, then took up the second of the blankets I'd brought over earlier and wrapped it around her own shoulders. The wool was a pale blue, very much a colour she favoured, with a satin ribbon edging. She tucked her feet up on the chair, her slippers curling under her in a way familiar from so many winter evenings at university. I relaxed against the back of the chaise longue, smiling at the great secret I had just entrusted her with.

"I'm sure that would make more sense if you were less foxed," she said frankly. "I'm glad you're better, anyhow." She saw the *New Salon* on the side and made a face. "What a to-do there is about you in the paper, Jemis. It's not much fun, is it?"

"No, it isn't," I agreed.

She plucked at a loose edge of the satin ribbon on her blanket. I reached over precariously to add another piece of wood to the fire, causing a brief flurry of quite ordinary orange sparks to go up and fall down extinguished.

"Was it a surprise to you, to become the Viscount St-Noire? It seems like it from the reports, but you can't always believe what you read ..."

It was, alas, all too easy to believe that my terrifying grandmother had greatly enjoyed causing scandals in her youth.

I rallied myself for another strangely ordinary conversation. "It was. My mother was estranged from my grandmother, the Marchioness, and I had never realized she was the heiress to the Woods Noirell, nor I her heir after her. My grandmother denied all relation when I wrote to her after my mother died, and it wasn't until Hal came to visit this autumn that I realized that as an Imperial title it descends through primogeniture whether male or female."

"And then you had to slay a dragon."

"It asked me a riddle first, and I thought that was all that was needed to prove myself. There are some strange magics in the Woods Noirell ... They used to be the approach to Ysthar on the road to Astandalas, and it's always been perilously easy to stray in amongst the Good Neighbours. My mother told me many stories."

Hope glanced up at me through her long lashes. "Do you believe in the Good Neighbours?"

I was drunk enough to say what I thought. "Yes."

"The tales seem so fantastical."

She didn't know there was a unicorn foal—Ballory—a few doors down the hall. "I didn't particularly believe in dragons, but there one was. Mr. Dart and Hal were both witnesses to its riddling, and half of Ragnor barony to its death, as it happened at the Dartington Harvest Fair. It destroyed the whole cake competition. Hal was very disappointed. We were so sure our cake was going to place."

Hope giggled. "You and Hal entered a cake competition?"

"We were often on kitchen duty together, you know."

"I remember." She sighed. "I miss Morrowlea, don't you? It seems like a dream sometimes. All that time to read and talk and think, all the *variety* of things we were doing, gardening and cooking and sewing and cleaning, but also art and music and archery, and such wonderful Scholars to study under, and no one thought it impossible that a man and a woman could be *friends*."

I nodded sympathetically. "I miss that, too, though the end of last year was difficult for me."

"All that mess with Lark. I know."

She was silent for a while. The wind howled outside, possibly even stronger than it had been earlier. There were a lot of rattling noises and a heavier repetitive clunk, as if something had gotten loose and was now banging against the roof or the outer wall.

I put another piece of wood on the fire. It was a little too long and the end stuck out, but I ignored that in favour of sipping at my wine and watching Hope look down at her hands. She had on a ring, a heavy silver thing set a large aquamarine surrounded by tiny diamonds. The aquamarine might have been scratched, or perhaps there was something engraved or etched on it, but I couldn't see the shape in the uncertain light.

It seemed incredible that she had sneaked into my room simply to reminisce—we were friends, but not *that* close, I had thought—but I was a little befuddled, and now starting to feel tired, and was surely missing hints. I tried to think of what she'd told me when we first encountered each other that afternoon. "You said things were difficult at home?"

My words were nearly drowned out by a shockingly bright light followed almost immediately with an inordinate clap of thunder. We both jumped.

"Do you think that hit the house?" Hope asked in a small voice.

I shook my head. My ears were ringing. Hopefully there was a lightning rod grounding the roof, or some magic left over from Astandalan days to protect against lightning-sparked fires. This was not a night to want to fight a fire.

—I had entirely forgotten about the poor folks at Finoury's Inn. I hoped that they had managed to put out the fire and find safe accommodation for the night before the storm hit hard.

"I'm sure it will be fine," I said reassuringly to Hope, who patted me on the hand in reciprocal compassion.

There was another flash of lightning and near-instant thunderclap. I caught my breath at how close it was. I'd been caught in summer thunderstorms on the plains around Morrowlea, but never in a winter storm complete with lightning. The windows were rattling louder than ever, and the clunking noise was getting almost frantic.

A third lightning bolt and *boom* the thunder, and with a shrieking howl something broke at my window and the wind barrelled in, extinguishing all the candles and making the fire flare halfway up the chimney.

"Good Lady," I said, making to get up and getting tangled in the blanket Hope had half-dropped.

She grabbed my shoulder with an iron grip, her fingers digging deep into my shoulder. "*Jemis*," she hissed. "Something's coming in the window."

CHAPTER TWELVE

I might have been foxed, but I was not so impaired not to be able to respond to *that*.

The wind was howling so loudly through the now-open window that I could barely hear anything else—but yet—there were crashes coming from behind me, by the door, as well as whatever was squeezing itself through the gap, barely visible in the shadows against the snow as the curtains billowed wildly.

Despite the radical equality espoused at Morrowlea, both Hope and I knew that her reputation would be seriously damaged if she were to be found alone in my room in her night-gown.

The bath-room was tiny and had no other exit, which made it a bad place to hide.

Hope herself said something faintly, but I couldn't hear her over the wind. I shoved her in the direction of the bed alcove and the door; she picked the bed, tumbling through the four-poster's curtains and jerking them closed behind her.

I cast around for anything resembling a weapon. There wasn't anything but the half-full third bottle of wine and the priceless glasses. Dominus Lukel had spent many classes talking about improvised weaponry and the difficulty of breaking glass without damaging one's own hand. I wouldn't break the bottle, I decided, grabbing it by the neck, but I could use it as a club.

Something made a noise at the window. Not the keening wind or the banging shutters or the scrape of something along roof-slates, but a deep-throated grunting.

My eyes were adjusting to the dimness but all I could see was the dark curtains snapping in the wind and a darker shape behind them, against a pale blur that must be the snowstorm through the unblocked side of the window. The fire behind me cast light only a short distance, and that erratic as the flames were flaring and nearly going out as the gusts caught it. My nose was irritatingly cold and starting to run.

I gripped the bottle in one hand and carefully squatted down until I could grab the last piece of wood I'd placed on the fire, trying not to take my eyes off the window as I did. The wood had only caught at one end and I felt better with something approximating an actual weapon.

Most uncanny things feared fire, didn't they?

I tried not to imagine what might be in the woods of Western Lind that would decide to come hunting inside human dwellings in the midst of a raging blizzard.

I really ought to have chosen *Myths and Legends of the Linder Mountains* instead of the *New Salon*.

I had the smouldering firebrand and the bottle of wine. Hope was hidden in the bed. Whatever was happening in the hall outside the bedchambers hadn't yet made it to my door, which left me and the window.

My father had told me over and over again to *think* before I thrust myself into death-defying situations. But surely I had to do something? Whatever it was would be compromised by the exertions of entering—

I found myself crossing the room without further conscious thought. I couldn't let it get its feet under it. Some uncanny things needed invitations to enter ... as I hadn't given any, nor any permission, surely this wouldn't be a vampire or one of the lesser Fae.

Both would be afraid of fire. I swallowed and switched hands, so the firebrand was in my right, my dominant hand, and the bottle in my left. The deep-throated grunting continued, along with a scrabbling noise audible even over the wind. I edged closer to the curtains, which fell suddenly still, as if the window had been blocked.

If something were coming *in* … My thoughts were moving too slowly. I backed away again, so I could set down the bottle and pick up the spare blanket instead. I needed to get an advantage, and I didn't know what it was.

Hope, apparently unable to bear the suspense, poked her head out of the curtains on the bed. Her face was a dark blur, her nightgown a pale one. She whispered, "What is it?"

"Shh," I said, not taking my attention off the window.

She ignored my gestures, sliding out instead and padding over to me. She did not have particularly light steps, did Hope. Thankfully there was still a lot of noise coming from outside the room.

I thrust the blanket into her hands. When she took it, I leaned against and whispered into her ear, "When I pull back the curtain, jump on it."

"Right," she said, in a resolute voice. I spared a thought to wonder where *this* Hope had been all last year. She wasn't soft at all, underneath her fluttering pastels and gentle eyes.

We went forward together, the firebrand flaring up and down in the draughts. A high-pitched wail started up, suggesting that whatever-it-was had come further into the room and left a gap for the wind to come through.

I swallowed again. Perhaps my tendency to a glorious fugue state in the course of mortal danger had been a magical gift, now sacrificed and gone. Or perhaps it was that I was drunk. Either way I did not feel calm, collected, focused.

O Lady, why were my thoughts wandering so?

I reached out with my left hand and grasped the edge of the curtain. Hope elbowed me and in one motion I tugged the curtain down and thrust the firebrand out, while she jumped forward with a sudden yell and tackled the shape in front of me with no hesitation whatsoever, then sat on it.

It said, "*Oof.*"

I paused. Sticking out from under the blanket were a pair of absurdly extravagant boots, visible even in the dim half-light cast by fireplace and the sputtering brand and the strange white light coming in from the window along with a tolerable deal of snow.

I knew those boots. I had spent several hours staring at them a week or so ago, when the person dressed as the Hunter in Green had hailed our coach and requested delivery of his person to Yrchester.

"Well?" Hope said, *sotto voce.*

"One moment," I murmured, handing her the firebrand. Stepping carefully over our captive, who was keeping still for the moment, I fumbled with the window until my fingers froze but I did manage to close the sash. That done, the draught lessened considerably. I took back the stick, which was still burning, and went around the room righting and then lighting various candles.

Then I went back to see that yes, the boots *were* dyed green.

I nodded at Hope. "I think I know him."

There was a sudden jerk under the blanket and a familiar odd-accented voice said, "Jemis Greenwing!" And then he started to laugh roisterously.

~

Three minutes later, the Hunter in the Green and Hope were hiding behind the bed-curtains while I answered the door and informed a doubting Henry Coates that my window had come loose and let in a great gust of wind, and nothing else.

"I heard laughter," he said suspiciously.

I blinked as guilelessly as I could at him. "I was reading today's *New Salon*."

That appeared to be an acceptable response, for he gave me a grimace of acknowledgement. "My apologies, Lord St-Noire."

I gave him a sketch of a bow in return. "No matter, Coates. Was there anything else?"

He looked up and down the hall, which was empty of any other people; though who knew what had been going on while Hope and I were otherwise preoccupied. I wanted to ask about the hullabaloo but something stopped me from opening that box of trouble.

Coates bit his lip and shuffled his feet and gave every indication that he did want to say something else, but instead said, "No, no, it's late and I shouldn't keep you from your bed. I'm glad to hear all is well. Did you need any assistance with the window?"

"No, thank you, I believe I managed to get it fixed well enough for now."

"Very good then."

He hovered a few moments longer, rubbing his shoulder absently while I watched him politely and also curiously, very aware of the highwayman and the chaperone hiding almost in plain sight behind me. The wind howled outside, with a high-pitched keen, but the candle-lanterns weren't guttering quite so badly as before.

"Did you mean it?" he blurted suddenly.

"I beg your pardon?"

"Did you mean it, that you think that the mercantile class are equal to the gentry?"

"Is it so unusual a belief?" I replied lightly, knowing from my own experience that yes, yes it was. "I went to Morrowlea, sir," I said more seriously.

"So did Miss Garsom, and she doesn't hold with such nonsense."

Perhaps that underlying distaste for Morrowlea's radical egalitarianism was why I had never liked Anna. Or perhaps it was just that she didn't particularly like me.

"I believe in the equality of all people," I said firmly. "Neither wealth nor name makes either righteousness or joy."

"You're a very odd man," Mr. Coates muttered in a low voice, which I wondered if I was supposed to hear. "Thank you, sir, and good night," he said more loudly, and gave me a just-appropriate bow before sauntering off down the hall. I watched to see that he went into another room, hoping it was his, then shut my own door firmly and turned back to my unexpected guests.

The Hunter in Green pulled open the curtains and stared at me. "Was that Henry Coates?" he demanded. "What are you doing speaking with *him*?"

～

After introductions ("Miss Stornaway, this is the Hunter in Green; Miss Stornaway"; "Charmed, I'm sure"; "Likewise"), Hope carefully folded the blue blanket, set it on the back of the wingback chair, and said that she was going to bed. "I do hope we can speak further before you continue on your journey, Jemis," she added.

"Of course," I replied politely, and watched to make sure she made it safely to her door, the opposite way up the hall from Henry Coates'. She lifted her hand in acknowledgement to me before she closed her door, and I closed mine and turned to the Hunter in Green, who had claimed the chaise longue and was investigating the bottle of wine.

"Excellent vintage, what," he said approvingly.

"What, indeed," I replied dryly, taking the chair. He had taken off his gloves, revealing pale skin and well-tended nails, along with a golden ring I was fairly sure was a match of my own, and denoted him a member of Crimson Lake. Whatever that organization *was*, exactly, which I had *still* not yet fully discovered despite nearly three months ostensibly a member. "Dare I ask what brings you to my window this dark and stormy night?"

"It's a foul wind that blows nobody good."

"It's far too late for proverbs," I retorted, yawning. "Will you give me an explanation I can use to soothe myself to sleep?"

"Never too late for gnomic utterances," the Hunter said, seeming to grin behind his mask if the tone of his voice was anything to go by. He was wearing clothes similar or the same to what I'd seen him in before, green tunic and hose, with a cowled green yoke over his head and shoulders. This time both mask and matching codpiece were formed of green-dyed rawhide shaped into leaves, the mask a Green Man face such as you might find tucked into certain groves or back gardens around Ragnor Bella. He was also quite wet, though not as sopping as I would have expected.

Well, he could have a gift—or been given a gift—of magic to protect him from the worst of the elements. I rubbed my own Crimson Lake ring with my thumb, wondering how far I could push it. This was the first time I'd seen any of his skin; previously he'd been careful to keep all identifying features but his height and musculature hidden. Even the skin of his eyelids was smudged a shadowy green.

He laughed, more softly than before. "You're a canny one, aren't you!"

"And you an uncanny one, to be out in this storm."

And I must be drunk, to state something like that so flatly. All my mother's stories made it clear that you *never* confronted someone you thought one of the Good Neighbours, for fear they might be. If they were in disguise, it was for a reason.

He laughed again. I threw the blue blanket at him. "Here, sir, unless you won't catch cold?"

"The storm is centred on this house," he informed me, accepting the blanket and snuggling into it as if he were a child seeking comfort. It had a most ridiculous effect given his imposing height and physique.

"A mile out in every direction and the squall is passed. The closer-to the house, the higher the wind. The road is blocked with a foot of snow, but the drive to the house rises to seven-foot drifts. Why, I was quite able to climb up a snowbank to reach your window."

"Fighting the wind and the shutters all the way?"

"Ach, there aren't any shutters on this style of house. I knew this window was easily opened from the outside. I made sure of that, last time I was visiting here."

I raised my eyebrows at him. "And when was that?"

"Recently enough to know the Master doesn't put just anyone into his favourite son's room," the Hunter replied, imperturbable. "Fetching outfit, by the way. Suits you."

"Thank you!"

"Mind if I take a sip of your wine? It was a cold journey, all in all."

He was starting to shiver despite the blanket. I frowned at him, wondering how he expected to drink while wearing a full face-mask, but let him take my glass and the half-bottle remaining, and instead worked to mend the fire with the remaining wood in the basket next to the hearth. "Does the Master know you've come visiting?"

"I've hardly had the opportunity to greet him," he pointed out, and then sneezed abruptly. "Excuse me!"

"And bless you," I replied sardonically.

I was sure he was grinning again. "Mind if I kip down on your couch, Greenwing? I won't keep you from your bed any longer, but I don't fancy disturbing the *rest* of the household tonight."

I rolled my eyes at his pun. "What of your business?"

"What of it? I came to see what the storm was about, and here I find you at the centre of it."

My thoughts flashed to Mr. Dart, two rooms down, with a unicorn foal at his hearth and magic in his eyes. And—while I didn't think this was *actually* the Hunter in the Green, consort of the Lady of Summer, nevertheless he had chosen that divinity as his costume, and that surely meant something. And—there was always that chance.

I watched his body language carefully. "Does the name Ballory mean anything to you?

The Hunter dropped the bottle. I was grateful it landed on the hearthrug. He leaned forward intently, every muscle taut, eyes shining behind the mask. "You found her! Thank the Lady!"

I grinned at him. "Not I."

And where was *that* name written?

He radiated puzzlement for a moment before a whole slew of things seemed to fall into place. I could watch his blue eyes, inward-turned and thoughtful, and the way his shoulders first tightened and then relaxed until he was slouching back in the chaise longue. He put his feet up and reclaimed the bottle, frowning at a splotch of wine on his hose.

"It was Mr. Dart all along, then. Thank the Lady. He's a sensible man."

I would have been offended at his clear relief, but for the fact that I felt much the same.

"This'll put the fox among the ducks," the Hunter went on gleefully, and then, when I raised my eyebrow at him, added, "Come now, I'm sure you heard of Mr. Dart's ducks this autumn?"

"I hadn't realized they were objects of such gossip."

"Well, until you returned there wasn't much else to speak of." He sneezed again. "Excuse me."

I regarded him more narrowly. Perhaps he didn't appear soaked because the fabric of his tunic and hose didn't show how wet they were. He wasn't wearing a coat, or even the many-caped great-cloak he'd sported on our last encounter, and he'd lost his hat somewhere. The cowled yoke covered his head and shoulders, but that was definitely damp if not wet. And my room was cold and draughty.

I said firmly, "Let me draw you a bath. You're chilled through and it's not as if you could fit into my clothes. If we hang them by the fire they might be dry enough by morning to be going on with. If not, some of the other guests are large men, and their clothes might fit you."

"I'm not wearing anything Henry Coates has touched," the Hunter muttered indignantly, but the effect was spoiled by another sneeze.

"Come on," I said, going into the bathroom and starting the taps running, as hot as I could cajole them to. "They've got the new boilers, there's still plenty of hot water."

He hesitated, one hand going to his mask, even as he turned his head longingly in the direction of the bath.

I rolled my eyes. "I promise I won't reveal your identity unless you give me permission," I said. "It's not as if I know who you—oh!"

For the Hunter in Green had removed his mask and there, grinning sheepishly at me, was the Honourable Roald Ragnor.

CHAPTER THIRTEEN

M y first wild thought was one of sheer vindication.
"I *knew* you couldn't possibly have become as
stupid as you were pretending!" I cried, and then blushed with
embarrassment when he laughed hard enough to start the tears
in his eyes. "That is—"

"Oh, I heard you."

His accent had shifted back to the familiar one of home. I
raised my eyebrows at him, willing my blushes to subside. "I
do appreciate your mimicry, sir! What accent was it supposed
to be?"

"Central Zunidh," he replied promptly. "There was
someone from Solaara in the year above me at Tara. Fascinating girl."

"I'm sure."

He grinned unrepentantly at me, with a sharpness to his
eyes and expression that had been sadly missing in the
Honourable Rag's face when I'd seen him at home. That made
something slide into my mind, solid and certain as an axiom. I
said, "I have a message for you from your mother."

His eyes narrowed, the green paint around them like a
raccoon's mask. "My mother is dead, Greenwing."

"Call me Jemis," I said absently. "So am I Or was, that is," I added as he spluttered. I tapped my chest, Crimson Lake ring chiming gently on a silver-and-gemstone button. "Definitely *was*."

He stared at me, this young man I'd known since childhood, and did not know at all. "Define *was*."

"I died yesterday, or perhaps it's the day before yesterday now, of a wireweed overdose, but by the Lady's grace was returned to life to spite the Dark Kings. Now, would you like your message? I assure you I shan't recall it after I've told you. It's not for *me* to know."

He blinked at me and said nothing further. I spoke for a few minutes, as best I could tell, though what I was saying fell out of my mind like a dream dissolving into morning wakefulness. He frowned and smiled and chuckled and looked uncertain by turns, and at the end appeared utterly flabbergasted.

"There you are," I said, relieved to have that message given, and turned to see the bath was nearly overflowing. "The water! One moment."

I hastened to the bathroom, where I turned off the taps and discovered another towel left beside the ones I'd used earlier. I went back out into the main room to see that he was still standing with one hand on the back of the chaise longue, where I'd left him. His expression was bemused.

I yawned, covering my mouth desultorily. "Do you mind if I wash up before your bath? I won't be a moment. Then I can go to bed ..." He was starting to smile again. "What? I have multitudes of things I want to ask you, but I'm half-foxed and suddenly exhausted. It's been a long day."

His smile grew to something like I expected from the Hunter in Green as I'd met him, snarky and good-humoured. "Somehow you always manage to turn things around on me," he complained. "I do something dramatic and you up the game. We must confer; we'll set the continent on fire."

"We'd best get Mr. Dart involved in *that*, as he's the Lady's chosen Champion. I do not disparage your choice of costume, but I have it from the Lady's mouth that She chose him."

"And he found Ballory. — No, go to bed, Jemis! I shall warm myself at your bath and fire — "

"You may share the bed after, so long as you promise to try not to kick."

"No one has ever complained I do so."

I laughed and went to fill the ewer with warm water so he could make use of the bath. "I'll hold you to that, Roald, Hunter or no."

~

He didn't kick, but he *was* a snuggler.

I woke up to find six feet of nobleman in disguise curled up against my back, one arm draped heavily over mine. He was toasty warm, which I have to admit was very pleasant given the ambient temperature in the room and the fact that he'd stolen half the covers away.

I felt thoroughly disinclined to move. It was morning, judging from the light coming through the gap where the bedcurtains hadn't quite met, and the wind had ceased. It was, in fact, eerily silent. I was rather grateful for the broad and lightly snoring bulk beside me. Yestereve's events had apparently not been entirely a dream.

The conversations I'd had after Hal's departure made little sense, as I lay there going over them in my mind. Even sober and rested, I couldn't think what Hope and Henry Coates were about. Both so desirous of speaking to me, alone and in the middle of the night, but saying nothing more than commonplaces. Even Jullanar Maebh's odd concern about Roald Ragnor made little more —

I stopped on that thought, as Roald Ragnor himself snorfled and rolled over without waking, freeing my arm from where he'd pinned it. I would have to ensure he knew she was here before he did whatever he had actually come here to do. Surely there was more to his arrival than hazarding the oddly-localized storm to find out its origin.

There was a soft creaking noise as the door opened, followed by light footsteps. I tensed, listening warily, before the sounds resolved themselves into someone mending the fire and clearing away the dirty glasses we'd left out. A scraping noise and a soft tut, and the light at the edges grew noticeably brighter—the curtains at the window being drawn.

I debated the proprieties of waiting versus getting up while they were still there, but the thought of an over-solicitous servant drawing back the bed-hangings to reveal me in bed with a stranger who must be immediately known to have broken into the house in the middle of a raging blizzard galvanized me upright with a jolt.

The telltale aroma of coffee had nothing to do with this, I assure you.

The Honourable Rag snorfled again, but quietly and into his pillow so I left him to wake on his own, hopefully discreetly —a word I had never hitherto thought to use in application to him—and I slid out of bed myself. I passed through the curtains without opening them, and discovered the butler just setting down a tray.

The room was back to rights, all the blankets folded and returned to their chest, which he now closed with a quiet snick. The fire was burning brightly, still new but already taking the edge off the chill. I glanced at the window, where a small scurf of snow edged the inner sill. It was too bright to see anything else but what I thought was blue sky.

I blinked my eyes hard against the dazzle-spots. "Good morning."

"Good morning." The butler gave me a short but solemn bow, which I returned in like fashion, trying not to yawn. A small headache had formed in the bridge of my nose, and I wondered how rude it would be to fall on the coffee like a ravening wolf.

"Breakfast will be served in the dining room downstairs in an hour or so," he informed me.

"Thank you."

I brushed my hair back from my face as best I could. I hadn't taken it out of the queue properly last night and it was horrendously knotted. I eyed the tray the butler had set on the table between the chaise longue and the wingback chair. It contained a large silver pot of coffee, a glass jug of water, two cups and two glasses, and an assortment of scones, jams, and what seemed to be whipped butter. There was also another bowl of quinces, this one a fine enamelled affair.

"I have taken the liberty of removing your visitor's garments to be cleaned," the butler said demurely. "His mask I have left here. I presume he will not be joining our other guests downstairs, but the robe should fit well enough and the slippers also."

Somehow this was far more mortifying than if I'd smuggled in a doxy and been caught *in flagrante delicto* with her. "Thank you," I managed stiffly.

The butler gave me another of his austere smiles. "It is good to see a young man hewing so well to the old ways."

"Er—"

He ignored my unarticulated question. "I fear you will not be able to continue on your journey today, as the drive is snowed in and we must wait for a crew to clear the road as well, but I trust you will find enough to amuse you for day's sojourn here."

"It is a fascinating house," I said tentatively.

The butler inclined his head with a pleased expression and shuffled out. I watched him go, confused at his phlegmatic acceptance of the extra visitor, until I recalled that the garments he'd taken to be cleaned were those of the Hunter in Green.

Not that that made any more sense, taken logically.

I performed my ablutions automatically, my thoughts focused on reconciling my various encounters with the Hunter in Green and those with the Honourable Rag since my return to Ragnor Bella in September.

About all I could decide upon was that he was being deliberately provoking and obtuse in his proper persona, and deliberately provoking in an opposite way as his alter ego. But he had saved my life, when it counted.

I had so many questions.

I dressed not in my own clothes, which were nowhere to be seen, but in a variation of yesterday's outfit. A new linen shirt and silk hose (these in pearl-grey), the same embroidered teal waistcoat and slippers, and a different outer coat, this time black and grey with silver and teal embroidery. It was a sensible way of extending what had to be an expensive wardrobe. Someone had been to court, clearly, without the full fortune of a great lord but the need to be seen as wealthy and of the Quality.

After tying my cravat and arranging the jabot to my liking, I returned to the inglenook and sat down in the wingback chair to enjoy the coffee, a restorative glass of water, and a scone. The neatly folded *New Salon* from yesterday caught my eye. Ignoring the three-page essay on myself, I turned to the back and the crossword puzzle.

By the time the Honourable Rag emerged from the bed, I had done the puzzle and made a good start on cracking the code being used in the *Etiquette Questions Answered* column. I had been suspicious for weeks but now that I was fresh from the successful interpretation of *On Being Incarcerated in Orio Prison* as a guide revealing how one might escape the supposedly-inescapable cells, I was more certain than ever that there was something there.

I took several sheets of paper and a positively antique quill and inkwell from the box on the writing desk, along with a lap-desk with a convenient container for said inkwell. I sat down again on the chair, feet warming at the fire, and started playing with combinations.

I was a little disappointed to realize, a quarter of an hour in, that it was the Elmsdale variant of the Ajiricano code, which Violet and I had used for most of the winter term in second year to leave notes for each other in the library.

I looked down at the notes. Which *Violet and I* had used. And Violet was a double spy.

Had she expected me to decipher these? She must have known I was never as good as she about realizing the presence of a code. Still, it was a decidedly odd coincidence if not.

"So," the Honourable Rag said. I jumped, nearly tipping over the ink, and hastily screwed the lid back on. He grinned at me and flung himself down in the chaise longue. He was enveloped in the thick woollen robe and with warm sheepskin slippers on his feet, and accepted the coffee I offered him with professedly ardent gratitude.

"So," I repeated, setting down the *New Salon*. I had seen a stack of older editions somewhere ... downstairs, that was it, in the maze of stuff before we had found the crates of tea and the box of unicorn.

"I have questions," he said, grinning at me over the cup. "I imagine you do, too."

"So many," I agreed.

We regarded each other for a moment, before he said tentatively, "One for one?"

I began to agree but was interrupted immediately by a knock on the door. I looked at the Honourable Rag, who sighed and shrugged elaborately. He then retuned to the bathroom and shut the door after picking up the Green-Man mask along the way. I went to the hall door and opened it to find Mr. Dart standing there, visibly anxious.

"Jemis," he said in a low voice, "let me in. I have dire news."

"Dire?" I opened the door so he could scuttle inside. "Did something happen to Ballory?"

He shook his head vigorously. "No, no, she's fine. What isn't fine is that—is someone else here?"

"Er, yes, but don't worry, it's confusing but nothing to be worried about."

Mr Dart stared at me. "Jemis, someone was murdered last night."

CHAPTER FOURTEEN

"**M**urdered!" I said. "Who?"
"I don't know."

That stopped me dead. (So to speak.) I coughed and directed him to the seats; he took the chaise longue. Hoofs clattering on the wood floor drew my attention downwards, to where an alert and playful unicorn foal had decided to make its presence known. Ballory's liquid black eyes showed no hint of fright or even wariness as it took the hem of my borrowed coat in its mouth and started to suckle on it.

"She's been like this for two hours," Mr. Dart explained, briefly distracted from his gruesome news.

I, however, wasn't. "How do you know there's been a murder, then? Did someone see something?"

"I found the murder weapon."

I looked at his empty hand. He flushed. "I didn't take it with me! I went downstairs to see if breakfast was being served—how did you warrant it up here, anyway?—and one of the knives on the wall told me it had been used to kill someone last night."

Right.

"And then what?"

"What do you mean, and then what? I sought you out, obviously." He shifted, visibly agitated, and wrung his hands slightly. I eyed him for a moment and then pointed towards the coffee. The headache between my eyes was back and gathering reinforcements, but he seemed to need it more. I didn't correct him when he picked up the Honourable Rag's cup, however.

"Well," I said with an attempt at sang-froid, "at least this time I have witnesses to show *I* didn't do it."

"Is that my cue?" the Honourable Rag asked in his own accent. All three of us looked up: myself in resignation, Mr. Dart in shock, the unicorn in glad eagerness. Ballory bounded over to him, only to stop splay-legged a foot or so back from where he was leaning against the bathroom door.

"Roald Ragnor!" Mr. Dart cried. "Whatever are you doing here?"

"House-breaking," I replied. The Honourable Rag's attention was largely fixed on the unicorn, but he spared me a mock sneer even as he extended his free hand for Ballory to sniff. His other held the Green-Man mask.

Mr. Dart opened his mouth, took a breath, shook his head, and made directly for the breakfast tray and the coffee pot. The unicorn left off sniffing the mask and bounded back over to him. He set down the coffee so he could stroke its head. It leaned into his touch, then picked up one of the quinces — just at a height it could reach by craning its neck — and carried it over to the hearth, where it lay down in a rather dog-like fashion to eat it.

After swallowing down half the refilled cup coffee, Mr. Dart's colour improved. He watched the Honourable Rag saunter over with what I considered excessive theatricality (but see: his disguise as the Hunter in Green; his alter ego's career as a highwayman; his own general giant blondness and propensity for wearing scarlet and black and excessively dramatic boots) to take the wingback chair. He set the mask down next to the silver tray. Mr. Dart followed the motion and slowly sank back until he was half-reclining on the chaise longue.

"We were just about to start a question for a question," I said, unable to resist a smirk. "Want to play?"

Mr. Dart frowned at me. "Should it not be an answer for an answer?"

"I knew I was forgetting something," I acknowledged.

"Then, by all means, yes." Mr. Dart rolled another golden quince across the floor to Ballory, who ate half of it and then slumped down to rest after all the exertion. Mr. Dart himself put his legs up on the chaise longue and rested his stone arm on the cushion with which it was furnished.

I brought the bench back over from where the butler had replaced it by the bed. The Honourable Rag made himself a plate of scones, jam, and what on closer inspection appeared to be some form of clotted cream. I watched him, a little queasy and disinclined to eat yet, but not as delicate as might have been the case after sharing several bottles of wine.

I cleared my throat. "So, do we start with the most urgent, or the most important, or simply what we are most confused by or curious about? We have about three-quarters of an hour till breakfast, or so I was informed."

"You're the one who can question the servants about this murder," Mr. Dart muttered. "You're clearly on the best terms with them."

"Yes, about this murder," the Honourable Rag interjected. "How exactly do you know about it? You found the *weapon*, you said? What makes you think it was used for such a crime?"

Mr. Dart looked at the now-sleeping unicorn foal, and at me. I gave him an encouraging smile. The Honourable Rag obviously had some splendid secrets of his own to reveal, if we paid in appropriate coin.

Mr. Dart began in an oblique fashion. "All things know when they've fulfilled their purposes. It was a stiletto dagger, and it was rejoicing in the life-blood it had drunk. It wasn't doing it at supper yesterday, so it must have happened overnight."

I nodded as if this all made perfect sense (and after my experiences with Mr. Dart's ability to hear the inanimate, it rather did), rejoicing in the politely befuddled expression on the Honourable Rag's face. He appeared somewhere between his persona as the Hunter and the vacuous-but-good-natured version of himself he'd been performing, and not quite sure how to respond to two people who had, after all, been intermittent friends since childhood.

While it was disturbing to contemplate the joy a knife might take in its work, it was hard to feel tremendously exercised by a murder for which we had no victim nor murderer. It didn't feel real to me, even if it evidently did to Mr. Dart.

"My turn for a question," I said, ignoring the Honourable Rag's half-articulated complaint. "You've already had one, *and* an answer." At his expression—and bearing in mind what I wanted to ask *him*—I added, "Part of our Mr. Dart's magic is to hear the voices of the inanimate." I grinned at his incredulous, awed response, and went on. "So tell us: why have you been going around dressed as the Hunter in Green half the time and otherwise pretending to be a total idiot?"

"Now, now, don't be catty," Mr. Dart murmured.

"You know exactly what I mean."

"I reckon I do," the Honourable Rag said, laughing. "I put effort into that, I'll have you know."

"That is good to hear," I said blandly.

The Honourable Rag moved his Green-Man mask a little away from the tray so he could put his cup down. "There are some things I can't tell you, as they are not my secrets to tell, you understand. What do you know about the situation in Orio City?"

"Too much and too little," Mr. Dart muttered.

I sighed. "We were caught up in it, alas—well, I was, and

the others as a result of being with me. Are you familiar with the name Lark?"

"The Indrilline's heir and bride-to-be of the governor-prince?"

"She was at Morrowlea with me, and, er ..." I trailed off. The whole situation with Lark seemed distant and somehow no longer fraught, though I was still righteously angry at being so *used* by her.

Mr. Dart sighed extravagantly. "She and our Mr. Greenwing here were paramours, until the spring when her efforts at stealing his magic by means of continuous wireweed doses were spited by his love for his father, whom she made the misjudgement of criticizing publicly. He responded with challenging her final paper, to the point where she failed out of Morrowlea and Jemis was awarded First place. Her retaliation was, first, to hire the Erlingalish playwright Jack Lindsay to write *Three Years Gone*; secondly, to hire him to write a sequel, due out shortly at her wedding; and thirdly, to capture him and his companions and imprison them in the palace. Did I miss anything salient?"

"We escaped the palace-prison," I said, with what I thought was acceptable smugness.

The Honourable Rag responded with as much intrigue and surprise as I could have wished. "No one's ever escaped! Were you not in the cells?"

"We were," Mr. Dart said, giving me a long-suffering look. "Jemis wrote his final paper at Morrowlea interpreting Ariadne nev Lingarel's *On Being Incarcerated in Orio Prison* as a cypher giving the clues necessary to escaping. We were all somewhat astonished to find he was correct."

"This perhaps explains what you meant by saying you were dead of a wireweed overdose."

"A sacrifice was required," I explained. "Returning to your question—and a sneaky way this was of getting further questions of your own answered, don't think I haven't noticed!—

144

the general situation has changed considerably as a result of our escape. We took with us Ruaridh of Nên Corovel."

The Honourable Rag sat back with an oath. "And in an unexpected stroke the political situation of the continent has changed."

"You should probably talk to Hal. He's been muttering about what the unicorn—Ballory, sorry—signifies."

Ballory opened one eye, ears pricking, at the sound of its name, before sighing, shuffling around a little, and relaxing again. I smiled involuntarily.

"Hal ...?"

"The Duke of Fillering Pool."

"Your allies are remarkable," the Honourable Rag murmured. "And your knowledge more extensive than I had suspected. Very well. In short, while I was at Tara I fell in with some folks none too pleased with the way Orio City was going, and very much on the side of the Lady."

"Which one?" Mr. Dart enquired.

The Honourable Rag gestured at his mask. "Both of them. I was fortunate," he added, looking wryly at me. "I found the revolutionaries before I fell *quite* too far into the dens of iniquity run by the Indrillines. A few weeks the other way and it would have been a much more difficult situation. Fortunately I had been given a warning by someone I respected, and even if I had been extremely angry to be seen as needing it ... I did. I give you thanks, Jemis. It was not easy to hear and I did not treat you well at the time, for which I most heartily am sorry. Your warning saved me from great peril."

Well. That was as handsome an apology as I'd ever received. "You are very welcome," I replied. "Unfortunately I didn't realize I was deep in the thrall of wireweed until I was cut off. Although I am, by the Lady's grace, healed from that affliction, I shall need to be vigilant for the rest of my life that I do not fall into another such thraldom."

There was a bit of an uncomfortable silence; this was heavy

conversation before breakfast. Finally the Honourable Rag cleared his throat and continued.

"There are strange things going-on in and around Ragnor Bella, and not *just* to do with the two of you—though they do seem to have accelerated after your respective returns home, which now that I know about your magic makes a great deal more sense, Perry."

"I have decided to go by Peregrine now," Mr. Dart said firmly, then gave me a sardonic smile. "I have had a message from the Other Side, you see."

"It is a strange sort of largesse you scatter, Jemis. Well then, Peregrine—it suits you! And not just because of the companion unicorn."

"Go to, sir Hunter."

"I proceed, I proceed. Welladay. Given the many mysteries of the situation in Ragnor Bella, I agreed to be the point of contact for those, ah, of my persuasion, and also to see what I could ferret out on my own. As I did not wish to make a stir— not knowing that Mr. Greenwing would soon be home to kick the hornet nest with a vengeance—oh! I do apologize."

I had jerked a little at the infelicity of the phrasing; my stepfather had been stung to death by a hive of enraged wasps in the summer. I waved at him and added a splash more coffee to my glass. It could have done with some of the chocolate and spices with which the coffee house in Tara had adulterated its brews. The mountain folk of Lind appeared to like their coffee like coal-tar.

"Anyhow, as I did not expect such an ample sufficiency of misdirections for my own investigations and activities, I decided on a twofold cover. One," and he touched the Green-Man mask affectionately, "one was to indulge in a bit of play-acting suitable to my temperament and the role, and the second was to, ah …"

"Indulge in a bit of play-acting suitable to your temperament and the role," I supplied for him, grinning at his faint flush. "Fair enough. I can hardly complain when you saved my life so adroitly."

"This answers the obvious half of the question," Mr. Dart said thoughtfully. "We shall need to confer further, with Hal and Major Greenwing as well, to understand what else is happening and what my declaration will do for it."

The Honourable Rag opened his eyes wide. "Your declaration?" He glanced down at the unicorn foal and back up at Mr. Dart with rising awe. "You don't mean ..."

Mr. Dart nodded solemnly. "The Lady's heir, Ruaridh, is grievously injured from his long incarceration. We spoke, after we escaped, when ... when we were sitting vigil over Jemis."

He cleared his throat awkwardly, though I found this more fascinating than not.

(There was something incomprehensible about the idea that Jullanar Maebh had washed and laid out my body, and Marcan and Hal and Mr. Dart and Violet had all prayed over it, until Mr. Dart went to sleep and in his dreams fought against the Dark Kings to keep them from entering the world through the door made by my death.)

The Honourable Rag looked at me askance, but gestured at Mr. Dart to go on, which he did after a moment.

"Ruaridh said he could see my magic, and he told me I was coming to that cross-roads between one possible life and another. My first thought was to reject the idea—but then Jemis came back from the dead and it was if the world shook to its foundations."

I smiled at him, feeling a breath of cool air like the zephyrs in that far country, at the edge of our true homeland. Both Mr. Dart and the Honourable Rag flushed and looked away, and I wondered what my expression showed that I did not know.

"It's a bit uncanny, what, that holy light," the Honourable Rag said in a low voice.

"You're one to talk," Mr. Dart returned, gesturing meaningfully at the mask.

"So," I said, trying to return to the present. "If I haven't mistaken, you mean to say you're going to declare yourself a great mage?"

"A great mage, a wild mage, and a Peregrine with a unicorn," Mr. Dart said, smiling brightly.

There was a longish pause. Then the Honourable Rag said, "I *quite* see why you wanted him here for this discussion. Welladay and the Lady bless! What is your brother going to say when he loses his steward?"

"Oh, he'll be busy training his daughter in all her new duties," Mr. Dart said airily.

"His *daughter*?"

"Yes," I said, "Jullanar Maebh Ingridsdottir Dart. I believe you know her?"

And the Honourable Roald Ragnor, all six feet of him, swooned.

CHAPTER FIFTEEN

The only problem with our cunning plan to see who was missing at breakfast, and thereby begin to narrow down the identities of the murderer and their victim, was that only Mr. Dart and I showed up.

We had, naturally, left the Honourable Rag behind. He claimed his swoon was due to a dearth of food and an over-abundance of exertion in the past day, so we left him the scones and the remainder of the coffee, as well as Ballory to keep him in line.

I was inclined to grant him his excuse, as I had enough to think about already. As Mr. Dart felt a familial protectiveness for Jullanar Maebh, he was more insistent on an explanation.

"The reasons are our own, and none of your business!" the Honourable Rag finally said in exasperation, the most honest emotion I'd ever seen on his face.

"As she is my niece, and under my protection—"

"Miss Ingridsdottir—Miss Dart, that is—is entirely capable of protecting herself."

That sounded rueful, and as if there was a story behind it. I raised my eyebrows—half the continent was well aware of my family's supposed peccadilloes—and he flushed a fine pink. "She broke it off," he finally muttered, shamefaced. "I couldn't let her know I was playing the fool, and so ..."

"And so she thinks you *actually* a fool, and accordingly broke off with you because she assumed you were up to your neck in debt to the Indrillines, and therefore in no way as good a prospect as you might seem on paper?" Mr. Dart shook his head. "Did you not realize this would be a result?"

The Honourable Rag squirmed, but Mr. Dart was persistent, and after a short while we learned that he had not realized the depth of his attachment until it was broken; and also that he *did* truly believe in the necessity of his work as the Hunter in the Green.

"You need not harrow hell, surely?" I asked, doubtfully.

"We may need to harrow the land, if what we fear happens. The news you've brought may head off the unrest, but then again ..."

"It might precipitate it," Mr. Dart said, with a thoughtful glance at the still-sleeping Ballory. "And a lovely misdirection! Be you on your good behaviour with my brother's daughter, Roald!"

"She will not know I am here," he promised. "And I will hardly be back home this Winterturn." He nudged the mask with his slippered foot, but added nothing further.

I looked at Mr. Dart, who frowned but eventually accepted this, and we made our way downstairs to see if we could determine who the murder victim might be.

～

Bessie served us coffee and seed cakes and the local variant of the Linder sauces, these coiled links like a pig's tail, which were apparently eaten for breakfast alongside little cakes made of grated rutabagas and potatoes. I quite liked them, and working out whether they were pan-fried or baked occupied my attention for a few minutes.

The table was set with places for ten. It was not as elaborate as the night before, but there were still the bowls of golden quinces and red apples. The curtains at the windows had been drawn back. Before sitting down I went to look out, finding the snowdrifts had come up high enough to be visible against the glass panes.

It was blindingly brilliant outside, all pristine white snow and blue sky. I squinted against the sun, as the windows faced east, and made out a building across what was presumably usually a courtyard. The snow was nearly over the top lintel of the only visible door.

Mr. Dart and I took seats next to each other on the side facing the door through to the sitting room. Mr. Dart stared at the door, crumbling his seed cake in his fingers. I quite like seed cakes, myself, but less so for breakfast. They're more of an afternoon food, in my opinion. I glanced at Mr. Dart and decided not to enter into such an inconsequential conversation, for fear he might unravel completely.

He had pointed out the stiletto as we passed through the sitting room. It was the dagger I had noticed the evening before; it was more disconcerting than I had expected to look at Mr. Dart's green complexion and realize the knife was silently rejoicing in the blood it had drawn.

I gave up on the rutabaga cakes and pouring myself more coffee instead, from the jug Bessie had left on the table. It was not a usual custom for gentry houses, at least not in South Fiellan, but I didn't mind not having to ring for a maid to come replenish my cup. Mind you, it was also odd that the housekeeper herself was acting as parlour-maid, but little about this house seemed as well-run as one would expect.

"No clues about, er, who?" I asked in a low voice.

Mr. Dart started violently, nearly tipping over all the cups and the jug. Before I could do more than lift up my hands a swirl of air—of *magic*—righted them. I eyed the splash of coffee frozen in midair, all glinting black-brown droplets and fantastic curls, and swallowed hard when it siphoned itself back into Mr. Dart's cup.

"No," he said after a moment. His good hand was clenched. "There's no … situational awareness, usually. They're not … people."

"That's a relief," I joked, or tried to.

He nodded solemnly. "It is."

Indeed.

"I say," I said presently, as a certain particularly heavy-browed figure in one of the etchings opposite me reminded my of the butler and what the man had told me the evening before.

"Yes? Do tell."

"I was told that only the family or those granted permission by the Master can lift the weapons. An enchantment my grand-mother cast, apparently."

Mr. Dart sighed. "Sadly, that does not narrow the question overmuch."

Except presumably it exclude our party, Hope, and Henry Coates himself, who if he hadn't been the victim was the most obvious suspect.

After a while Bessie returned to take away out plates and ask us if we needed anything more. Mr. Dart obviously yearned to say something about the putative murder, but I forestalled any blurted indiscretion (ignoring the fact that I am much more prone to them than he) by asking whether we could expect any of the other guests, or even our mysterious host, this morning.

"The Master is indisposed," the housekeeper said with a curiously flat intonation, as if of a rote line. "Madam Veitch is usually an early riser, but she is unwell this morning, I under-stand. That storm!" She shuddered expressively.

"Yes. Is the drive snowed in?"

"Aye, sorr, it'll be another day afore the men can dig us out. No one's even reached the house yet from the stable! But don't you worry, sorr, they know what to do."

From which I deduced that the 'men' were not in the house itself, except perhaps the unseen Walter of the night before, and the butler of course. And ... I smiled at her. "Is this amount of snow common around here?"

I thought this an innocuous question but Bessie clammed up immediately.

"It's not unknown," was all she said, before curtseying and firmly telling us to ring the bell if we wanted any more coffee.

I sat back and considered what the Honourable Rag had said about the storm being centred on the house. Could the master be a weather wizard?

Unlikely, as it was well known that weather wizards had been among the worst affected by the Fall of Astandalas. I couldn't think there were *any* accounts of any surviving with both sanity and magic intact.

I glanced at Mr. Dart, who continued to stare with a pale, distracted face at the door. The Interim was long since over, and what magicians I had met of late all seemed to find their powers working as they expected. Mr. Dart's power was a law unto itself, but that was the nature of wild magic, not a result of the broken enchantments and unloosed magical bindings resulting from the Fall.

If not that, then what?

I looked around the room, at the monstrous insects in their glass displays cases. The blue butterfly was behind us now, and instead I was facing several dragonflies, their wingspans close to a foot across. Green, red, striped with yellow, their wings clear and blotched, like the colours used in a horse race.

There could be an artefact of some sort, buried in amongst all the other treasures and junk the Master had collected in this strange cabinet of curiosities. Perhaps even the Heart of the

Moon, the stone the cult had been searching for in Ragnor Bella back in September.

There could be a curse, twisting weather around the house, though I could not imagine to what end.

(But then again, what had been the cause of the curse on the bees and the people of the Woods Noirell? Because I had not known to do the dances my mother had done, and no one else had, bees and people alike were frozen in time. When I had performed the dance the bees had started to move and so had the people, who discovered they had lost three years. *Why* no one knew; or was saying.)

This could, conceivably, have something to do with the Good Neighbours. I knew Marcan scoffed at them, but that was the prerogative of the second sons of kings. This part of Lind was too close to the Woods Noirell, on the other side of the mountains, and the Farry March, in the vale between northern Lind and central Fiellan, for the country folk not to be aware of the Gentry.

Or, of course, it could be all three, or neither. I had only studied a term's worth of History of Magic, and we had spent most of it discussing historical forms of divination, the professor's particular interest. I could wax eloquent about the history of haruspexy (I had written a paper on it before absconding to Classical Languages and Literature); I did not know the history of curses in Lind.

"Will you stay in here?" Mr. Dart asked suddenly.

I blinked at him. "If you wish, but why?"

"Or in the other room," he went on, gesturing to the sitting room with the ominous dagger. "To see if anyone else comes down and watch their reactions if they do."

"I see," I said slowly. "And what will you be doing?"

"Were you off in the clouds? I shall return upstairs to see how my cousin is this morning."

And Ballory and the Honourable Rag, I presumed, and agreed to his plan. We both went into the sitting room, where he shuddered minutely at the sight of the dagger and then went on upstairs, leaving me — the horrors — alone without a book.

I circled the room. Unusually for an Alinorel house, there were no books to be found. There was a desk over to one wall, between two windows and below the array of daggers. I contemplated it for a moment before deciding that I could not bear the thought of sitting *below* the stiletto with my back to the door and any incomers. If I were a murderer, I couldn't imagine I'd be too pleased to find someone so close to my weapon of choice.

Of course, the murderer had returned the knife to the wall, clean and apparently innocent of any crime, so perhaps he or she would be pleased as a mummer to find it so disregarded.

While I was still hesitating, the butler entered. He approached me directly, and I wondered uneasily, for a fantastic moment, whether he was going to snatch the stiletto off the wall and attack me with it.

"Good morning," I hazarded, stepping away from the wall.

"Indeed," he replied, more quickly than before, and paused attentively.

He wasn't holding anything, nor did he give any indication of why he'd come over, besides the attentive demeanour. I cleared my throat as the silence stretched on awkwardly. The amused gleam in his eye was surely a figment of my doubtlessly overwrought imagination.

"Er, there was quite a hullabaloo last night in the hall ... do you know what caused it?" At his blank stare I added, even more awkwardly, "I was, er, distracted from attending immediately."

The butler softened minimally and inclined his head. "Of course, young sir. I fear young Mr. Garsom and his friend Mr. Coates were well-lit when they retired last night, and were not appreciative of others' rest when they did so. There is a suit of armour at the top of the north stair, which they toppled down, to much, as you say, hullabaloo."

He pronounced the word with mild disdain. I stifled a nervous grin. "Ah. I see. They were uninjured, I hope?"

Certainly Henry Coates had seemed so, when he had come to my room shortly after to ask me of my political views.

"A few bruises, I believe," the butler said, tone dismissive. "Is there anything I can assist you with this morning, sir? Alas that the post cannot be expected until the drive is cleared."

The thought of the post led to the post-rider, and that easily to the *New Salon* up in my room, and that to the collection in the main hall of the house. "Actually, yes. I noticed on our entry yesterday that there was a stack of back issues of the *New Salon* in the, er, hall. Would it be possible for me to look through them? I have a mind to do some research. I'm particularly interested in this year and last year's issues."

Research is one of those magic words to a certain type of mind, and the butler lit up with vicarious interest. "Indeed, sir!" he exclaimed, or as close to it as his tortoise-paced words permitted. "I will see to it. Will you take them in your room?"

I sought an excuse for remaining downstairs all morning. "Ah," I said, and then thought of several customers at Mrs. Etaris's bookstore, who talked at length about how important it was for them to own pristine editions of books: they came into the store to look through her copies, which, they claimed, 'didn't mind being read'.

I should have to ask Mr. Dart whether this opinion was justified.

"I shouldn't like to discompose the Master by taking them out of sight. If it doesn't offend, I shall look at them in here and make my notes. The light is good."

"It is, sir," he allowed, but gave me a pleased smile. "Will you have tea this morning?"

Tea was such an incredible luxury I faltered on the honour he was showing me; and then remembered the crates and crates of it we'd found. "Thank you," I said gravely, and he proceeded slowly out of the room.

In remarkably short order a boy arrived with a huge stack of papers. He was a hearty, likely-looking lad of about sixteen, who introduced himself as Wally. On my polite enquiry he informed me shyly that he was working in Hillend Towers — apparently the name of the building, though why I couldn't imagine as it was not in a style running towards any form of conspicuous erection — while he studied for the Entrance Examinations.

"The Master is so knowledgeable," he said, rather starry-eyed. "And so generous! He has me to sit three times a week and tells me stories about all his things. And he lets me borrow books, and answers my questions. My da's ever so pleased."

"That's wonderful," I said, even as Wally briskly rearranged the room without any word from me so that the desk was away from the wall and two leaves extended on either side of it. "There, that'll see you right, sorr," he said in satisfaction. "There's paper and a blotter and quills in the drawer there, like, you see?"

"Thank you."

"Where did you go, sorr, if I may ask?"

"Morrowlea, like, er, Miss Garsom." Wally looked suitably impressed. I looked at him and added, which I didn't normally, "I was the Rondelan Scholar in my year, actually, so if you have any questions about studying for the exams …"

"That's very kind of you, sorr," Wally said, grinning at me as I trailed off. I wondered what on earth I was thinking.

Well, random people had given me much advice when I was studying for the Entrance Examinations, and some of it had even been helpful.

I settled down at the table thus made out of the desk, with the stiletto dagger safely behind me (and a few feet back; it was not going to fall down on top of me) and the three doors in the room — the one to the hall, the one over to the dining room, and the one that both Wally and the butler had used — in plain sight.

After finding an ancient set of quills and an even more ancient but nevertheless exceedingly sharp pen-knife in the drawer, I cut a nib to my liking, stirred up a pot of black ink, and started investigating a year's worth of ciphered notes concealed in the *Etiquette Questions Answered* column while I waited to see who might come tiptoeing in.

CHAPTER SIXTEEN

Naturally, I had to start with that most boring yet essential stage of research, transcribing notes.

If they had been *my* copies of the *New Salon*, I could have just cut out the relevant passages, but since they weren't, and short of enquiring at the company's offices for which university might be archiving their issues, this seemed to be the best source. It was, after all, quite possible that Master Boring *was* the person archiving them. At least according to everyone else.

I had spent a good deal of time at Morrowlea copying out passages from Ariadne nev Lingarel's unpublished notes, so I was familiar with the rhythm of transcription. It was significantly faster this time. The script was printed, first of all, and secondly was in Modern Shaian, and thirdly involved nothing but the most obvious and common abbreviations.

I didn't try to do any actual decoding, but I couldn't help but catch strange glimpses of what I imagined were ciphered messages, running parallel with questions of deportment or courtesy or precedent.

In the second of the February issues, for instance, I read:

A Reader Asks: My mother-in-law owns her own business, and I recently learned my brother's wife is one of her favourite customers. My sister loves the business but hates the proprietress. I had invited both sides to attend a dinner party celebrating the birth of my first son before I learned this. What do I do to keep everyone happy?

The Etiquette Mistress Answers: My dear, warn your sister! Then sit her beside the most interesting person at the table (besides yourself, your husband, and your darling new son—congratulations!—that is), well away from your mother-in-law. If the conversation shows indications of turning sour, begin discussing the state of the roads; all persons have opinions thereon.

The Ajiricano code in its Elmsdale variant utilized a double substitution. The recurring nouns—in such a column as this I presumed family members and certain forms of behaviour—would have set definitions or parallel meanings, while there would be some alphanumerical substitution going on using the length of words, or the prevalence of certain letters, or the like, to give details. One of the great features of the Elmsdale variant (over, say, the Lofthouse or Pikaroon) was that part of the message was left unencoded.

It was tantalizing to suspect that this particular message involved a warning about the state of the roads and the likelihood of *someone*—the 'mother-in-law'—being a present danger.

Regretfully I left the specifics aside. For all I knew 'warnings' were actually good things, and 'most interesting' was the key word here. It would have to wait for an extended period of leisure uninterrupted by murder investigations. It was a stroke of good fortune to have found the complete run, and I wanted to make the most of it while I could.

I got as far as the middle of April before anything changed. The butler shuffled in with a tea tray mid-morning, and slowly and lovingly detailed to me its contents.

There was a kind of cardamom-flavoured soft roll, like a Linder variant of cinnamon buns. I eyed the plate with intrigue. Cardamom was not a flavour used much in Fiellan, though I knew it from my stepfather's Charese Winterturn traditions.

(I wondered briefly, even as the butler laid out a beautifully ironed snowy-white linen napkin for me, whether there would be 'cardy biscuits' for him in that glade where the souls of the dead refreshed themselves before heading to the Mountains. I couldn't remember if there had been food and drink, there. — Well, I could leave them as part of my solstice offering at his grave.)

"And this, young sir," the butler intoned, "is a very *special* tea. It was the young master's favourite."

I thought back to the *Peerage of Lind*. "Would that be one of Master Boring's late sons?"

The butler's eyes kindled with a remembered pride and still-present grief. "Aye," he said. "Richard the Younger. He was a brave man and make no mistake! It's his clothes you're wearing. And very well you carry them, too, if I say so myself. It's a much nicer fashion than the young bloods nowadays."

I had to agree, and, smiling, did so. Evidently I reminded the butler of Richard the Younger — he was the mountaineer, not the soldier, if I recalled correctly — but as it had not led anywhere worrisome except for my still-missing clothes, I saw little harm in going along with him for the moment.

"This tea," the butler went on in a dryer voice, straightening as if to indicate that the unwonted moment of tenderness was over, thank you, "is called *Love in a Mist*. Regard." And he opened the lid of the silver teapot, revealing a mass of leaves hovering in the midst of the liquid.

At first it looked very odd, but then the leaves resolved themselves into something like a complicated flower in full blossom. The fragrance wafted up, leafy and floral and astringent and delicate all at once.

"Do you see it? The tea makers bind the leaves in such a way that when the boiling water is poured over they unfurl into a flower. *Chrysanthemum*, this shape is called."

I recalled the name from illustrations in old books from Voonra and Ysthar before the Fall. Hal always pointed out the images of flowers foreign to our Northwest Oriolese eyes. I smiled at the butler, who was giving me something of a conspiratorial smirk. There was something wonderfully extravagant about a hidden beauty such as this.

"Aye, there it is," the butler said, replacing the lid with a faint chime of silver on silver. The pot was burnished bright, accentuating its glorious simplicity of line, which was quite unlike the encrusted epergnes and other silverware on the dining table.

"Thank you," I said. He poured the tea for me before he left me alone to drink it. My cup was made of porcelain so fine I could easily see my fingers through the walls. It was all white, with fluted walls and a simple beaded design along the rim. I could imagine a great lady—even *the* Lady—taking tea with it.

Dying seemed to have removed certain forms of embarrassment. The idea that this was a particularly delicate, even feminine, piece would have embarrassed me in the past; now it seemed simply something to note, and enjoy. Why could a man —*I*—not appreciate such beauty? Clearly the Master of the house did; or at least his butler.

I liked the tea better this time. It bore a resemblance to what Professor Aurelia Anyra had served me in Tara, but was much more floral, and I had not been offered milk with it. The liquor was a deep, burnished copper, almost the colour of Jullanar Maebh's hair.

A murmur and a half-stifled laugh alerted me to visitors. I looked up to see Hal and Hope come into the room. They were arm-in-arm and Hope was looking up at Hal with shining eyes, her whole face luminous. Hal himself was smiling down at her with tender regard.

My matchmaking services were obviously going to be entirely unnecessary. Hal checked when he entered the room and saw me, then smiled sheepishly even as he guided Hope to a seat on the sofa, which was just to my right.

"You seem to have settled in for the morning," Hal observed pleasantly. "Did we miss breakfast?"

"You and everyone but for Mr. Dart and myself," I agreed, and then stopped. If it had been Hal by himself, I would have launched into a discussion of the putative murder and missing murder victim. If it had been Hope by herself, I would have continued on last night's conversation as best I could, and no doubt have urged her towards confiding in Hal. With the two of them together, I wasn't sure what to say. Despite her unexpected resilience last night, no gentlewoman would be that keen on being informed of a murder.

"Are you looking for anything particular in all those *New Salons*?" Hope asked.

In their entry I had half-forgotten what I was actually doing. I looked down at them doubtfully. "I'm transcribing the *Etiquette Questions Answered* columns for the past year."

"We've only been snowed in for a morning so far," Hal pointed out. "It's not as if we need busywork to get us through the whole winter."

"I shouldn't be transcribing them if I thought I'd have access to them all winter," I retorted.

"Oh, don't, Jemis," Hope said, slumping out of her proper-young-gentlewoman's posture against the padded back of the sofa. Her skirts, all layers of white ruffles, puffed out around her. She closed her eyes and seemed to soften all over. "I have the head-ache this morning."

She hadn't had much of the wine, but then she never had, at Morrowlea, and perhaps it had gone to her head. I grimaced apologetically. "I'm afraid I was only given the one cup, but I can ring for another, if you'd like?"

"What are you drinking?" she asked without opening her eyes.

"A tea called, ah, *love-in-a-mist*, if I recall correctly."

Hal had been hovering solicitously over Hope, finding a knitted throw to tuck around her shoulders. He looked up at me with a curious smile. "That's the name of a flower ... nigella is another name. So is, er, devil-in-a-bush."

Even Hope giggled at that, then raised her hand to her forehead. I thought it an intriguing name for a plant and resolved to ask Hal why it had such divergent names.

It would have to be some other time, I realized. Hal had clasped Hope's hand with his own and regarded her with an entirely besotted look. I watched him for a good three minutes before he realized I was sipping my tea and doing so.

He laughed, not the great whoop but a more polite snicker. I grinned unrepentantly at him.

"So why *are* you transcribing the *Etiquette Questions Answered* column? You must know that there are books for that sort of thing."

"I do work in a bookstore, yes," I replied with an effort at serenity.

Hope opened her eyes to squint at me. "You do?"

"I told you last night that the viscountcy was both very new and very unexpected," I reminded her.

Hal mouthed, *Last night?* But didn't actually vocalize the question. I shrugged—I would likely be telling him all of last night's news shortly, when we were in private—and answered the earlier question. "It's all ciphered. I plan on transcribing the year's worth and seeing what messages are being sent."

I didn't say I thought Violet was the one doing the ciphering, or at least involved in it. She was hardly in a position to have been doing the actual coding in our last term at Morrowlea; though there were always letters. Hal frowned but left it at that. "Any news about the roads?"

I suppressed a snicker at this unintended reference to *all persons have opinions thereon*. "We're snowed in until the men in the stables clear the drive, I'm told. I'm also told that they know their work, and that this sort of weather is not unknown hereabouts."

Hal sat down on the chair next to Hope's sofa. His eyes strayed towards her semi-recumbent figure, his expression adoring but also slightly troubled. He was back in his travelling clothes, and looked every inch an ardent young lover out of a play, of good family but impecunious. Hope had implied last night that she came of merchant stock. If he were what he appeared, it would have been marrying down for her; in reality, Hope was nowhere near the List of eligible brides Hal's Aunt Honoria had compiled.

"That's a lovely dress, Hope — Miss Stornaway, that is," I tried.

She smiled without moving her hand from her eyes. "Thank you, Jemis. It's the first of December. The tradition in my part of Chare is to wear white in honour of the Lady of Winter today. We'd be lighting the Winterturn candles today, too. Three weeks from the solstice."

"Where exactly in Chare are you from?"

"I was raised in a place called Mollen, which isn't far from the border with West Erlingale."

"That's part of the Ironwood lands, isn't it?" Hal asked.

She hesitated, which I thought interesting. "Just south of there, yes. It's contested by the counts of Shavaren."

Hal made a face, presumably as a result of some encounter with the count (or counts) of Shavaren in the past. Possibly at his club in Orio City. Our club. He had sponsored me for membership before we'd been captured and escaped from the city.

"What was it like for you, when the Ironwood heiress was found?" I asked curiously. "When I was declared the viscount it was deucedly odd. Everyone was suddenly even *more* interested in my doings than they had been."

"Was that even possible?" Hal asked, grinning at me.

"The Greenwings," I informed Hope, "are the major source of gossip in Ragnor barony. I wish it weren't true, but alas it is. According to Tadeo Toynbee's guidebook, the only things of note in Ragnor Bella are the Talgarth's country house, the unparalleled racehorse Jemis Swiftfoot, and my father's career."

"They'll add you to the next edition, I expect," Hal said.

"And here I thought you a friend!"

Hope giggled. "Are you really named for the horse?"

"My father lost a bet. My mother let it stand because she liked the name; it's common in Pfaschen and Harktree, apparently. I think she was untowardly influenced by Mr. Dart's mother, who chose very old-fashioned names for her sons, but they assure me it wasn't so."

I realized that I had chosen the wrong tense of verb a moment too late. Hal caught it, with a sudden twist to his lips; so, too, did Hope. She said softly, without accusation, "I thought your mother had died?"

We'd had a conversation or two at Morrowlea about being orphans, she and I. "Yes, when I was fifteen. I … misspoke."

Hal's expression eased. I think he didn't want me to start talking about my experiences in the afterlife again, though how could I not, when my whole existence had turned inside-out so suddenly? But it was a very personal sort of thing, really, and even without the assistance of the *Etiquette Questions Answered* column or any relevant book I did know it wasn't exactly proper topic for general conversation.

I cast around for another topic. "So," I said, "devil-in-a-bush?"

"It's a reference to the flowers and seed-heads," he replied after a brief startled moment to reorient his thoughts. And then he spoke for a few minutes about black cumin and *kalonjee* and culinary usages, borrowing my quill so he could sketch flowers like antique paper lanterns and seed-heads like jester's caps in the margins of my transcriptions.

Then Mr. Dart came bursting into the room, face stark white, and said, "It's Henry Coates."

"The murderer?" I said, forgetting all my resolutions.

Even as Hal and Hope sat up in shock, Mr. Dart shook his head. "The victim."

CHAPTER SEVENTEEN

The room felt very odd after that blurted declaration. I sat back against my chair, feeling a tug from the odd length of my coat as it bunched against my thighs. I shifted awkwardly to loosen it. The room was much draughtier than it had been earlier, the flames in the hearth roaring loudly. I looked at Mr. Dart's strained white face, his hand gripping the edge of his own coat, and realized why.

"That's ... quite the statement," Hal said, staring from Mr. Dart to me and back again. "From your expressions you already suspected a death?"

"But how?" Hope asked, returning to her proper seat, spine straight and held well away from the back of the sofa. Her large brown eyes were worried. "If you thought Mr. Coates the murderer ..."

I had to confess that Mr. Dart's face had convinced me of the reality of this crime. I hadn't liked Henry Coates, not with my friends' deep dislike and his own sneering personality, but the memory his beseeching eyes, last midnight, puzzled me. He had been fretting over something, that was clear.

"How do you know it's a *murder*?" Hal asked, in a voice I abruptly suspected was his lord-of-the-manor one.

Mr. Dart glanced at Hope and bit his lip, then straightened his shoulders. "I am a wild mage, Mr. Leaveringham. The dagger informed me." He gestured at the wall behind me, where the stiletto hung in its seeming innocuousness.

I watched their faces. Hal stilled; Hope started and frowned and looked entirely disbelieving. But not guilty and not caught-out in any fashion, and I felt myself relax minutely. I had not even realized I suspected Hope, but then ...

"That is not evidence one could present in court," Hal said slowly, almost apologetically.

(I was sure I was missing something about what Mr. Dart's declaration meant in the here-and-now. Hal's sudden deference to him indicated ... what?)

"The stab wounds are," Mr. Dart replied tartly.

"So you have seen the body," I said, after a few minutes of shocked remonstrations and reassurances of poor Hope, who did not, after all, know Mr. Dart as I (or even Hal) did. "Where did you find it?"

"Him, surely?" Hal said faintly. "I did not like him, but common decency ..."

"From my perspective, there was a distinct separation, and some sort of spiritual form responding to the maturation of the soul, not the body," I informed him.

Hope whimpered. Hal took her hand, glared at me, and said, "I don't know that we needed to know that, Jemis. Carry on, Mr. Dart."

Mr. Dart was regarding me with an uneasy eye, but shook himself at this request. "Quite. I went up to see my cousin, who continues unwell this morning; I believe she has caught a cold. However, at first I mistook the door—they're all quite similar. The one I knocked upon was unlatched and swung open under my hand."

"Odd," Hope said, leaning forward in interest. I noticed that she was still holding Hal's hand, and suppressed a smile. "Given the storm," she went on, a little flustered when she noticed us all looking at her. "I should have thought the draughts would shut any door."

"Indeed," Mr. Dart agreed. "I called out and looked within, to see if aught was amiss, and ... it was. Mr. Coates was laying face-down on the floor. He'd been stabbed in the back."

"No doubt, then," I said.

Hope uttered a low, distressed cry. We looked at her again, more in sympathy than surprise, but she shrank back against the arm of the sofa in distress. Tears were starting to shine in her eyes.

"I'm sorry," she said brokenly after a moment. "I did not like him, but to die from being *stabbed in the back* ... how utterly horrible! Who could have done such a thing?"

"Who, indeed?" Hal murmured quietly.

There was a pause. The light pouring in from the two outside windows seemed inordinately brilliant. I was starting to be even more inordinately discomfited by the stiletto dagger on the wall behind me. After a moment Mr. Dart rallied.

"We should make a list of the occupants of the house," he said.

Hal nodded briskly. "And a timeline of where they were, last night and this morning. Who the last person to have seen Mr. Coates alive was, and all that."

"What about motives?" Hope ventured.

Hal shook his head. "Motives are a tricky business; people lie. Better to come up with opportunity and method first, and then see what secrets there are to uncover."

Hope regarded him with startled eyes. "You seem to have thought through what to do?"

I could see Hal debating with himself what to say. I could guess that he *had* been responsible for sitting in judgment and hearing the results of such investigations by the constables and other authorities in his demesne, but he could hardly say so without revealing that he was the Duke Imperial, and he seemed still disinclined to do so, presumably for fear that Hope would react ill to the revelation.

"I've read any number of mystery novels," Mr. Dart proclaimed. "Mrs. Etaris—Jemis's employer, that is—has a goodly selection in her bookstore."

"Really?" I said, surprised.

"You've been working there for two and a half months," he pointed out.

I made a face at him. "I've been preoccupied. Where are they?"

"Past the History books, in the back room. Next to all those three-volume-romances."

I had dusted the three-volume-romances, and their neighbours, but avoided looking too hard at the titles after I was caught out deeply immersed in one by the Honourable Roald Ragnor, who'd thought it hilarious I was so engrossed in *Eilonwy of the North, Or, Patience Rewarded*, as to have entirely missed his entrance.

I coughed. Mr. Dart smirked—he, like most of the town, had heard about this soon thereafter—but sobered quickly in the face of our present circumstances. I drew a fresh piece of paper towards me. The ink had dried on my quill, so I spent a few moments re-shaping the nib with the pearl-handled penknife that had been in the drawer.

"So, current occupants of the house?" I said. "Us, of course." I wrote down *Peregrine Dart, Hal Leaveringham, Hope Stornaway,* and *Jemis Greenwing* in a column to the left of the page, quite as if I were beginning a complicated translation-and-expansion exercise of Classical Shaian poetry.

"There's Anna, and her brother Ned," Hope put in.

"Jullanar Maebh."

"Mr. and Madam Veitch. And our as-yet-unseen host, of course," Hal added.

I wrote all these down, including *Master Boring*. Mr. Dart nodded approvingly. "What about the servants? There's Bessie, and I've heard about a maid named Hattie, is that right?"

"Hettie," Hope corrected. She looked sidelong at Hal and Mr. Dart, then said delicately, "And your, er, visitor?"

"Ah yes," I said, and wrote down *The Hunter in Green*.

Hal peered at the paper, which was upside down to him, and frowned mightily. "When did *he* arrive? And how did you know, Hope?"

"I went to talk to Jemis last night," Hope said softly. "That … man … broke in through the window."

"He's up in my room at the moment," I said. "Mr. Dart's spoken to him as well."

Hal seemed slightly perturbed, but whether it was because of Hope coming to talk to me, alone, in the night, or because of the appearance of the Hunter in Green I wasn't sure. "He does get around, doesn't he? Other servants? There's Walter."

"Wally, who's about sixteen," I put in.

Hal and Mr. Dart were looking at me with decidedly queer expressions. "He's forty if he's a day," Mr. Dart said slowly. "He brought my clothes this morning."

I blinked at him, having somehow not noticed that he was indeed wearing his proper clothes, plum and grey and neatly, unostentatiously, of excellent quality and fit. He no longer looked like a foppish hanger-on, but like what he was, a young scion of the solid country gentry.

"Perhaps Wally's his son. He brought my papers in to the parlour earlier." I surveyed my list. "There's also the butler."

Hope uttered another exclamation of shock.

I looked at her sharply. "I beg your pardon?"

"There isn't a butler. Anna told me—he died two months ago, not from anything untoward, he was old and it was his heart, apparently. Anna was complaining that her uncle was too miserly to replace him, even with guests coming for

Winterturn. There's only Walter and the grooms in the stables for menservants."

"Then who have I been talking to this whole time? Hal, weren't you there when he brought the wine in? Yesterday, when we were waiting for everyone to come down for supper."

"I'd gone to freshen up," Hal said. "When I came back you had that excellent wine."

"The butler brought it to me. And the wine when we went to Mr. Dart's after supper, and the tea service this morning. And he lit my fire—"

"Don't go into a fuss!" Mr. Dart said sharply. "There's probably a simple explanation. Has he spoken to you?"

"Yes—"

"About anything personal? To him, that is?"

I hesitated, going back over our interactions. I gestured down at my clothes. "He was fond of the Master's late sons, and pleased Master Richard the Younger's clothes fit me well. It seemed harmless so I didn't complain about my clothes not reappearing yet."

"Those aren't yours?" Hope asked in disappointment. "When you didn't change this morning I was hoping you'd decided to start a new fashion. Anna is already planning on writing to the *New Salon* with an account. She thinks it's marvellous."

"There have been worse things written of me in the *New Salon*," I said absently, still stuck on the notion that no one else had interacted with the butler. "It's true I simply *assumed* he was the butler. He hasn't exactly said. So he could be another servant—perhaps Master Boring's man?"

Hope was shaking her head again. "Walter's his man. He was only assisting on our side because Anna told Bessie, the housekeeper, not to let the maids alone with Mr. Coates."

It struck me what an unsavoury reputation the man had, though all he'd done in my presence was to make a few objectionable comments and smirk unpleasantly.

173

"We shall add it to the mystery," Mr. Dart said, fishing in his pocket and then frowning. "I left my pipe upstairs. Also, I shouldn't mind speaking to, er, the Hunter again. Has *he* seen the butler?"

I thought back to this morning. "I don't know about *seen*, but he must have heard him, when the butler—or whoever it is —came in to mend my fire and bring the tea and scones this morning."

"Well, write down *The Butler*," Mr. Dart said practically. "And there's probably a cook and perhaps a scullery maid as well, I expect. Walter served us last night at supper, along with —was that Hettie again, Miss Stornaway?"

At Hope's nod of agreement I wrote those three job titles down, with question marks beside them, and finally added *Henry Coates* at the end.

"That's a long list," Hope said.

Leaving aside the four in our party—or six including Hope and the Honourable Rag (or rather Hunter in Green)—that left a round dozen suspects. Even without accounting for the enchantment on the dagger—and the servants might have the master's permission to take it down for cleaning, of course—I felt fairly sure Hope was not involved; but could not say the same for Anna Garsom.

"What should we do now?" Hope asked, looking from Hal to Mr. Dart and then to me with a plaintive expression. Her thoughts had apparently been following mine, for she said: "I cannot bear to go up alone—not when we know someone in this house is a murderer, but not *who*!"

"How I want my pipe," Mr. Dart muttered, using his left hand to adjust the sling supporting his stone arm with a disconsolate expression. "Jemis, what do you think?"

"I am still contemplating the butler who isn't," I replied. "Oh—you *did* see him—he answered the front door to us yesterday!"

Hal said slowly, "Jemis, no one answered the door. You opened it and went in."

It took me a long moment to compose myself. "I introduced you."

Except that they'd been thoroughly occupied with assisting Jullanar Maebh, to the point of rudeness, I'd thought and dismissed at the time.

"We came in after you opened the door, and Miss Dart fair swooned," Hal said. "I didn't notice anything until you rang the handbell on the table—"

"And the housekeeper, Bessie, came," Mr. Dart put in.

My head was whirling. "The *butler* opened the door and rang the bell for Bessie. We talked about my grandmother and he questioned me about our arrival. You didn't hear any of that? What did you think I was doing?"

"Looking for a way to summon the housekeeper," Hal replied promptly.

"I was focused on my cousin, and ... the house," Mr. Dart added.

Hope was listening to this with her mouth parted in astonishment. "How very odd," she said, in her usual soft way, which made everything sound mildly delightful. "What on earth could have caused such a thing? Magic?"

Hal tapped his fingers on the chair. "I should have expected either myself or Mr. Dart to notice magic afoot. No, I suspect this is something to do with Jemis's ... background."

"You don't mean it was a ghost, do you?" I asked uncomfortably.

Hal quirked his mouth and exchanged a glance with Mr. Dart, who was leaning moodily against the desk, looking the very model of a proper young gentleman of Chare. "That, or—we *are* close to the Woods Noirell, and the Farry March, and as you have pointed out, the Fair—"

"Don't name them!" I hissed. "Not if you think they're *here*. If they haven't named themselves it's for a reason."

"You have their blood," Mr. Dart said reasonably. "Apart from this week's events, they might recognize you. Did he seem to care about your name?"

I thought back to my initial interaction with the butler. "More my grandmother's."

Down which line came the fairy blood, my mother had told me. I considered the matter uneasily. I wasn't sure whether I would prefer ghosts, or the Good Neighbours, or an arcane magic neither the Schooled nor the wild mage could feel.

"Someone should stay down here, in case anyone comes by," Hal said, with the air of one happily relinquishing an uncomfortable subject. "You're not finished with your transcribing, are you, Jemis?"

"No; I'm only on April."

"I'll help," Hope volunteered, looking relieved. "I expect Anna will be down soon; she was looking for her embroidery earlier."

I wondered vaguely how that had gone astray, but the nuances of needlecraft were not something I had spent much time on. I hadn't minded the Sartorial Arts classes at Morrowlea, but embroidery had required a deftness of fingers that I hadn't enjoyed.

Hal and Mr. Dart agreed, Hal a little less enthusiastically, and they returned upstairs together.

I reshaped my quill nib with the penknife, and frowned at my papers with their copies of the *Etiquette Questions Answered*. And what answer would I receive if I wrote in to ask what one should do when one suspected someone at the house in which you were an unexpected and probably unwanted guest of being a murderer?

Hope arranged herself on the opposite side of the table to me, with a portion of the *New Salons* at her side and her own fountain pen in hand. I regarded this a little dourly. The Honourable Rag had borrowed mine, and not given it back despite several requests. This wouldn't have bothered me except that it had been a gift from my stepfather last birthday, and fountain pens were still rare and expensive. I was surprised Hope had one, in fact, unless she had some connection with the inventors, who were Charese if I recalled correctly.

I mused on this topic, and the difficulties facing Hal's and her courtship, and more pleasing rumination on my fair Violet. I was engrossed in these happy reflections (and to a lesser extent, the accuracy of my transcriptions) when Hope suddenly stirred and said, "Jemis."

I looked at her to see that she'd finished her stack and was staring intently at me. A quick glance around the room was sufficient to demonstrate no one had come in while I was inattentive, so I finished off the paragraph I was copying and set down my quill. "Yes, Hope? What can I do for you?"

She twiddled her pen in her fingers. Her voice was very soft, almost inaudible, as she spoke. "Jemis ... do you think it's wrong of me to think that Hal's likely to propose?"

I leaned forward, as she clearly didn't want to speak such a personal conversation loudly, and lowered my own voice. "If I may judge by the way he's looking at you, no." She did not seem relieved by this; quite the contrary, in fact.

My heart sank. Poor Hal! "Can you not see your way to accepting?"

She turned her head, lips firmly pressed together, and stared blankly down at the pages she'd copied. She had neat handwriting, copperplate feminine; my guess was it was the style taught in the Charese equivalent of Rondelan kingschools.

"I don't think it would be accepted," she said at last, her shoulders slumping.

"By your family?"

She looked up at my tone, which was not particularly sympathetic, as I realized. I flushed, not quite sure how to say that Hal was the single most eligible bachelor in Northwest Oriole, and *she* was the one likely to have difficulties.

"By the terms of my inheritance," she said slowly, with a careful, dull, precision to her tone. "I am required to marry a man who proposes to me by my full name."

I blinked at her. "I fail to see —"

"Henry Coates is the only one who knew it."

CHAPTER EIGHTEEN

Hope sat back, face averted, and spent a few minutes trying to compose herself after this admission. I made a bit of a production of shaping the quill nib again.

(It was quite remarkable how often I had to do so, really. Modern metal tips were much more convenient. I was grateful I'd learned how to do the old-fashioned method at Morrowlea, much though we'd all ridiculed the class at the time. But we all could do at least basic calligraphic forms by the end of first year.)

My thoughts were whirling. That had sounded uncomfortably close to a confession of motive.

"It's an odd sort of inheritance requirement," I said at last. Something told me not to dig deeper, and though it must be said I'm not always that good at following such intuitions, in this case it was quite obvious.

"It's an odd sort of inheritance," she replied bitterly. "More trouble than it's worth."

"I know that sort of heritage."

She looked sharply at me, then flushed darkly. "I had forgotten. I'm sorry, Jemis—and here I'd thought, when I first read about the dragon, how much I wished I could talk to you! If anyone would understand, *you* would, I thought."

I tried to look attentive and interested, which wasn't difficult as I was in fact both; and unconcerned, which was harder. Hope straightened her stack of papers. "How far did you get?"

"Ah, middle of June, I think."

"I'm to the end of August."

Hope had started with the beginning of July issues. Which left only the extraordinary events covered between the beginning of September and this week, the first of December. I cast my mind back to what was happening in early September. I'd been in Ghilousette, heartbroken and recovering from wire-weed withdrawal, when I'd finally received word of my stepfather's death. I'd travelled home, to be immediately set up with a job by my stepfather's second wife, at the bookshop.

Most of what had subsequently occurred in Ragnor Bella had not made it into the *New Salon*, thank goodness. Those early issues, before the Dartington Harvest Fair and my slaying of the dragon and consequent acquisition of the viscountcy, had been much taken up with the unexpected discovery of the Ironwood heiress.

—Surely not.

I looked at Hope, sitting there uncomfortably. Hope, who had wanted to talk to me; who had sympathized strongly with being in the *New Salon*; who thought I, of all people, would understand her situation.

I could remember Mr. Dart reading out the news, and the Honourable Rag claiming that the Ironwood heiress *must be quite the antidote, if she's not called a beauty with all that fortune behind her.* I thought Hope rather pretty, myself, but I could admit she wasn't exactly a beauty in the classic mode.

"I was a foundling orphan," Hope said suddenly, keeping her eyes on the paper. Her colour was still high, cheeks dark with her flush, and she held her hands clasped before her. "Found literally in a basket at the door, if you can believe it."

Had there been a fad for such things at some point? Magistra Aurelia, Professor of Magic at Tara, had told me *she'd* been found in a basket at the door of the Faculty of Magic.

I made an agreeable noise and sipped some of my stone-cold tea. It was surprisingly good.

"I was raised in Mollen, as I told you. My parents—adoptive parents—were a weather-witch and a physician. Very respectable, well-educated. I had excellent tutors. They died in the Fall."

We had talked about this, she and I, a few times when we'd been placed together on work duty in the gardens or kitchens or like. There were many orphans or half-orphans from the Fall and the Interim afterwards, and she had not explained the double tragedy of her family history. Of course, neither had I explained the double tragedy of my father's twice-reported death and unexpected return and seeming suicide; and who knew what other secrets there might be in anyone's lives?

"I was taken in by my father's brother, who owned the general store in Mollen," Hope went on. "My uncle was—is— very kind, and we rubbed along well together. He was an old bachelor, you see." Her voice was very fond and I smiled.

She smiled back, then faltered. "I studied—it would have been possible for me to go to one of the lesser universities, with the money my parents—my adopted parents, that is—had left for me, but I had always wanted to go to Morrowlea, ever since I first heard about it. I liked the name, and I liked the philosophy of the place. I did well enough in the Entrance Examinations to go on merits."

Her voice was very proud of this accomplishment. I grinned at her. "Congratulations!"

"You're not—jealous?"

"No! Why—oh, is Anna?"

She gave me an unimpressed look. "Everyone is, Jemis. Unless—oh, were you the Rondelan Scholar? I suppose you're also irritated that it was one of the aristocracy born—even if not raised—who placed so high."

I was deeply gratified that she grasped this without my even having to mention it. "Yes, exactly!"

She laughed softly. "We *are* very similar, aren't we?"

"I'm really not as interested in rocks as you," I said, meaning it as something of a jest but her face fell.

"I wish I wasn't," she said passionately, if lowly. "If only …"

I didn't know what to say to this. There didn't seem to be any obvious way a scholarly interest in geology would lead to social disaster. There had been no hint of an unexpected land-slide caused by unwise excavations, for instance. "Er, may I ask what happened?"

"My uncle married this past year, to his widowed neigh-bour, who had two daughters of her own. *They* were jealous," she spat bitterly. "Always going on about how much prettier than me they are, because they're slim and graceful and good at dancing and have lovely hair. No matter that they didn't even pass the Entrance Exams enough to go anywhere! *We just want to be good wives*, they say. *We have all the education we need for that. Who needs university?* All that."

"I thought there was a movement towards more parliamen-tary representation for Charese women?" I was sure Mr. Dart had mentioned something about it.

Hope scoffed. "Among the university set, yes.—The upper gentry, that is. There's a movement amongst the merchant classes for women to stay at home. Be domestic. Run house-holds, not businesses, and never mind any sort of intellectual or political ambitions. That's not our sphere, you see."

I was beginning to. "And so, since you studied geology …"

"About the least feminine topic possible."

And she'd gone to Morrowlea, the most radical of the Circle Schools, perhaps of all of them. I regarded Hope with new interest. *Soft* and *gentle* and *kind* were the adjectives I'd

always used to describe her; this sort of spitfire anti-reac-
tionary sentiment seemed new.

"I can see why you said you were finding things difficult at
home and decided to come here when Anna invited you."

"When Anna *condescended* to invite me, so I could see how
the *true gentry* lived," Hope corrected.

This was definitely not the Hope I was accustomed to.
"Ah," I said elegantly and appropriately.

Hope deflated with a giggle, which was more like what I
expected of her. "Oh, Jemis, am I scandalizing you? It's just ...
it was so *free*, at Morrowlea, didn't you find? Oh, I know there
were differences and distinctions, and of course Lark insisted
she was in a class all by herself, but we all experienced the
same things, did them together. I miss that."

I looked down, at her tightly clasped hands, and realized
how hard it was for her to articulate all these things. I reached
out and laid my own hands over hers.

"Thank you," she said quietly. "I've been so unhappy this
summer. It was all a shambles at the end, wasn't it? The dream
ending like a blown-out candle, leaving just smoke and ashes
behind. I didn't even think to talk to Hal about writing before
you and Marcan left. I thought there would be all the time ..."

Her voice faded and she clutched my hands tightly. "Jemis,
you understand, don't you? I went home, and all my cousins
could say was that I had wasted three years, and who was
going to want me now? *Plump and plain Hope Stornaway, who
knows better than everyone else.* I didn't have enough money to go
on with a second degree, not at Essanen, and no one in Mollen
would marry a girl who had such ideas in her head."

"I think," I said carefully, "that you should talk to Hal
about this."

"Oh, Jemis, I *can't*. Don't you see? If I were only Hope
Stornaway I could run away with my beau to Ronderell and
we could ... I don't know. Hal's such a good gardener. We
could start a plant nursery, with all the new plants coming in

from the West, and use what I had from my parents—my adopted parents—to buy a bit of land, and we could build a grotto and a garden and it would all be so lovely, don't you think? *You'd* come visit us, wouldn't you? No matter that you're the Viscount St-Noire! You'd come collect eggs and milk the cow and peel onions in the kitchen and bunk in the loft, wouldn't you?"

I nodded dumbly. I had my own small dream, of the Dower Cottage on the Arguty estates, with a cat and a child and Violet in the chair beside me. It was a beautiful dream, as beautiful in its way as Hope's; and because I was the Viscount St-Noire, and Violet the daughter of the Lady of Alinor, too small for the lives we would be required to lead.

"Just over the county line, into the Ironwood lands, there was a ruined stone tower. It was said to be haunted," Hope said, talking faster now, her hands gripping mine tightly. Her silver ring, with its blue stone, pressed against my Crimson Lake one. "The story was that whoever spent a night in the tower would be granted a wish—any wish—but no one ever made it the night through."

"You went?" I asked, trying to mask my surprise. Violet I could easily imagine doing such a thing—even Lark—or Red Myrta—but Hope?

(Given the other women in our year at Morrowlea, perhaps I had underestimated Hope. Had we all also underestimated Anna?)

She blushed. "I was never brave enough to try. I was out blackberry-picking one afternoon, trying to get away from my cousins and my aunt, and I got lost in the woods between Mollen and the old Ironwood place. You know I don't have a good sense of direction. I could never figure out how you always knew where you were, running," she added parenthetically. "I thought that was the most fantastic ability."

"My father taught me how to pay attention."

"I was caught by sunset," she said. "I found this tower … I

didn't even think about the legend. I went in, and gathered the stuff for a fire. I might not have been as good at self-defence as you, but I *did* learn always to keep a fire starter with me!"

"Dominus Lukel would be proud," I assured her.

"Not as proud as of you slaying a dragon."

I dismissed that tangent. "You spent the night in the tower?"

"I built a fire on the ground floor, but it wasn't quite dark yet, so I went upstairs. I didn't like the idea of not knowing if anything was up there ..."

"Quite right."

"I went up, with a firebrand—just like you last night going to the window!—and I went up the stairs. The tower was hollow, the bottom one big room, with an iron stair around the outside wall. One room at the top, with a trapdoor to the roof. There were windows there, big glass ones, Astandalan work. The sunset was quite magnificent."

"Was anything in there?"

"In the centre of the room was a big square stone. I went up to it—how could I not? It was sitting there on a raised plinth, like a decorative pot or a statue or something. I went up to it and there was an inscription all around the top of the stone."

This was getting intriguing indeed. "What did it say?"

Hope spoke solemnly. "*Whosoever lays rightful hands on this stone will inherit all the lands visible from this tower and all that pertains to them.*"

I went over this in my mind several times, but could determine no obvious cipher or riddle. "And the unrighteous?"

She shrugged, her hands damp and warm in mine. "There was no direct indication. Just all those tales of those who fled the tower in fear and fright ..."

"But you are a sensible woman, and went down safely to spend the night beside your fire?" I asked without any (hah) hope.

Hope smiled ruefully. "It was a very interesting stone, Jemis."

I sighed. "What happened when you touched it?"

"The tower lit up like a beacon, I was told later, and unfolded from a ruin to a castle, like something out of a fairy tale, all white and pink and silver. I couldn't see that at first, of course. All *I* could see was that the room was lit up like day and the stone had turned into a table, with a book on it. The book was open to a page that laid out a family lineage. ... My family lineage. Oh, Jemis, can you imagine? You knew you were related to the Marchioness, even if you didn't know you stood to inherit. I was a foundling! I had no idea!"

"It was a grimoire, then?"

I had never been as interested in recent history—apart from my father's—as in that pertaining to the Classical poets whose works I loved. I tried to think what I knew of the Iron-woods, which was almost nothing: just that it was a title that had been lost until their heiress was recently found. I had assumed that they were lost in the Fall, but perhaps not.

"It was.—You don't know anything about this? Oh, Jemis!" She laughed a little. "The Ironwoods were enchanters in Astandalan days. They were famous for it—you should see the castle. Full of all sorts of strange contrivances. I'm no practitioner, so this surprised me a great deal. Apparently the family was cursed to a hundred years of obscurity and three generations without magic, and all their castle and lands were forbidden them, and also their name."

That was quite the curse. I wondered what or whom they'd fallen afoul of, but before I could ask, Hope went on.

"My grandparents were the ones who were cursed. They went out into the world, penniless and friendless. No one knew them anymore, you see. The grimoire said they were too proud to have friends for themselves; all they had were those who admired their enchantments and their wealth and their name. Without those ... they were nothing. They were eventually assisted by a Traveller community, and lived out their days with them. They had a son, who married a Traveller woman, and eventually they had me."

"If your family were Travellers, why were you abandoned as a baby?" I asked in surprise. I didn't know much about the Traveller communities—they didn't tend to come into South Fiellan except in story—but I did know they were reputed to be close-knit and protective of their own.

Hope shook her head. "I don't know. The Mollen parish records say that a group of Travellers passed through the year I was found, and that some of them took ill and died, and that a baby was found after they had left the district. I'm still trying to track down which group it might have been, but they were hard-hit by the Interim."

"And so ..."

"So you see," she said earnestly. "Touching the stone and being of the rightful lineage was only the first step. You had to break a curse too, didn't you? Mine is half-broken—the rest comes when I marry. But there are rules to the inheritance."

"And one of them is that you must marry someone who knows your true name."

Her voice lifted out of its low murmur in her aggravation. "Exactly! So you see that I can't marry Hal!"

There was a movement over by the door, which I feared very much indicated that someone had been listening to the end of this conversation. I wasn't at all sure who I hoped it might be. Hope looked over, following my glance, but returned her anxious gaze to my face without seeming to notice anything.

I cleared my throat. "Surely since Henry Coates is dead, you needn't worry?"

Hope looked at me with patient incredulity. "*He* knew my full and true name—but *I* don't!"

CHAPTER NINETEEN

Reaching towards her in sympathy, I knocked over the inkwell. Only a hasty application of mostly-blanks sheets of paper saved all my careful transcriptions. After a few minutes spent mopping up the mess, which left me with black marks all over my hands—Hope, in her white dress, quite miraculously managed to avoid being splattered more than in one or two spots—I recovered sufficiently to ask questions.

"But how would he find that out?"

She shrugged miserably. "I don't know. I don't even know how he learned I am the Ironwood heiress—I haven't told Anna, or anyone, really. No one could believe it at home ... They all thought there must have been a mistake."

"I'm sorry to hear your family were so ... unhelpful."

"My uncle—adopted uncle—was lovely, as he always is," she said. "It's his wife and my new cousins. If they were unhappy with my being the Charese Scholar to Morrowlea you can imagine how they reacted to my being the Ironwood heiress! They say it must all be a Traveller cheat, now they know my mother was one. I don't even know her name! I was so grateful when Anna wrote to invite me for Winterturn I didn't even hesitate."

"I can understand that."

Hope gave me a small smile. "I'm sure you can, Jemis, if anyone. It's so lovely to see you and Hal still friends ... Everything ended so unhappily that I wasn't sure of—of anyone. I am so ashamed I didn't stand with you," she rushed on. "I knew it was wrong, I knew Lark was bullying you, but I didn't —I shouldn't have come to see Anna. She turned on you just as much as everyone else! I just don't have any friends in Mollen and—"

She started to cry. I regretted for the first time that I was wearing the grand teal-and-grey suit, for it had not come well endowed with handkerchiefs. As I usually took care to supply myself with several—my recovery from the wireweed addiction had involved a tedious amount of sneezing—I felt the lack.

Eventually I found a linen napkin brought with the tea and cardamon rolls that hadn't been stained by the ink, and presented it to Hope. By this time she'd almost managed to compose herself, and gave me a watery smile.

"Thank you."

"Think nothing of it."

"Oh, Jemis, you're too kind."

It had not taken long, I was afraid, for me to fall away from the joy and serenity of the Wood of Spiritual Refreshment. I gave her a wry, noncommittal shrug. "I see no reason why you should not maintain your friendship with Anna. I'm still friends with Marcan, and he didn't say anything, either."

"Hal did."

"Very few people possess Hal's moral courage, Hope."

Her face fell. "Oh, how I *want* to marry him!"

I reached forward to clasp her hands in mine, the damp napkin crushed between us. "You shall, if I can help at all!"

That made her giggle even through her still-falling tears. "And you *have* slain a dragon, so this should be a—a piece of cake."

"Beesting cake," I agreed, grateful withal that she decided to ignore the reference.

She sighed. "I suppose you've had to start thinking about *appropriate matches*, haven't you? You were on the list—or, well, not *you*, since you hadn't yet been acknowledged, but *the heir of the Woods Noirell*, if found and if a male, was."

"The list?" I asked, mind racing. Hal's Aunt Honoria had such a List ...

"Yes, Lady Honoria Kental, the aunt of the Duke of Fillering Pool, came to see that the terms of the inheritance were met. She was such a bulwark," she added, in fond tones that surprised me. "She said she'd take me under her wing, when I come north for the Duke's Winterturn Ball. She said she'd thought I'd be a good match even though that's ridiculous. But it was very kind of her to say so."

"It's not ridiculous," I said, with more truth than she yet knew.

Hope gave me one of her softly disapproving glances, as if to say she knew I was smarter than *that*. "It's only the fortune and the title that gives me any capital on the marriage market, Jemis. If I were plain, pudgy, poor, too-well-educated Hope Stornaway, twice-orphaned foundling, can you imagine the Duke of Fillering Pool would look twice at me?"

I rather hoped my face did give my true thoughts away, but from her unhappy expression it didn't. "I think you sell yourself short," I said. "You went to Morrowlea on merits, and even if you're not classically beautiful—"

She laughed wetly. "You're so sweet, Jemis. I know you prefer the 'classics'—Lark and Violet were the great beauties of our year."

"Nevertheless," I persisted.

"It doesn't matter, anyway," she said, shaking her head. "If I can't find out how Henry Coates found my true name, I can't marry anyone. There's a magical binding on the entailment;

even if I tried to give up the estates, I still couldn't. I wish I
could."

Her voice was uncertain enough that I squeezed her hands.
"Do you?"

She looked up at me and gave me a small smile. "It *was* a
very interesting rock, Jemis."

Before I could come up with a satisfactory response to this
(I did utter a sympathetic if nonsensical sound), the door
opened and Anna flounced in.

Unlike Hope in her demure white, Anna was wearing a
dark red gown that struck my eyes as being a dinner dress,
hardly suitable for midmorning. She had her dark hair up in
ringlets tied back by a red ribbon that didn't quite match the
gown.

I let go of Hope's hands in what I hoped was a natural
fashion as I stood and bowed slightly in greeting. "Good morning, Miss Garsom."

Anna swept me a deeper curtsey and gave me a somewhat
perfunctory titter. "Good morning, Lord St-Noire. I hope you
found your accommodation to your satisfaction?"

I bowed again in lieu of answering that honestly. "Thank
you."

She was fortunately not attending carefully to me, instead
coming over to Hope and grasping her by the arm. "Hope,
dearest, will you come with me? There's—" At Hope's look
over to me, Anna tittered again. "Oh my dear Jemis—Lord St-
Noire!—you will excuse us, won't you? I need Hope most
particularly, I'm afraid."

"Of course," I replied blandly, though equally *of course* I
was madly curious to know what had occasioned this kerfuffle.
It might be something quite ordinary—Anna had always been
a bit of a dramaturge—but then again, it might not.

Hope had been resisting bodily, but when I said nothing to
urge her to stay she gave in to Anna's tugging and followed her
out of the room. I waited a moment, but though I could hear

their voices in immediate conversation, I couldn't hear any words. I moved over to the door, just in time to see them exit not up the stairs but through another door down the hall that seemed, from the brief glance I had through it, to lead into the main room with all its multitudes of clutter.

No one else was in sight or hearing. I positioned the door just short of closed, in the thought I might hear the next arrival coming, and put a piece of wood on the fire before returning to my desk and the *New Salons*.

My thoughts were not exactly on the *Etiquette Questions Answered* column's mystery.

~

I had caught up to where Hope had begun transcribing, checked her work (which was perfectly adequate, thank the Lady), and continued on with September's issues by the time of my next visitor. This was Madam Violetta Veitch, who came with a bag of yarn and two large knitting needles she brandished like weapons when I cleared my throat to wish her good morning.

"Oh!" she cried, swinging around from where she'd been looking towards the fire, not me. "I—I—I do apologize, sir. I failed to see you there."

I assured her it was no insult, and gave her a bow halfway to a court 'leg', to fit my clothes and make her smile. She did smile, though it didn't seem to reach her eyes.

Overall she looked quite like her cousin Anna, being olive-skinned and dark-haired and fairly short—both easily over-matched even by my height, which was on the short side of average for a man, and quite close to average for a woman. Madam Veitch was bony and angular, her hair greying in irreg-ular streaks. She was wearing a dove-grey morning dress that did little for her colouring, with a knitted black shawl over her shoulders. Her most striking feature were heavy black brows, which made her eyes look oddly deep-set in her face.

She murmured something presumably polite if nearly inaudible and sat down in the chair by the window. Her work bag was a hefty thing and made a solid-sounding clunk as she set it down on the floor beside her. I tried not to be obvious as I watched and listened to her settle herself into position. From what I could remember of the thread-craft enthusiasts at Morrowlea, there was nothing one would expect a knitter's bag to contain that would make a sound like that.

I re-organized my papers, cut the nib on my quill again— almost as good an excuse to stop and pretend to be otherwise engaged as Mr. Dart's pipe—and what was *he* doing just this moment?—and surreptitiously watched Madam Veitch pull our thick wool yarn in soft umbers and blues, as well as a partially-begun item and the heavy knitting needles.

"It's a scarf," Madam Veitch said pleasantly, more calmly than before, as she shook out the tail of the knit work and arranged her yarn and her shawl to her satisfaction. "My dear husband has a tendency to catarrh, you know."

"Ah," I said weakly, hoping my face wasn't burning red at being caught out.

"You're probably not too familiar with such homely things," she went on, catching a loop with one needle and then plying them both with the dexterity of long practice.

I'd been much more interested in the looms and the art of tailoring at Morrowlea, and hadn't done any more than the required classes on darning and basic sewing. My mother, like any noblewoman of her day, had been accomplished at needle-point, and though I remembered her trying to knit in the isolated days of the Interim, I also remembered her laughing and using her effort at a sock as a washcloth instead, and telling me she would *sew* us new socks instead.

Which she had. They had been more like slippers than

stockings, but they had been warm all through those long, hard, winters.

"My mother preferred tapestry," I said aloud, making Madam Veitch nod in a kind of condescending agreement.

"As one would expect from a lady born."

There was nothing I could say to that that wouldn't sound snide, so I turned back to my transcriptions. The knitting needles flashed in the corner of my eye, distracting me every now and again.

It occurred to me, as I copied out the questions and answers from the issue that Mr. Dart had read to me so long ago, the one announcing the discovery of the Ironwood heiress, that if I didn't *know* the stiletto on the wall behind me was the murder weapon, those steel knitting needles would cause suspiciously similar wounds.

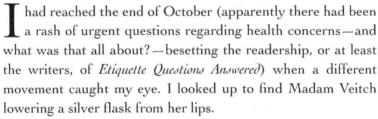

I had reached the end of October (apparently there had been a rash of urgent questions regarding health concerns—and what was that all about?—besetting the readership, or at least the writers, of *Etiquette Questions Answered*) when a different movement caught my eye. I looked up to find Madam Veitch lowering a silver flask from her lips.

She smiled at me with a strangely delighted expression. "It's a tonic," she said demurely. "My physician prepares it for me."

A draught brought a definite wash of lilac over to me. I sneezed briefly and smiled at her apologetically, my mind jumping back not to October but to the end of September, to an encounter with Domina Ringley, Mrs. Talgarth's sister, in the Ragnor Bella bakery. *She* had been drinking a lilac-scented *tonic* from a flask, as well; Kilromby wireweed tonic, in point of fact.

"It's that time of year," I said nonsensically, and returned to my work as best I could.

So Madam Veitch was taking wireweed. I considered her thin frame and the clear increase in the speed with which she was knitting. Domina Ringley had been overly thin, too, and she drank her 'tonic' almost constantly. Madam Veitch had either been much more circumspect or else hadn't taken any the rest of the time she'd been sitting there. Seemingly, she was still in early enough stages of the addiction to not be entirely compromised as of yet.

She continued knitting, her steel needles flashing faster and faster in the sunlight coming in through the window. The sun had shifted over the course of the morning, and seemed to be reflecting more and more brilliantly as the day went on. The needles occasionally flashed directly in my face and made my eyes water.

I paged through the November issues of the *New Salon*, whose lead stories were familiar to me, and slowed down as I came at last to a second copy of this week's edition, which I was already rather too familiar with from last night's reading.

At last I stacked all my transcriptions neatly together, with a few extra sheets of paper in case there wasn't enough in my room, and refolded the *New Salons* as tidily as I could manage without ironing the paper flat, as Hal's butler did for him every morning.

Hal had claimed this was his father's institution, and that the butler had continued of his own initiative all through Hal's childhood and adolescence, and it wasn't until he'd gone to Morrowlea that he'd realized papers did not usually come in so pristine a condition.

"Have you finished?" Madam Veitch asked. Her voice was light, curious but curiously unconcerned at the same time.

I could not pretend I did not know exactly that sensation. Had I not been the same way half the time at Morrowlea?

I smiled at her with a little difficulty. She was waiting for an answer. "Yes. I'm ... pursuing a course of research this winter. It was fortuitous to find the full year's worth of papers here to assist."

"I believe Ciradon has the archives," Madam Veitch said unexpectedly. "It's a bit out of your way, I suppose."

Ciradon was one of the universities on the Silver List, notable chiefly for having its own, rather prestigious, vineyard. It was located somewhere in the contested lands south of Chare, I seemed to recall.

I was a little relieved to know that Master Boring was not the presumed archivist for the *New Salons*, just an ardent collector of ... well, everything, it seemed like.

Including unicorns.

As if my thought of Ballory had summoned him, Mr. Dart came in the door and made swiftly to me. He nodded politely at Madam Veitch, who hummed and selected another ball of yarn to work with, this one in a rather intense pink that clashed with the green and orange she'd previously been using.

"Je — Lord St-Noire, are you finished with your morning's work?"

I was glad I was, for obviously I would have gone with him regardless. "Yes, just now," I replied. "If you'll excuse me, Madam Veitch?"

She waved one of the needles in the air in a vague blessing. I returned the quill, inkwell, and penknife to their drawer, and collected my stack of transcriptions. Mr. Dart was hovering by the door, his face in a parody of his usual cheerful smile. I followed him out, shutting the door firmly behind me, and let him lead me upstairs.

"Well?" I said once we were away from the parlour.

"My cousin is sadly unwell. I fear we may be obliged to stay here for a day or two longer, Lord St-Noire."

I blinked at him, wondering if this were true or an excuse to stay. "I am sorry to hear that," I replied eventually, as we came to the hall at the top of the stairs. Ned Garsom was

standing there, looking lost. "Good morning, Garsom," I said
as pleasantly as I could.

He nodded distractedly. "St-Noire. You haven't seen Henry
—Coates, that is—have you?"

Mr. Dart carefully didn't say anything. I hoped my face
didn't reveal too much. "Not this morning, I'm afraid."

"Damn," the young man said, and, unprompted, added:
"We had a bit of a set-to last night. I hope he hasn't gone and
done anything foolish."

"Yes, I heard the suit of armour go over."

He grinned awkwardly, rubbing his backside uncon-
sciously. "What a crash that was! I was hoping the storm
disguised the noise. I was a trifle foxed, I'm afraid. Curse this
house! We've been here a week and nothing to do but drink.
My sister's friend's a cold fish, which you wouldn't think with
all that flesh on her, but she's hardly *our* sort, is she?"

"No," I agreed coolly, thinking of how wonderfully Hope
had surprised me yesterday and today.

Garsom shuffled around, peering with dull, darting eyes at
the closed doors lining the hall. He did not share Anna's
striking features. "What a mausoleum this place is! Henry
must've gone looking for sport down in the kitchen. We had a
bet—"

He stopped abruptly, receding flush darkening again. A
wash of scent hovered in the air around him, not lilac but
something like clove-gillyflowers. He tittered almost identically
to his sister. "I'll see you at lunch, I guess. If you see Henry, tell
him I'm sorry for leaving him with the armour, will you?"

I inclined my head, not at all sure how to answer that
otherwise, and we watched as he dithered for a few moments
before deciding to descend the stairs. I looked around to see
that both suits of armour were in their places. Even from this
end of the hall the distant one looked decidedly worse for wear,
a goodly number of its spiky protuberances bent or snapped
off.

Mr. Dart waited, still silent, until the door at the bottom had closed again, and then he hustled me across the hall and into not his or my or even Hal's room, but that occupied by the late Henry Coates.

Hal and the Honourable Rag—once more in his costume as the Hunter in Green, complete to the gloves and the green eyeshadow and the codpiece (and why were *his* clothes dry so fast?)—were there, standing on either side of a desk on which was laid out an assortment of items.

I looked around the room even as they murmured distracted greetings to us. Henry Coates' room was much like my own, if noticeably smaller and more plainly furnished. The colour scheme combined a bluish grey and a dull rusty orange, which was surprisingly cozy in effect. There was a curtained bed in a wall alcove, the curtains drawn.

"The body's there," Mr. Dart said briefly.

"I see," I said. A large wardrobe stood along from the bed, the doors open to reveal various clothes and accessories in various states of put away. One door had a long mirror on the inside. Two travelling bags sat next to it, along with a pair of riding boots.

Henry Coates had brought a great many boxes and baggage with him for his country repose. As he had not been granted a greatly furnished room, the corners were full of untidily stacked luggage. Apart from one upholstered chair by the fire, and a small side table, there was the small wooden writing desk and the chair that went with it, and a stand with an ewer and basin, and that was it. There was also one window, tightly shut and covered with snow all along the edge of the panes.

"No one came in or out that way," the Hunter in Green said, lifting his head from the table to look at me.

It was jarring to hear his mimicked accent, the buoyant but yet intelligent tone, and know who was behind the green mask. I smiled easily at him and could swear that his shoulders relaxed the barest trifle. "You would know the ways thereof," I said.

"There's a fifteen-foot wall this side of the house, anyhow," he went on. "Come look here."

I crossed the room obediently and regarded the objects laid out on the desk. A stack of letters, opened. A stack of letters, sealed. A penknife the match of the one I'd used in the parlour, which actually was quite interesting given the antiquity of the rest of the set.

A small notebook covered in black leather, just the size to fit easily in a waistcoat pocket, and an exquisite new-style fountain pen with a silver cap.

A pile of coins, mostly the marks and pfennigs used in both Linder and Chare, along with a smaller pile of Rondelan coins, and one gleaming Astandalan gold sovereign.

And most curious of all, a jade-green dragon scale.

I considered this display, and the dead man hidden in the bed behind us. "What do we reckon, then?" I asked. "Was our Mr. Coates done in for blackmail or theft?"

Mr. Dart looked at me with a quick, mirthless smile, and from his pocket drew out his pipe. While I watched him he lit it, drew a deep draught, blew a rather splendid smoke ring, and then half-chanted, "Either, neither, both, and—"

We finished the children's counting rhyme together. "When the wind blows, we'll know where you stand."

"Wish that were so," Hal said, and set down two rings: the seal of the governor-prince of Orio City, and that of Crimson Lake.

CHAPTER TWENTY

I stared at the rings for a long moment, mind working ineffectively as I tried to determine whether they had any significance for the murder or not. The air was cool, and held a bit of the same clove-gillyflower aroma Ned Garsom had sported, though that was quickly being masked by Mr. Dart's fragrant pipe tobacco. Unlike my draughty room, there seemed no movement to the air. The fireplace was burning surprisingly well, actually.

Perhaps my friends had tended it as they searched the place.

Hal crossed his arms and took a step back. "Well? Children's rhymes aside, any thoughts?"

I glanced at his mulish expression and knew immediately that he had been the one to hear Hope's anguished cry that she absolutely *couldn't* marry him. I sighed inwardly but decided that would have to wait until we had a quiet moment together. Hope had not outright demanded my secrecy on the matter of her true identity, but it was as obvious as Hal's own charade that she wanted to tell him in her own time.

That made me sigh inwardly again, that their respective desires to be loved for their own sakes—hardly unwarranted!

—were leading them to believe the other an inadmissible match.

I turned my attention to the table. We were going to be here at least until the snow was cleared and we figured out a way of safely returning home. Long enough, surely, to find time to help Hal and Hope find their way to happiness together.

And to solve the mysterious death of Henry Coates before the murderer turned his or her eye on anyone else. Though presumably no one else was blackmailing half the household, if my suspicions were correct.

The objects sat there in their seeming innocence. I turned to Mr. Dart first. "Any, er, inklings on your end?"

He shook his head and blew another smoke ring, which he sent to hover with the first just above his head. I wasn't sure how I felt about this sudden embrace of his magic. It was a good thing, I was sure—my discussions with Magistra Aurelia and general knowledge of wild magic (such as it was) made that clear—but it *did* seem a remarkable volte-face.

Three days ago he'd been vehemently denying any need to work on it, and now he had a unicorn and an almost cavalier acceptance of it. Surely whatever message I'd brought from the afterlife hadn't been *that* life-altering?

I went over that thought again in my mind and inwardly winced.

I examined the objects again. A dragon scale, from all appearances one taken from the dragon I had slain. I hadn't thought to ask for one, myself, before the Scholars took the carcass to Morrowlea for anatomizing and study, and rather wished I had.

"Do you think I could have that scale?" I said aloud, touching it gently. I couldn't feel any magic that it might have, not anymore, but the buttons on my waistcoat warmed very gently. "It has magic on it …"

"It's made of magic," Hal said in a snide tone. I forgave

him, given that he thought his potential love had rejected him, and moved on to look at Roald—the Hunter in Green.

"You knew Henry Coates—"

"And loathed him," he interrupted, sounding every inch the possibly-a-minor-deity.

"He tried to blackmail me," Mr. Dart interjected. We all looked at him. "Regarding my brother's relationship with Sir Hamish. It's illegal in Chare. I told him to tell everyone and be damned."

"And did he?" I asked.

Mr. Dart blew another smoke ring, which joined the others hovering above his head. "Yes."

And that, unfortunately, probably explained the lack of friends mentioned from Stoneybridge. The only person Mr. Dart had mentioned to me by name in the past three months was his tutor, Domina Black.

"Hmm. How fortunate you have a unicorn to vouch for your moral rectitude," Hal murmured.

"I wonder how he came by those two rings," Roald said thoughtfully.

I raised my eyebrow at him. "Is Crimson Lake not *your* organization?"

I was sure that behind his mask he was laughing at me. "Now, how would you come by that idea?"

"Oh, I can't think. Well?"

He shrugged massive shoulders. "Ha'penny truth, I make it. I did not found the group, but I have been active in recruitment."

"But not to the point of Henry Coates?"

"Not I. I know too many he's *written* to, to trust him."

"So the question becomes, is it *his* ring, or another's?"

"Not the only question," Hal put in. "Where did he get that scale you're admiring? And *why*? He could hardly think to blackmail you for it."

That stumped me, but Roald said, "There was the accusation that you murdered Fitzroy Angursell in the form of a dragon...."

Mr. Dart blew another smoke ring, then said, "Which came from Yellem, so even if there has been no hint of the upstanding Mr. Coates in Ragnor Bella, there needn't have been. As for the scale ... the Scholars crossed the Coombe pass into Chare on their way to West Erlingale, did they not? If we need to, we might enquire whether they had any suspicious interactions along the way."

"A possible motive for you, then," Hal said, gesturing at me. "And one for Mr. Dart. He could not have known of the Hunter in Green's arrival—unless you came to a rendezvous?"

"Not with him," Roald stated, rather to my surprise. I raised my eyebrow at him again, and was sure again of his hidden laughter. "Your face is a study, Greenwing."

"Oh, do call me Jemis."

"You can call me Hunter," he returned immediately. I quirked a smile at that. He gave me a ridiculously extravagant half-bow, all flourishes, which I knew was in imitation of my own not-so-subtle reaction to people *putting me in my place*, back when they all thought that place far below them.

"Enough," Hal said sharply. "This tomfoolery is of no assistance. We have a dead body that no one knows is dead—"

"Four—no, five—of us do," I pointed out. "Including Hope, that is. I don't imagine she's told Anna."

Hal pursed his lips unhappily. "I expect not. We'd all know by now if Anna knew."

"Tendency to hysterics, has she?" Roald enquired.

"Dramatics, rather," I replied blandly.

"We have a corpse and a murder weapon—and someone in this house is a murderer. So far we can but hope none of the four of us were involved."

I was surprised Hal had stated that so baldly. "Hal," I began, but he turned sharply away under pretext of picking up the unopened letters.

"These letters are of interest," he said stiffly, holding them out. "Consider."

I dutifully considered. Each were addressed in the same masculine hand, in a thickly drawn ink that remained clear despite a propensity to uneven lettering. I fanned through the handful, noting the names were those of the family along with that of Hope. *Mr. Veitch. Madam Veitch. Miss Stornaway. Miss Garsom. Mr. Garsom. Master Boring.*

"Intriguing," I ventured, turning the letters over to see that they were all well-sealed, each with an untidy red blob of sealing-wax set, not entirely surprisingly, with the seal of Orio City. The buttons on my waistcoat warmed as my finger brushed against the wax.

"Look at the open ones," Hal directed.

I did so, finding the envelopes addressed the same but the contents all blank. The buttons remained warm against my stomach.

"I confess to a degree of confusion," I said eventually, when the three of them simply looked expectantly at me. "There is magic here, so my enchanted waistcoat buttons tells me, but other than that?"

"Oh, give those here, Jemis," Hal said, and promptly snatched the envelopes out of my hand. I stared even as he lit a candle with a murmured word of magic and held the letter addressed *Mr. Veitch* up against the flame. Faint grey words began to appear out of the blankness.

... I write as a party most interested in your recent activities in Orio City ...

"Definitely blackmail, then."

"Assuredly," Hal replied grimly. "Sit down, and let us tell you what we discovered while you were busy in the parlour all morning."

I thought that a little unfair—they had asked me to stay, after all—but had begun nevertheless to oblige him when there was a distinct rap at the door.

We all exchanged alarmed glances and scattered to corners hopefully out-of-sight, although the room afforded few besides the curtained bed, and that was already occupied. Mr. Dart and I ended up on either side of the door.

"Henry?" Garsom's voice came through the door, sounding anxious and surprisingly thin for such a large man. "Henry, are you in there? — This isn't funny, man," he added in a lower voice. "Those—visitors—you were worried about are poking around. What if they find—hell. What are you doing, Anna?"

"Same as you, I expect," she said in a cool voice. "What happened to your *friend*? Did he finally slope off?"

"He can't have gone far," Garsom whined. "There was a blizzard last night."

"Aren't I aware of it!"

"Anna—"

There was a thump, as if one or the other of them had backed up against the door. I was glad I'd latched it behind me on entry. Mr. Dart and I, who were closest, edged nearer so we could hear what the siblings were saying. Hal approached more slowly, leaving only Roald in the midst of the room. The baron's son had always had sharp hearing, I remembered out of nowhere.

There was silence at first, before Garsom said reluctantly, "Anna, I know you don't like him, but we need him."

"What we *need*, brother mine, is for you to get your head out of your arse and suck up to our uncle so he gives you the inheritance."

"He won't see you either?" Garsom said, a malicious edge in his voice. "Is that why you've turned to St-Noire? Still angling for a title, since you missed Belfort's despite all your efforts? I can't see what else you see in him."

"He's not so bad as all that." Garsom just laughed, and Anna went on in a hurried, disdainful tone: "Honestly, Ned, he's as even more easily led than you. Now that Lark's dropped him he's practically begging for it."

"He's too short for me. But if half a pickle pleases you, sister—"

There was the distinct sound of a slap, followed by an unrepentant chuckle. "Don't think I don't know what you get up to, Anna. My friend Henry was full of *all* the gossip."

"And maybe he's met the end that deserves," Anna said, with vitriol, and stamped off.

Mr. Dart lifted his hand to his mouth and wouldn't meet my eye. My face was burning. They say eavesdroppers never hear what they'd like—too true!

Garsom tapped again at the door. "Were you listening, Henry?—Henry? Oh—Miss Stornaway."

"Mr. Garsom," came Hope's soft voice. A hand came down on my shoulder—I startled and half-turned, to see that Hal had come up behind me and was now pressed close. "Is something the matter? You seem distressed."

There was a most unconvincing chuckle. "I was looking for my friend. Have you seen him?"

"Not—not recently."

"When?" he said eagerly. "Did you see him this morning?"

Surprising strength of body and character or not, Hope was not a good liar. We could not see her, of course, through the door, but we could hear Garsom's suspicion.

"*When* did you see him, Miss Stornaway?"

"I—I didn't mark the time—it was morning—there was a noise in the hall—I came out to see what it was—and he was coming up from downstairs. We didn't speak," she added, too quickly. "He went into his room and I returned to mine. I haven't seen him since."

"I can't think where he's got to," Garsom said disconsolately, thumping against the door again. "Nothing for it—I'll have to move on with it myself."

"I beg your pardon, Mr. Garsom?"

"Nothing—nothing. Anna's gone to her room, Miss Stornaway."

"Ah, yes, it's nearly lunch, isn't it? Perhaps you'll see him then."

"Perhaps, unless—Never mind that. Let me accompany you to your door."

"Th-thank you."

Two sets of heavy footsteps went down the hall, followed by one coming back. I saw the key in the door and quickly turned it before Garsom could come back. He did try the handle, which rattled.

"So you *are* in there," he said through the door. "Look, Henry, this isn't funny any more. I don't trust these strangers —who know what they're really here for? They might have— hell!—they might be here the same as us. I wouldn't put it past my uncle to set the whole thing up—There's something fishy about all of it. You'd best stay away from downstairs till the visitors go. We don't want them looking too hard into—Hell. I've got to go—there's my cousin."

He stomped off, leaving us to move as quietly away from the door as possible even as another, lighter, set of footsteps came by. We reconvened by the table full of oddments.

"That was a convenient turn," I said, noticing again the little black notebook, and wondering what was in it.

"A little too much so, perhaps," the Hunter said. "That door doesn't block the sound as one would expect. We might have been heard earlier ourselves."

"You were," said a voice.

CHAPTER TWENTY-ONE

I spun around fast enough to knock Hal back a step and cause Mr. Dart to drop his pipe.

There was no one else in the room but for the four of us around the table.

"Who said that?" I asked sharply.

"Who said what?" Mr. Dart said, bending down to pick up his pipe. "And keep your voice down — someone might hear."

"Someone *did* hear," I said uneasily, moving around the room. "A voice just said, *You were*, after R — the Hunter said we might have been heard."

They were all regarding me worriedly now. I pulled back the curtains on the window, but they concealed nothing. There was no bathroom, which left the curtained bed and the open wardrobe.

I moved the coats and other items in the wardrobe to be complete, but nothing was there. That left the bed.

"Jemis," Hal said, in warning or in doubt.

"Someone in this house is a murderer," I said through gritted teeth, and flung open the bed curtains. Nothing was there.

Including the corpse.

~

The bed was neatly made, quite as if a servant had come in that morning to do so. There weren't any obvious wrinkles from where the body had lain. Nor were there any bloodstains, which was a relief. A faint waft of clove-gillyflowers was all the odour. I frowned at that. Ned Garsom wore that fragrance, but I couldn't recall noticing it on Henry Coates yesterday, even at midnight.

The other three came to look over my shoulder in perplexity. "The body *was* there," Mr. Dart said slowly.

"I helped lift it," the Hunter in Green agreed.

Given Mr. Dart's stone arm, Roald had probably done most of the lifting, but it was reassuring that Mr. Dart hadn't started seeing things.

Less so that I had apparently started *hearing* them.

"Has someone been in here all morning?" I asked, letting the drapery fall closed again. For good measure I peeked underneath the bed, but all I could see was a prodigious quantity of dust-balls and a thankfully unused chamberpot. I extricated myself to see all three of them looking in various directions with evident embarrassment. "Your expressions indicate *not*. What *have* you been doing?"

"I only found the body an hour ago," Mr. Dart defended himself. "I came upstairs to talk with, er, the Hunter. Hal wasn't in his room so we sat in yours, Jemis, with Ballory."

"I was talking with Hope," Hal muttered, no longer shyly pleased but scowling. "Nothing improper, I assure you. We sat in the window-seat at the end of the upper hall the whole time. Full view of anyone coming along. The stablehands are clearing the courtyard, by the way," he added parenthetically.

I didn't recall seeing a window-seat anywhere along the hall. "So you saw Mr. Dart come up?"

"I didn't see you," Mr. Dart said at the same time.

Hal fiddled with the dragon scale on the table. "Well,

perhaps we were preoccupied. And there was a bit of a curtain."

"Not exactly *full view*," I murmured, but let off at his pained expression. "Hal—"

"Don't, Jemis. We have other things to worry about."

Given that we had come to the subject, however awkwardly, I persevered. "You should tell her your title, Hal."

He gave me an utterly disgusted look. "If that's what it takes, then no, thank you!"

"That's not—" I swore briefly. "That's not what I meant. I don't wish to speak what I was told in confidence, but there were several reasons why she thought I might have helpful advice for her, and being your friend is only one of them. She was particularly sympathetic to the strange inheritance requirements of—"

"Oh, leave off," he interrupted angrily. "There's a murderer about, and a vanished corpse, which are both rather more urgent, I suspect!"

I retreated for the moment. "Very well. You found the wrong door, you said earlier?" I said to Mr. Dart, who lowered his pipe, which he was puffing in moderate agitation.

"Yes—I was looking for my cousin's."

"All the women are on the other side of the hall," the Hunter pointed out, not suspiciously.

Mr. Dart flushed. "There was a strange feeling in the air on this side. And the corpse, when I came to open the door."

"It would be much more helpful if everyone were just a touch more straightforward in their stories," I muttered. "We need to work out a timeline, at the very least. And no one has finished stating what's in all these letters or the black book. Not to mention the suspicious conversation out in the hall just now."

The Hunter sighed gustily. "Not to mention *your* suspicious voice and the disappearing body."

"And the mysterious butler who isn't," Mr. Dart added.

There was a piercing scream, followed by any number of banging doors and thumping footsteps.

We all looked at each other. "I think," Mr. Dart said, putting the pipe back in his mouth, "that someone has found the body."

I rubbed my face in aggravation. "Why are there always so many things happening at once?"

∽

We left the Roald to take the various objects of interest back to my room. He promised to transcribe what he could of the hidden writing ("It's just lemon juice," he said disparagingly. "Surprisingly amateurish, but he *was* a fribble") while we found out what was toward.

He pocketed the black book without promising anything regarding it, which was probably to be expected. I ought not to forget he was here on his own agenda.

Our caution in exiting Henry Coates' room was probably unnecessary, as there was so much excitement downstairs that we could have made the noise of a hundred elephants and gone disregarded. We followed the babble of noise to the parlour, where most of the household was gathered.

I was second through the door after Hal, who ran in with barely a pause, only to stand a step back from Hope, hands out but face twisted with indecision. Hope looked at him with her heart in her eyes, even as she tried to comfort Anna.

The first thing I noticed, after the noise, was the over-whelming fragrance of flowers: clove-gillyflower and lilac. They sent me into immediate wrenching sneezes. Mr. Dart pressed a handkerchief into my hand, then set his on my shoulder in comfort or in warning before moving to one side of the door. I looked at him but he was intently examining the room. I followed suit as my sneezes dissipated and the door swung shut behind me.

Anna stood in full, heaving hysterics in the middle of the room, next to the desk where I had sat all morning. The *New Salons* were gone, but the extended leaves Wally had arranged for me were still outstretched.

Sprawled obscenely on the top of the desk was the body of Henry Coates. He was laying supine, head lolling back over the leather blotter. One of Madam Veitch's steel knitting needles was plunged deep into his left eye.

Next to Anna and with her back turned resolutely to the body was Hope, who was trying ineffectually to calm her friend down even as her eyes strayed towards Hal. Anna was keening a nearly-inaudible note and rocking slightly back and forth, apparently entirely unaware of Hope's arm around her shoulder. Her eyes were fixed on Henry Coates with a blank savagery.

Ned Garsom stood on the other side of the desk, staring down at Coates with a dumbfounded expression. He kept saying, "But how? When? *Who?*" No one answered him.

Madam Veitch herself was slumped in the chair where she'd been sitting that morning, apparently in a dead faint. Her husband, ruddy face pale with anxiety, knelt beside her, chafing her hands and urging her ineffectually to wake.

"What has happened?" someone said from behind me.

I turned to find that Jullanar Maebh had appeared. She was dressed in her own clothes from yesterday, and though still drawn seemed considerably better than last I had seen her. I hesitated in answering, and her face fell.

"That bad, is it?" she said, with an attempt at a smile.

"Henry Coates is dead," Mr. Dart told her quietly.

Jullanar Maebh staggered, putting her hand on the door-frame in support. "*Dead*! How? When? *Why?*"

That was a telling distinction to Ned Garsom's utterance. I was grateful Henry Coates had not managed to draw Jullanar Maebh into his unpleasant orbit.

"Those are all excellent questions," Mr. Dart murmured,

then blocked her instinctive attempt to enter the room. "No—it's not pleasant."

"*He's* not going to rise again, is he? Oh—*Lady*."

She had seen the body. Mr. Dart turned her bodily around; she buried her face in his chest. "Cousin ..."

My attention was drawn past the group in the middle, where Hal and Hope had nearly succeeded in stopping Anna's keening, to where Ned Garsom was surreptitiously going through his late friend's pockets, and Madam Veitch had just slipped something into her husband's. Beyond them, to the side of the door leading to the dining room, stood a tall, cadaverous figure in severe black and white, white-powdered periwig and all: the not-butler.

He was watching the scene with an expression almost of glee. I knew I shouldn't stare at him, but there was something so cool and calculating, something so fierce in those deep-set dark eyes under their thick black brows, something so *satisfied*, that I could not look away. No one else seemed to notice him; but he felt my attention, or something, for he suddenly looked up to see me watching.

He put a finger to his lips in the ancient sign for silence, then gave me a grotesque smile and a wink before retreating silently out the door.

It came to me that it was his voice I heard upstairs. Which solved one mystery but added to others. For one thing, he must move much faster than he pretended.

The door had not finished swinging shut when Bessie came hastening through, followed by the older serving-man from the evening before, who was carrying a large sheet.

The two made short work of shrouding the corpse, Bessie removing the needle without any visible squeamishness, which impressed me rather. The man, Walter I presumed, lifted the body with ease and started to carry it away despite Ned Garsom's protests.

"What—what are you doing, man?" Garsom made as if to

grab him, but caught only the cloth-wrapped foot. He let go with revulsion. "It's—it's undignified. We have to find out what happened!"

While I knew perfectly well that Henry Coates had not been killed in the parlour with a knitting needle, this was quite a sensible point—more sensible, in fact, than I expected of Ned Garsom.

"The master said," Walter replied, looking uneasily at Bessie.

The housekeeper nodded. Her face was set into stern lines, mouth firm and eyes shadowed. "Aye. He's to be put with the —he's to be kept cool," she amended. "Till his people can be notified."

I noted that the master had somehow learned what was going on; or at least that it seemed appropriate to the cool-headed Bessie to feign that he had.

"He was *murdered*," Garsom proclaimed. "We can't just— ignore that!"

"I sent young Wally out the window to summon the physician," Bessie said, gesturing imperiously at Walter, who nodded and carried his grim burden out of the room. "What can you expect to see that he won't?"

"There might be—clues? Letters, writing, who knows—"

"Who indeed?" Mr. Dart murmured very quietly beside me.

I wondered if Garsom also enjoyed mystery novels, and fancied himself a detective. Then I thought of his clumsy efforts to find whatever-it-was in Coates' pockets, and amended that to whether and to what extent he was implicated in Coates' business. Or indeed murder. That loud conversation outside the door might have been, as the Hunter in Green thought, *too* loud.

Garsom was looking at us with wild eyes. "I—I should go —look in his room—There might be—Any hint might—"

But Mr. Veitch had stood up from his wife and now crossed the room to address Garsom. "Might be *what*, Ned?"

"His door was locked," Garsom blurted. "From the inside. How did he get down here?"

Bessie sighed and jangled the chatelaine of keys at her belt. "The rooms lock both directions, sorr, and Mr. Coates was worried last night about his belongings as he had misplaced the key. As to how he came to be *here*—that is the question, aye. Now, if you'll excuse me, I must see to lunch. You'll all feel better for some soup."

And with that extraordinary pronouncement she stalked off. Even Anna had broken out of her hysteria—or stopped her dramatics, I wasn't quite sure which—and stared after the housekeeper.

A waft of pipe-smoke made me look to the side. Mr. Dart had not lit his pipe, but was tapping it against his stone arm. I was reminded that there *had* been a key in Henry Coates' lock: I had turned it to keep Ned Garsom out, not half an hour ago.

"You seem most concerned about Mr. Coates' belongings," Mr. Veitch said, with a suspicious frown at the unfortunate Ned Garsom.

"He was my friend!" Garsom spluttered indignantly.

"Come now," Mr. Veitch said with a twisted smile shadowing his otherwise pleasant face. "Leave off this undignified pretence. We all know he was no such thing."

It was obvious Mr. Veitch had hit a nerve, given how much Garsom was sweating. He backed away from his cousin, but couldn't go far until he hit the wall, with the boring etchings and the anything-but-boring display of knives. I looked around as discreetly as I could but no one but Mr. Dart was paying any attention to the stiletto. "I—I don't know what you're talking about."

Mr. Veitch gave him a disgusted sneer, which sat strangely on his pleasant face. "You *are* an idiot, aren't you? Surely you realized it wasn't just you he was blackmailing."

CHAPTER TWENTY-TWO

Silence fell in the wake of that statement; or near-silence. The turn of the key in the lock of the door through which Bessie had just exited was quite audible.

I was still standing nearest the other door, a couple of feet inside the room. I turned to grasp the handle, but before I could a patter of light steps sounded and the tumblers in that lock clanked into place.

So the servants had locked us in.

I turned back to the room at large. We had Ned and Anna Garsom, Mr. and Madam Veitch, Hope, Hal, Mr. Dart, Jullanar Maebh, and myself. The Hunter in Green, Ballory the unicorn, and all the household servants—and the enigmatic Master Boring himself—were on the other side of the locked doors.

"Are we to assume, then, that one of us did it?" Mr. Dart asked me quietly.

The odd, sharp satisfaction on the butler's face came to mind. "I wonder," I said thoughtfully. "Did you see the butler's expression, Perry?"

"I have yet to see the butler," he answered. "Was he in here?"

"On the far side of the room, the door Bessie and Walter came through—he left just before they arrived. He appeared strangely ... gleeful."

Mr. Dart examined his pipe. The tobacco in the bowl had a disconcerting violet-green tinge to its smoulder. "A point to consider, certainly. Especially in conjunction with what we found earlier ..."

"Which you didn't finish explaining to me," I pointed out as quietly as I could.

Mr. Dart smiled at me, his eyes very blue. "Follow my lead?"

I opened my mouth to reply, then sighed explosively as I was interrupted.

"—I'm sure *I* don't know what you're talking about!" Anna exclaimed sharply, flouncing to a seat on the sofa. She seemed remarkably composed for someone who had been keening hysterically not five minutes ago.

We'd been in a play together, first year at Morrowlea. She'd stayed involved with the Dramatics Society the whole time, mostly but not only because of the costumes.

O Lady, why did I have to be so suspicious?

"Don't you?" Mr. Veitch said, rubbing his hands almost jovially. Now that we were in trouble he was weirdly cheerful. "Come, come, my young friends, haven't any of you a penchant for mysteries? This is most excellent entertainment, isn't it?"

—Or rather, why did everyone else have to *act* so suspiciously?

"My friend is *dead*," Ned Garsom insisted, stomping around the desk to sit next to his sister on the sofa. I watched her rearrange her scarlet skirts with an indignant huff, and almost missed the fact that he used her movement to pass her something, which she promptly sat on.

What was it with these complexities? Why couldn't this be an easy case of injured pride or angered love or obvious self-interest?

I was sure Mrs. Etaris had mentioned something about nine-tenths of murder cases being obvious as a scalded cat.

Of course I would end up embroiled in the one that wasn't.

"Sit down, sit down," Mr. Veitch said, gesturing at the rest of us. "There's no sense in looming awkwardly, gentlemen — and ladies—and my dear *Lord* St-Noire, don't think I have forgotten you!"

I grimaced at him and drifted to the wooden chair in which I had sat all morning. I pulled it away from the desk, noting that there were no new stains on the blotter or the wood, and sat with my back to the stiletto dagger and everyone in clear view.

"I believe," Mr. Dart said slowly, "that you have some explaining to do, Mr. Veitch."

His voice was steady, his bearing calm, and he stood in the middle of the room, one arm in its sling, gently smoking pipe in the other hand, like a gentleman fully at his ease. But we could all feel otherwise. The air was suddenly heavy around him, wavering like heatwave mirages. The fire in both hearths flared up in silver sparks that did not fully subside, and a wind that was not a draught from the window stirred all our hair and clothes.

Mr. Veitch sat down beside his wife with an ungainly thump and a pallid face.

Hope sank into a chair beside one of the hearths, her face askance at the sparks. Hal's sentiments had overmastered his doubts, and he stood behind her, one hand protectively on her shoulder, the other on the back of her chair. Ned and Anna Garsom both pushed back into their seats with the force of their dismay. Jullanar Maebh was seated in a chair near the wall and looked passing confused.

Madam Veitch roused, blanched, uttered a small confused sound, and began straightening out her yarns and other knitting paraphernalia with shaking hands. I regarded her and was inclined to believe her swoon. Mind you, it could have been occasioned by the unexpected presence of the body with the knitting needle in the parlour, rather than the death itself.

It was hard to imagine anything further from the Mountains I had seen—was it only yesterday?

"Er, I don't know that I meant *you*," Mr. Veitch babbled. "That is—I shouldn't like to—impose—impress—impugn—impute anything, not of *you*, sir."

I really needed to learn what exactly Mr. Dart's declaration meant.

"I thank you," Mr. Dart said coolly. "Perhaps you might explain your accusation of blackmail? Come, we are all friends here," he added, with a mild edge, "save for the one who might be a murderer, of course."

No one moved. Mr. Dart blew a handful of smoke rings, each a different shade of grey, and set them hovering in a cloud above his head. They shifted position slowly, gently, weaving in and out of each other's loops.

Mr. Dart removed the pipe for a moment. "No one wishes to volunteer? Lord St-Noire, what say you of the events?"

Follow my lead, he had asked me. Welladay and good Lady, as the Honourable Rag might say. I inched my chair closer to the desk and retrieved paper, quill, ink, and pearl-handled penknife. Everyone watched me in silence. Once I had prepared my writing utensils, I dipped the nib into the ink and looked at Mr. Dart with an attempt at sangfroid nowhere as effective as his.

"I saw Henry Coates last at around midnight, just after a great clatter and crash of noise I was told this morning was the suit of armour falling down the stairs. He was on his way, he said, to his room, and as far as I saw entered it. Who saw him next?"

No one would meet my eyes. Hope had hers well down, on her tightly clasped hands. The silver-and-aquamarine ring glittered in the silver light from Mr. Dart's sparks. Hal caught me looking at her, and frowned mightily before leaning down and whispering something into her ear.

Hope looked up at him, her heart in her face, before she turned away, her eyes filling with tears. Mr. Dart cleared his throat, at first I thought to question her, but he turned instead to Madam Veitch. "Madam, it was your knitting needle we all saw," he said. "What interactions did *you* have with the man?"

"Now look here," Mr. Veitch said, half-rising angrily, but I saw Madam Veitch thrusting her flask back into her knitting bag and hastily swallowing. Her face changed within a few seconds: a mouthful of her wireweed tonic and she was now flying high above such things as prudence.

I watched her sadly, knowing where this led. It had been six months of a slow and painful recovery for me, and that was when I had no idea that the cause was a drug I had been given unawares.

If I had been taking it of my own volition? With a ready source?

"It from my spare set," Madam Veitch said, reaching into her bag to pull out the half-wrought scarf she had been working on that morning and demonstrating that two needles were stuck into the ball of umber yarn. She glanced across at her cousins. "I loaned them to Anna this morning, since she couldn't find her embroidery."

"What of your dealings with Mr. Coates?" I asked, making a note of this point, and recalling that Hope had said that Anna had misplaced her work-bag. Or had claimed to have, anyway.

Madam Veitch, with her needles in hand and her emotions lifted by her tonic, began to knit. Her movements were once again quick and deft. "He was a paltry sort of man," she observed. The needles flashed silver in my eyes, though the sun had moved on from the windows. "Always trying to act as if knowing all one's deepest secrets bought him entry into one's house. Well," she added with a humorous look at Ned Garsom, "I suppose it did."

"*Wife*," Mr. Veitch hissed.

She smiled placidly at me. "You understand, don't you, Lord St-Noire? It starts off so small ... a bet here, a wager there, a little flutter down at the races ... a game or two of cards of an evening ..." She laughed, apparently sincerely amused. "And all of a sudden you find out your husband's run through two fortunes and more besides. Mr. Coates was quite a favourite at our house, for a while, until he met Ned and learned I *wasn't* the sole heir to Towers."

Towers was this house, with its fortunes in tea and antiquities and who knew what else.

"And did he also supply you with your ... tonic?" I dared to ask.

Her needles did not falter. "He recommended it. There's an apothecary in Highbury who compounds it for us all. It's nothing *serious*," she added, almost gaily. "Just a little pick-me-up for when you're feeling down. Better than drinking all the time, don't you think?" She elbowed her husband, whose red nose suggested he was fond of his drink, and who smiled indulgently at her.

"It's been a miraculous difference," he said, almost fondly.

"I see," I said, wondering if I did. Mr. Dart sent up two smoke rings, one after the other, in peacock-blue and a blushing purple.

A cloudy sense of what this might all mean was starting to form, dimly, in the distant recesses of my mind. I needed more details. If the Veitches had made use of Coates' connections first as a lender (or perhaps to find a lender) on the strength of their prospects, and thereafter were being blackmailed—

—Could they really not know what the active ingredient in the tonic *was*?

I had spent nearly three years at Morrowlea, and not even the hospital matron had breathed a hint of suspicion. Wireweed was avowedly illegal in every country in Northwest Oriole, but before this autumn's revelations I had only the vaguest idea of what form it might take. The only druggery tonic I knew of was laudanum.

Yet within six months of the spring term whole swaths of the continent were known to be addicted to it. How had the Knockermen and the Indrillines worked so fast?

Ned Garsom guffawed. "And here we were thinking you were so upstanding! Anna, did you hear that? You're not the only one!"

"Ned, don't be a bloody fool," Anna retorted, then simpered immediately at me. "My apologies for my language, Lord St-Noire."

I raised my eyebrows at her in utter incredulity. The falsity of her advances rang suddenly loud in my senses. I *knew* she was an accomplished actress—had I not seen her in half a dozen plays?—this cloying, obvious act of toad-eating had to be deliberately bad.

But why?

"And what was your relationship with Mr. Coates?" Mr. Dart asked in a calm, soothing tone, before sending up another smoke ring, this one a soft red, to join the peacock-blue and purple ones.

Garsom looked at Anna, who crossed her arms and gave every evidence of refusing to say another word. He gave me a silly-looking smirk, then seemed to recall (with the assistance of Anna's foot jabbing into his calf, if the motions of her skirt were anything to go by) that he was supposed to be upset about Coates' death. "Well, we were business partners," he said proudly. "And Anna was his wife."

CHAPTER TWENTY-THREE

"It wasn't a valid marriage," Anna said sharply. Her cheeks had flushed deep red, and her deep-set eyes were flashing fiercely. "You contracted me, brother, without my knowledge *or* consent."

He twisted in the chair to scowl at her. "You agreed—"

"I *agreed* that I could hardly do worse!"

"You signed the papers, Anna—"

"Under duress!"

"Duress!" Ned Garsom laughed coarsely. "Is that what you call it? Your entertainments are too well known for that, Anna. Don't try to deny it, now."

From Hal's expression, he had a fair idea what Anna's *entertainments* were in this context. I was glad to see that Hope was as confused as I.

"Now, then, being blackmailed into marriage isn't so very awful, is it?"

Mr. Veitch was overflowing with ghoulish enjoyment at this scene. I could see that those of us less closely involved with the family were more than slightly uncomfortable with this airing-out of dirty laundry.

Anna gave her older cousin a disgusted sneer. "Would you care to share a bed with that creature?"

Mr. Veitch nodded in false empathy. "True, true. I can hardly blame you for recoiling."

"Too bad Belfort caught you in his stable with his groom before you could snare him," Garsom said, sniggering. "I'm still not sure how Henry got hold of that."

"Fortunately," Anna hissed, "it is now a moot point."

"And did you ensure that?" Mr. Veitch asked.

Anna said, "No," but it was without the ringing certainty of her prouder declarations.

I went to write down her apparent motive for the murder, but the ink had once more dried on my pen. I unsheathed the penknife and trimmed the nib, paying close attention to my hands.

The air was heavy with emotion and Mr. Dart's magic. It felt less threatening now, yet also somehow *sharper*, as if the pustule was being lanced.

∾

("**E**ver fancy becoming a physician?" Mr. Dart had asked me, one day not so long ago. He was visiting me at work in the bookstore, and had been drawn into a treatise on human anatomy while I dealt with a small onrush of customers.

I put the money in the till and answered truthfully. "Not especially. You?"

He set the heavy treatise—who knew there was so much to say about the skeleton?—back on its shelf. "No. Hamish studied medicine almost to the doctorate, did you know? He says it trained his eye in the particulars of the human form."

As Sir Hamish was a greatly skilled portraitist, this did not seem a poor trajectory.

"It would be good, I imagine," Mr. Dart had gone on, "to heal people."

I glanced at his stone arm, which had so far resisted all attempts to return it to normal, but answered him obliquely, lightly as he was himself speaking. "History not being quite so full of remedies?"

He laughed. "'I'll have you know that history is *entirely* full of remedies, if only people were inclined to take them. It's like a mystery novel: things are always either far simpler than you think or far more complicated than you would have imagined."

He'd borne a knowing expression, no doubt in response to my own half-pained grimace at the thought of the too-complicated history of my father's career and reputation. Yet on the other hand our relationship should have been simple, if only I could manage to let it be.

"Mrs. Etaris tells me that most crimes, in real life, are entirely lacking in mystery," I said instead. Mrs. Etaris' husband was the Chief Constable of Ragnor Bella, but half the town, as I was coming to learn, was certain she was the one who solved the majority of his cases.

"And for the rest?"

"One need usually follow the money—and sometimes wounded pride—to unravel the situation."

Mr. Dart laughed. "One could almost as easily apply that maxim to the understanding of history.")

W e were probably over-complicating things.

What did we—or I, since I could hardly confer privately with Mr. Dart and Hal, let alone the Hunter in Green on the other side of the locked doors—so then, what did *I* know?

Leave aside the notebook and the dragon scale and the money and the exact contents of the letters. They had not been stolen; they explicated Coates' life, but not his death.

What did I *know*?

Master Boring of Hillend Towers was a snobbish, eccentric man of wealth, apparently unwell. He had invited his surviving relatives—Anna and Ned Garsom, and their older cousin Violetta Veitch—to join him for Winterturn. The presumption was that he was evaluating their suitability to inherit his fortune.

Madam Veitch, in turn, had brought with her her husband; Anna her friend Hope, ostensibly as a chaperone and companion; and Ned his so-called friend Henry Coates.

Henry Coates was blackmailing all four, and had somehow inveigled the unwilling Anna into an unwelcome marriage. He was not exactly blackmailing Hope, but was certainly setting up some sort of extortion scheme with her as the victim.

Ned Garsom was indebted to him, but also attempting to work his own cunning scheme—even if I had no clear idea what *that* involved—possibly with his sister's assistance. The scheme might or might not be in open conjunction with Coates'.

The younger men had gotten drunk—or had they?—last night, and at the top of the stairs had an imbroglio with the suit of armour. If Coates had died subsequent to that, I might have thought he'd fallen and broken his neck; but I had seen and spoken with him shortly afterwards. He had been preoccupied with something, and interested in my views on the value of the merchant classes, but had gone off without much discussion.

I regarded the tableau of deeply uncomfortable house-guests. No one was looking at each other, including Hope and Hal, who both seemed miserable and very solitary despite his hand on her shoulder. Mr. Dart alone seemed composed, and he was standing in the middle of the room with a flock of multicoloured smoke rings above his head.

I fixed my attention on Ned Garsom. "What exactly are you doing here that you think a cunning scheme? Are you stealing from your uncle?"

The blunt question shocked him—though once again I

wasn't sure if it were the bluntness or the accusation that roused the response. Nevertheless, he spluttered indignantly. "Absolutely not—I am—it's my inheritance anyway—no!"

Mr. Veitch leaned forward with undisguised interest. "Then what? No need to be shy!"

Anna uncrossed her arms so she could scoff petulantly. "It'll be a grand failure, like everything he does." In a lower voice she muttered something that sounded suspiciously like, *Couldn't even get rid of the body*, but her brother talked over her before anyone else reacted.

"This time will be a success," he said rapidly. "It's a surefire plan—Henry said so."

"Henry is dead."

His grin barely faltered. "One less share, then. And really —Anna—he wasn't exactly Quality, was he?"

"*Now* you see it. What happened to 'we need him, Anna'. 'Keep him sweet, Anna.' 'We can't go ahead without him, Anna'."

Ned Garsom shrugged. "Well, you said it: he's dead. I know he brought his contact list with him—we don't need him now."

Was he even listening to himself?

"You see," Garsom said proudly, evidently eager to share a secret he had been hard-pressed to keep. "I had this absolutely *brilliant* idea—"

"Yes?" Mr. Veitch urged.

He spread his hands out wide, in exuberant revelation. "Revolution."

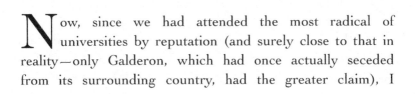

Now, since we had attended the most radical of universities by reputation (and surely close to that in reality—only Galderon, which had once actually seceded from its surrounding country, had the greater claim), I shouldn't have been shocked by Anna making this pronouncement.

Astonished, yes, for she'd come to study with a particular Scholar, not for the politics or the radical equality, but not *shocked*.

Ned Garsom, in his second year of Economics at Stoney-bridge, however, *was* a surprise.

"Revolution?" I repeated.

He lit up with nearly rabid enthusiasm. "Yes! It's time we took back what was *ours*!"

Despite the poor reception to his first speech, Garsom had spent half of supper last night discoursing on the problem of uppity merchants and their unworthily social-climbing daughters. (Which, come to think of it, was perhaps a *personal* bitterness.) I'd half-forgotten the rant in the course of the subsequent excitements; he'd evidently forgotten my reaction.

He was eloquent, in a bluff sort of way. I could almost imagine the Honourable Rag getting this sort of idea into his head—if I hadn't known that the Honourable Rag had an entirely different (and much more appealing) revolution in mind.

Ned Garsom said nothing about magic or wireweed or the increasing desperation of the lower classes. He mentioned nothing of pirates or press gangs or smuggling or the increasing danger of the roads. He seemed entirely ignorant of the moves to seize power by the Indrillines or the Knockermen or the Lady of Alinor.

No. According to this fount of wisdom, the real problem besetting Northwest Oriole was that the aristocracy needed to take back their power and, like good fathers, discipline their child-like wives, daughters, and tenantry.

I confess I didn't follow his entire argument.

In the Kingdom of Rondé, of which both Fiellan and Hal's Fillering Pool were part, parliament had just passed a new law permitting inheritance by primogeniture without distinction of sex. We all knew that this was because the male heir to the kingdom was unfit to rule, while his elder sister was not only well-educated but also had a healthy son (and was, moreover, usefully widowed, so there would be no troubles with a prince consort).

As a result of this both Mr. Dart and the Honourable Rag were out their inheritances in favour of their female relations. Their response had not been reactionary; rather the opposite.

Ned Garsom's plan seemed like a piece of fluff designed expressly to appeal to an uncritical young man who wanted a return to the glory days of Astandalan rule. Given the political situation of the continent—which I was slowly beginning to grasp—this was a serious warning sign. I glanced around the room. Hal and Mr. Dart were both listening very carefully indeed.

("Not even to stop Lark," Hal had said, "am I setting myself up as a petty emperor." It was becoming increasingly clear even to me that we were going to have to do *something* to ensure no one else tried to.)

Garsom finally wound down. He leaned towards me, visibly eager for my approval. "So you see, don't you?"

The attention paid to "Lord St-Noire" was beginning to make more sense. Also the need to secure Master Boring's fortune and resources.

I regarded him critically. "How did Henry Coates feature in this plan?"

"It was my idea, not his," Garsom said, as petulantly as Anna, then seemed to remember his friend was dead. He grimaced with exaggerated sorrow. "Poor Henry. He'll be so disappointed not to see the results ..."

"I'm sure," I said dryly.

"Codswallop," said Mr. Veitch. "He was a blackmailer and a good riddance to him, as I don't doubt you well know! If you think he was after anything but his own profit, you're even more of an idiot than I took you for."

"Look here, cousin —"

"No cousin of yours by blood, thank the Lady! What was he really after? That's what I want to know. He didn't start hanging on to you until he learned about our uncle, I know that. You didn't have anything he wanted, that's why. But after? Answer me that, and we'll likely found out why he was killed."

"Oh, as for that," Madam Veitch put in.

"You have an idea, wife?" her husband cried in unflattering surprise.

Madam Veitch reached into her yarn-bag for a skein of dark green wool. Her initial wireweed-induced exhilaration seemed to have settled into an unshakeable good-humoured placidity.

"Madam Veitch?" I tried, too aware of how easily I used to fall into a focus on my own thoughts and forget the exterior conversation.

Sure enough, she startled. "Oh yes. I expect he was here the same as the rest of us, to hunt the unicorn."

CHAPTER TWENTY-FOUR

H ope said, "Hunt—what—a *unicorn*?"
    She was convincingly confused. Jullanar Maebh,
whom I had nearly forgotten about, so quiet had she been in
her corner, said in a clear, if clearly unhappy, voice, "What
blasphemy is this?"

"No blasphemy," Madam Veitch assured her calmly. I realized with a touch of surprise that I was starting to like Madam
Veitch.

She pointed with one of her needles at me, or rather at the
wall behind me. Not the array of daggers, I saw after I twisted
around, but the two ancient tapestries on either side. One
depicted the Knight coming on the injured Unicorn; the second
the Unicorn and the Knight fighting side-by-side against a
mass of shadowy monsters, all tentacles and teeth.

I glanced at Mr. Dart, who still stood alone in the middle of
the room, apparently unperturbed. One arm was in the sling
and the other hand held his pipe, but his shoulders were
straight and his chin high and his eyes frank and level and
luminous. Very much as I had seen him, the Lady's Champion,
at the Grim Crossroads between this life and the next.

I looked at the tapestries more closely. Whoever had done

231

them had seen those same monsters. I was sure I recognized one in the background, with moth wings and claws. And the unicorn looked like Ballory upstairs, not the idealized horse or deer like creature seen in most depictions.

Madam Veitch started knitting again, needles picking up loops of yarn without her needing to look at them. "My mother told me the story," she said in a soothing, somewhat sing-song voice. "It was on our family's land that the unicorns first came to the world. There is a sacred grove, she said, hidden from view. That's why the house is here. To guard it."

And who, then, had placed the unicorn foal inside a box?

"The first one was found after Sir Peregrine came over the mountains from the Coombe." She smiled at me, needles flashing in an easy, swift rhythm. "All things of note here-abouts come over the mountains from the Coombe."

I did not want to disappoint her, but— "We were trying to return thence," I said. "Not coming over."

She smiled enigmatically. "And yet of all those in this house, it was the two young men from South Fiellan who found their way to the heart of the maze and the prize therein."

How did she *know*?—Or was she merely guessing, her mind dancing from intuition to intuition under the fizz and joy of the wireweed burning up her inner magic.

Mr. Dart had not moved, except to blow yet another smoke ring, this one silver as the sparks still foaming in the two hearths.

"It's hardly a sacred grove," I said.

"Isn't it?"

Jullanar Maebh broke the ensuing silence. "Even if this is so—and I'm not saying it is—someone violated all things that are sacred by murdering a guest in the house. No matter that he was an unpleasant and immoral man, no matter a black-mailer. It was a wicked act. *Who did it?*"

"That is indeed the question," said Mr. Dart. "It is

becoming clearer who had motive—but motives can be decep-
tive, as is also quite clear. Opportunities, however ..."

"But everyone had the *opportunity*," Anna said. "He was
killed in the middle of the night!"

We all looked at her. Hope said, "Anna, did you not find
him just this morning?"

~

I wondered what it said about my interactions with her that
I didn't have any difficulty in imagining Anna stabbing
Henry Coates. From Hal's expression, neither did he.

Hope, on the other hand, knew her far better. She was
tearful and accusing. "You said—oh, *Anna*, you said he
wouldn't be bothering me any more—"

Hal's face darkened, and his hand curved protectively on
Hope's shoulder. She cast him a quick, grateful, look, before
returning expectantly to Anna. "Oh, how could you?"

"I didn't," Anna protested, if weakly. "I meant ... I married
him, he could hardly also marry you!"

"I wouldn't put it past him," Mr. Veitch said, with a lech-
erous leer.

Hal gave him a magnificently disdainful look. Unlike his
wife, Mr. Veitch was not coming off well the longer we
knew him.

A sudden loud reverberation from a gong startled us all
into silence. I jumped up, nearly knocking over the inkwell—
not though I'd been doing much with my notes, after all, as the
conversation had never quite managed to centre on who was
where at what time—and found myself looking directly at
Bessie.

The housekeeper stood in the doorway leading to the
dining room. She held a padded mallet in one hand and
regarded us all dispassionately. "Lunch," she said with ominous
emphasis, "is ready."

Ned Garsom was the first to move. He pushed past the housekeeper, who raised her eyebrows at his rudeness and stepped back to let the rest of us through. We all did follow him, though I couldn't imagine anyone was truly hungry in the circumstances.

Garsom was rattling the handle on the far door ineffectually. "It's locked," he said, and made as if to confront the housekeeper. Mr. Dart, who was closest, stepped between them. Ned Garsom stopped immediately, wariness in his eyes even as he scowled at the uncaring Bessie. "Look here, you can't just keep us locked in!"

"The master has ordered it," she said, with the same curiously flat intonation she seemed to use whenever speaking of the reclusive Master Boring.

"Orchestrating everything from his sickbed, is he?" Mr. Veitch said with out-of-place cheer. "Will he be joining us for the meal?"

"He has not requested a place set for him."

"Good enough for me," said Mr. Veitch, and sat down at the head of the table without waiting for anyone else. I pulled out the chair for Madam Veitch, who thanked me absently, and continued around the table to the seat I'd had the night before.

Something was niggling at me, something she had said the day before about the master, but Ned Garsom threw himself into his seat at the foot of the table with a childish huff, and the almost-realization vanished.

We slowly took the seats we'd been given at dinner the night before. I was once more facing the monstrous butterfly, on the wall behind Hal opposite me. There was an extra chair between Anna and Ned Garsom, where Henry Coates had been seated last night. As we settled into our places I noted that his place had been set.

That seemed … curious, until I realized that Jullanar Maebh had not joined us last night. Mr. Dart assisted her into her seat before taking his own. Ned Garsom made a sort of excuse for not holding her chair that Jullanar Maebh rightly ignored.

The table was again set elaborately. The mahogany was covered with a snowy white linen tablecloth, as ancient and fine as anything I'd seen at Hal's castle in Fillering Pool.

We each had great round platters at our seats, apparently solid silver. They were unadorned but for a floral motif around the edges, the centres mirror-polished. My face looked pinched and pale; I consciously tried to relax. Despite everything, it did seem as if the murderer had no inclination to perpetuate the habit.

Down the middle of the table were four silver bowls of aromatic golden quinces. Before each of us were the fanciful salt cellars. Mine was still the dragon, and Jullanar Maebh's the mermaid, but Anna's was not the trident-wielding seagod, but rather a golden snake curling around a red glass cup. I couldn't see if anyone else's had changed.

To the side of the silver chargers were various sets of utensils. I considered them in light of what I'd learned at Morrowlea. It appeared we would be lunching on fish, soup, sorbets, and at least two other courses.

"Oh, doesn't this look nice," Madam Veitch murmured, and smiled up the table. "Do say the grace, husband!"

It was a toss-up whether the others took that as gratefully ordinary or appallingly tone-deaf.

"May the Lady bless this food to our use," he intoned without apparent self-consciousness.

"And ourselves to her service," said Mr. Dart, with an odd glint in his eye.

"Amen," Jullanar Maebh, Hal, Hope, Madam Veitch, and I all chorused together, followed more raggedly and reluctantly by the three currently most likely to have murdered Henry Coates.

The far door opened before we had to make any further conversation. Bessie stood beside it, as if on guard, while the same servants as last night—Walter and Hettie—brought in the first course, the soup.

It was served in golden bowls that would hardly have looked out of place on the Emperor's table, for all I could imagine, but the soup within was beet and cabbage. It was a sumptuously rich purple, and smelled delicious; but it was peasant food.

My mother had cooked a version of this during the Interim, when most of our food was what we could grow in the Dower Cottage garden. Beets and cabbages both grew and stored easily. I wondered if Hal had ever had it before.

"Ah," said Madam Veitch, taking a small sip of the broth and then smiling almost radiantly. It appeared she'd sneaked another mouthful of her tonic while I wasn't paying attention. "Uncle keeps the old ways, you know." She fixed her deep-set eyes on Hope, whose white garments seemed almost to shimmer. "Why are you wearing white today, my dear?"

"In honour of the Lady," Hope replied in a small voice, setting down her spoon while she spoke. (White was not the most practical of colours to be wearing while eating beet soup, it had to be said.) "It's the first of December. Candlemas."

"We keep Candlemas too," Madam Veitch said in a pleased voice.

"We'll be lighting the candles tonight," her husband agreed.

"Did your mother teach you the family traditions?" Madam Veitch asked Anna, who started so that a few drops of purple fell from her uplifted spoon to stain the white tablecloth next to her plate.

"I didn't know there were any around Candlemas."

"And yet you came in good time for the Hunt?"

Anna exchanged a slightly frantic glance with her brother; Ned had slurped down his soup and was pushing his spoon sadly around his empty bowl. It was good soup.

"I don't know what you mean, Cousin Violetta. Uncle

Richard asked us to be sure we arrived by yesterday. He didn't say why."

Madam Veitch smiled around the table. "Look at all your rapt faces! Quite a marvellous sight, I do say, to see the young folk so interested. Now my dears, since you all arrived before midnight Candlemas Eve, you are entered into the Hunt."

I finished my soup, wiped my mouth with my napkin, and said tentatively, "You surely don't mean an actual hunt for a unicorn, Madam?"

"No, no, Lord St-Noire—that *would* be blasphemy. It is a hunt in *name of* the unicorn. We are the guardians of the sacred grove, our family. Surely you know the story?"

"I'm afraid not. We don't get much news of Lind on our side of the mountains."

"And yet we hear all about the Coombe." She gave me a glowing smile, her eyes lit not like Mr. Dart's, but more like the butler's fierce black gaze. Her eyebrows were almost as darkly abundant as his. Plucked brows must not be in fashion for middle-aged women in Chare; Anna's were much narrower if almost as striking.

"All sorts of stories come over the mountains. Tales of dragons and the Good Neighbours, of witches and quests and the high road that once led to Astandalas but always led to adventure. Have you never heard why the road went through the Woods Noirell?"

I shook my head, though I knew a few things about the result of all the magic Astandalan wizards had used to impose their will on Fiellan and the entirety of Northwest Oriole. "I presume because that was where the Border was."

"The Woods is a shallow place between worlds," she said. "A ford, you might say, or a pass. It has always been special. You should ask your grandmother for your family legends. They might be truer than you think."

I had already come across dragons and curses and

enchanted bees ... I wasn't sure I quite wanted to know what else might be in those woods.

The two servants came in. Walter cleared away the soup bowls and Hettie replaced them with tiny fish-shaped dishes, cloisonné enamelled with silver and green scales. Each contained a singular brown trout, broiled and presented whole, with a knob of butter the only sauce.

I sprinkled salt from my jade-dragon cellar over the fish and began to debone it with my fish knife and fork.

Madam Veitch ignored her fish entirely. "Earth and Water to begin the meal," she said. "Air next, and Fire last. And then ... the Hunt. It began many centuries ago, when Sir Peregrine came over the mountains from the Coombe and found the Unicorn in the sacred grove. He assisted with its healing, and they became friends."

It was a familiar story, often told as an encouragement to be kind to the injured and the weak, though I'd never heard an actual specific location being given before. Sir Peregrine had rescued the unicorn out of pity for its injured beauty, and the unicorn had come to be his constant companion. They had started to return over the mountains when they were caught by a storm—having now experienced the ferocity of a winter storm in these parts, I understood this part of the tale rather better—and were given shelter by an ancient crone.

When the storm passed and they were ready to move on, she asked him to do her a small favour.

Anything, he promised her unwisely, and she charged him to find and bring her a certain flower that grew only in the mythical Summer Country.

Their adventures were many and changed with the speaker (in her account, which was short, Madam Veitch skimmed over the journey, though most of the songs allocated many verses to it) but eventually Sir Peregrine discovered the way to Nên Corovel, the Summer Country, and fixed it in its place in the sea past the Tarvenol peninsula.

(Previously, my mother had said, it had wandered the oceans of the world, now in the far north under the arctic lights, now in the farthest west where no one from Astandalas had ever been, now in a lake that was only a mirage in the middle of the southern desert.)

Sir Peregrine and the unicorn found the flower required by the crone, and they fought against many evils and troubles along the way to return across what was then mostly wilderness to reach again the crone at the edge of the mountains to the Coombe.

But he could not find her. He searched all the mountains, he and the unicorn, but all they could find was a beautiful young woman, a shepherdess in the high pastures leading down into the Coombe. Sir Peregrine had grown old in his journey, and his hair was grey and his beard long (so said the tales), and he could only assume the ancient crone had died.

He came in the end to the place where he had first met the crone, and there he planted the flower, for he knew not what else to do. The flower took root and sprang forth into a great many-branched tree, all bedecked with flowers, and Sir Peregrine and the shepherdess tended it, while the unicorn graced their hearth and home with good fortune.

In the versions I knew, that was the end of the story. It was said that the shepherdess was actually the crone, and had been under an enchantment till he returned; or that she was herself the enchantress, and had disguised herself to test his character. It was always implied and sometimes outright stated that them tending the flower was the establishment of her as the first Lady of Alinor, and he her consort and champion.

Madam Veitch had a different ending to relate.

We had finished our fish when she came to the end of the story. "They were very old indeed when the flower-tree finally set a seed—just one—a fruit like a golden apple," she said. "Sir Peregrine and the Shepherdess watched as it ripened over the course of that year. And then, on the anniversary of the day Sir Peregrine had first met the unicorn, it fell."

"And?" Ned Garsom said, almost despite himself, when she stopped there.

"And it rolled down from the mountains until it lodged itself in the sacred grove where Sir Peregrine had found the unicorn, and Sir Peregrine and the Shepherdess followed after, hunting for it."

"So this Hunt of which you speak," Hal said slowly. "Is after the golden fruit?"

From my end of the table I could see Mr. Dart was eating his fish without fanfare or apparent difficulty. He appeared to be listening politely, but his eyes were forward, whether at the strange insects on the wall or the air I couldn't tell.

"After the noon meal on Candlemas," Madam Veitch said, "all the guests in the house have one hour in which to seek the golden fruit."

"And if we find it?" I asked.

"Oh, no one has ever found it," she said complacently. "It's just a story and a family tradition for the start of the Winter-turn season—a little bit of fun. You might as well speak of finding a unicorn, or unmooring Nên Corovel from the seabed, or a revolution. But my uncle did say that anyone participating in the Hunt this year could keep one item that they find."

"This is assuming we are permitted to leave the dining room," Anna said snippily.

Madam Veitch cast her a disappointed look. "My dear Anna, will you stop with this silliness of yours? Once you admit you killed him I'm sure they'll let us go."

CHAPTER TWENTY-FIVE

"**H**e was already dead when I found him," Anna cried. "I did stab him with the needle—you can't imagine how *angry* I was—"

She stopped there, no doubt at the incredulous looks on all our faces.

"Well," she amended in a more normal tone of voice, if anything could be normal about this subject. "He *was* dead."

Walter came in again to clear the plates, and Hettie with tiny porcelain egg-cups filled with a very light and frothy composition the colour of whipped egg whites. When I lifted the sorbet spoon to taste it all I could think was that it *was* whipped egg whites, very lightly salted.

"The dish of Air," Madam Veitch said, in what she probably thought, through the haze of wireweed euphoria, was a mystic tone.

I set my spoon down and directed my words to Anna. "And where was the body, when you found it—him?"

"In the parlour," she said, pointing with her spoon at the pass-through fireplace. The silver sparks seemed to cow her, for she shrank away from them, even though Mr. Dart was simply listening, and was at the other end of the table besides.

"To be clear," I said, "where had you come from when you found him?"

Anna flushed and lowered her eyes until she was well focused on the whipped egg whites, and said nothing. The silence went on for a bit, and then Hope said, "She had asked me to help her look through Mr. Coates' room while he was busy with her brother, but the door was locked. We went instead to her room, and discussed, er, personal matters, until I wanted to refresh myself before lunch. That must have been a good quarter-hour before she screamed."

"I had to be sure he *was* dead," Anna said.

Indeed.

Knowing it was probably fruitless—but who knew, given the extraordinary willingness of these people to admit to, nay to boast of, major crimes?—"Who saw him last this morning?"

Sadly, no one answered.

After the egg whites we were served with two braided loaves of rustic bread and two large wheels of farmhouse cheese, one pale straw, the other with a visibly sticky pinkish-orange rind. Hettie set these down at each end of the table, moving the silver bowls of quinces to a cluster in the centre to make room. Walter followed with two knives, one for each cheese. My end of the table had the sticky pink cheese, and a thin, narrow knife like a filleting tool. Or indeed a stiletto dagger.

Surely not coincidence?

Madam Veitch said nothing about the cheese being somehow connected to the element of Fire. I was a little disappointed.

Before Walter left the room Hal asked him, "Do you know when the physician is expected to arrive?"

I had nearly forgotten about the outside world's likely interest in this murder. From the expression on Mr. Veitch's face, who was in my line of sight to Walter, so had he, and he wasn't best pleased about the reminder.

Walter gave Hal a short, correct bow. "Soon, sir. Our Wally said the road crew has cleared to the Inn and up to the Edge, and the groundsmen and grooms have nearly excavated the drive. There is one great drift before the trees that is proving tiresome."

Walter's accent was almost as well-educated as the butler's. I recalled, even as Hal thanked him, that he was Master Boring's man, pressed into assisting the guests because the master was too miserly to hire anyone else. Or so claimed Anna as reported by Hope.

No one made any move towards the bread and cheese, nor said a word. After a moment Hettie and Walter came back in with plates of smoked sausages, served with more of the grated rutabaga-and-carrot cakes I'd had at breakfast, and yet more cabbage.

"Ah," said Madam Veitch. "The dish of Fire."

What was the point of the peasant food served on frankly excessively grand nobleman's plates? It had to be a deliberate choice.

Everyone poked at their food desultorily. Only Ned Garsom and Mr. Veitch seemed able to eat with any semblance of normal appetite.

I considered my cabbage and sausages and root vegetable cakes. What *did* this tell me?

—That Master Boring, for all his absence, was very much in control of the situation.

And following that, that the shared physical feature of his three relations were the same deep-set dark eyes and heavy dark brows that were in half the boring (hah) age-darkened portraits on the wall.

By Madam Veitch's account, this house was built on and around a sacred grove, which the maze of hoarded objects in the main hall somehow guarded. By the Hunter in Green's witness, some power had caused a great blizzard to centre on the house and trap us here, just in time to participate in the

Candlemas tradition of *Hunting the Unicorn*, which actually meant *seeking a mythical golden seed that no one has ever found* but was reputed in the stories to be somehow connected with the lordship of Alinor.

We had not yet performed the hunt, but yet, in the centre of the maze Mr. Dart had found a dust-covered box containing a live unicorn foal, and subsequently declared himself a wild mage coming into his power, and if that wasn't some flavour of magic or miracle, I didn't know what was.

Well, returning from the dead, obviously. Beyond that.

The near door opened quietly and the not-butler came in. He wore the periwig and clothes from earlier. They were a simpler variant of the style I was (still!) wearing, dark and sober but, as I could see now that I was not quite so distracted, of very fine quality of cloth and construction. The greenstone brooch gleamed on his breast.

I considered his features: the heavy black brows, the deep-set, dark, fierce eyes. His height was not shared by his kin but there could be no doubt of his relation.

So. For some reason, Master Boring was pretending to be an invalid but instead secretly acting as a butler, but only for me.

No one gave any hint that they had noticed his entrance. I pushed around my sausages, which were straight bangers instead of this morning's coiled links. I could not rationally believe there were secret meanings in *that*, though I had enough skill at the game that I could make up all sorts of punning riddles.

(Explosive revelations following on this morning's secrets leading on to yet more secrets, for instance.)

At the far end of the table, Ned Garsom stirred restlessly. On my either side, Anna Garsom sat rigidly, staring at her plate, and Mr. Veitch was jiggling his knee almost imperceptibly.

Madam Veitch, one over from Hal, was smiling entirely

unconcerned. But she was euphoric with wireweed, and I knew that while her reason was probably unimpaired—might even be improved—by the drug, her emotions were entirely compromised. There was no way one could trust her expressions to reflect her actions or thoughts.

I was so grateful to know that my emotions were now my own. And so grieved for the many who were burying their sorrows and despair in the drug or in drink. We could sit here in this rich man's house, dining off silver and porcelain, secure from the storm except for the dangers we brought with us. Too many others had nothing but the empty promises of criminals.

A soft whisper sounded in my ear, like a zephyr; it did not stir the air or the two candles on the table. It carried with it the birdsong of the Wood of Spiritual Refreshment, and the memory of Ariadne nev Lingarel telling me that no one knew, in this life, exactly whom we had touched.

I looked up at the strange quality of the silence to see that everyone was staring at me, including the servants and, over by the door behind Ned Garsom, the eccentric Master Boring himself.

Hal was seated directly across from me. His eyes were troubled, but he made the effort to smile at me. "You have had an intimation," he stated rather than asked.

I wondered what they saw in my face that they all looked at me with such burning embarrassment.

I myself felt no embarrassment, just an exhilaration that was far better than any euphoria the wireweed or mortal peril had ever granted me. "I was minded," I said, in a voice that was unaccountably husky, "that we none of us know what grace we might offer another, perhaps entirely unexpectedly."

If words could be a key, thus were mine, for half the table started speaking at once in an incomprehensible babble.

Mr. Dart said, "Be quiet," and everyone stopped.

He looked down the table at me. "I take it, Lord St-Noire, that you have solved the mystery?"

I blinked at him, nonplussed. He smiled.

Follow my lead, he had entreated earlier. But he must know I hadn't *solved the mystery*, surely? I would have indicated as much if I had!

Everyone was staring at me, including Master Boring, with various expressions of dreadful interest. I cleared my throat and temporized. "It does seem as if we need to clear the air before we could in any good conscience seek out a treasure guarded by a unicorn."

Behind Hope and Hal and Madam Veitch, Master Boring nodded. He had a strange smile on his face. I hoped I didn't look as nervous as I abruptly felt.

Mr. Dart said, "And so? Do *uncover* for us your reasoning."

Why was he putting this all on me? Master Boring was worryingly gleeful. *Eccentric* was only the beginning of it, I thought truculently.

I decided to treat this like a spontaneous oral exam on a difficult sight-read poem in Classical Shaian. What were the steps there?

Restate the problem, break it down into its components, then deal with those individually before a final concluding statement drawing all the elements together.

Perfectly straightforward, really.

I could wish I'd spent the morning investigating Henry Coates' effects rather than transcribing the *Etiquette Questions Answered* columns of the past year, but never mind that. Presumably Mr. Dart and Hal, who had, would have told me of anything that pointed explicitly to the murderer. And it had to be said that my presence in the parlour all morning meant that I'd had more interactions with the various parties under suspicion.

I cleared my throat again. "At some point between midnight and dawn," I began, "Henry Coates was murdered by being stabbed several times in the back with a narrow, sharp implement not dissimilar to this cheese knife."

I held up the knife in question so they could all see it. Anna shuddered visibly. Mr. Veitch's jiggling leg stopped, and he groped for a handkerchief in his pocket. Ned Garsom uttered a faint squeak. Madam Veitch smiled encouragingly.

Hal and Hope both seemed to be wondering where I was going with this. To be fair, so was I.

Mr. Dart nodded thoughtfully. *Follow my lead*, he'd said, and then done what? So far he'd done little but announce the murder, find the victim, and declare uncomfortable truths about his magic.

Well, I could do the uncomfortable truths.

"Mr. Dart found the body in Coates' own room approximately midmorning."

That occasioned a reaction. "What!" cried Ned Garsom. "He didn't tell anyone!"

I raised my eyebrows at him, pretending not to see how Master Boring had lifted his own handkerchief to his mouth to cover his laughter. "He told me," I replied. "We've known each other since childhood, and he knew I'd had neither opportunity or motive to kill the man. I'd never so much as heard his name before I met him yesterday."

I shouldn't have said that about *opportunity*, as it implied I knew the time of the murder much more precisely than was in fact the case. And I didn't exactly want to announce the Hunter in Green's presence in my room all night as an alibi.

(And—I'd been asleep. For all I knew Roald had had his bath and gone gallivanting around the house for an hour before crawling in next to me.)

The problem was—I smiled, or tried to, around the table, and decided to sail on right past my slip. "Anyone might have had the opportunity to kill Henry Coates, as our rooms are all along a hall, we know from the witness of the housekeeper that he had misplaced his key and so did not lock his chamber door, and we were all in our beds at the time of the murder. The wounds are of no assistance, for they could have been inflicted by anyone; with a sharp enough tool strength is unnecessary, and there was no sign of a fight."

Seeing as he'd been stabbed in the back.

"Thus, since *opportunity* affords us little means to narrow the suspects, we must consider motive."

I paused there, but no one tried to interrupt or interject anything, nor even to question why I was the one holding court. So much for the reactionary counter-revolution that Ned Garsom thought needed: my title as the Viscount St-Noire was the only reason anyone was listening to me.

Well, Hal and Mr. Dart might have done so on my own showing.

I hoped Hal did not think I truly believed him capable of murder.

"To begin with myself: I had no acquaintance with Mr. Coates and cannot say he gave me any great insult in the short extent of our acquaintance. Our only private conversation was held in the hall outside my chamber door, just before midnight. He knocked, as he'd heard me, er, laugh from something I'd read in the *New Salon*. We spoke for a few minutes only, mostly on the subject of Mr. Garsom's, ah, speech, at supper last night."

I wished for something to wet my throat but we had strangely been provided with nothing, not even water. I settled for placing my hands on the table. I nodded to my left.

"Thus Henry Coates was alive and apparently well at just before midnight."

Hope was visibly relieved, presumably because I hadn't mentioned her presence in my bedroom as confirmation of this point. Ned Garsom was even twitchier than earlier. Anna remained stiff and taut and grim-faced.

"And so we come to motives. Mr. Leaveringham, like myself, was unacquainted with Henry Coates before his meeting here, although unlike myself he'd had a conversation about the man with Mr. Dart, who knew of Mr. Coates from Stoneybridge."

There was a murmur of surprise at this, though I noted that no one looked at the motionless and faintly smiling Mr. Dart for very long. The air was not so crystalline and heavy as it had been in the other room, but the silver sparks in the two fire-places were mute witness to his barely-known magical power.

Uncomfortable truths, I reminded myself. "Mr. Coates had threatened Mr. Dart with blackmail, you see. However, as the 'shameful secret' is neither a secret nor a shame—at least not in Fiellan—Mr. Dart was not embroiled in Mr. Coates' criminal schemes of extortion."

Mr. Veitch jerked uncomfortably and his hid mouth with his handkerchief. I ignored him and went on. "While Mr. Dart was rightly disgusted and angered by the attempt at extortion, it was nothing recent and hardly grounds for murder."

Ned Garsom looked very much like he wanted to ask what the so-called secret was, but I went on before anyone could speak. The dim suspicions were starting to resolve themselves even as I spoke, though the idea was so absurd I wasn't sure how it could possibly be true. This was hardly a song by Fitzroy Angursell!

I regarded Hope, who was rather sick-looking but met my eyes bravely and gave a tremulous nod. My heart went out to her, but I kept my voice as cool and dispassionate as possible.

"We come now to Miss Stornaway."

Hal put his hand on her arm and glared at me. I nodded at him and chose my words with care.

"Miss Stornaway attended Morrowlea in a cohort with myself, Mr. Leaveringham, and Miss Garsom. She and I have much in common, more so than we suspected before the conversations we have had here."

Mr. Dart shifted slightly, pushing his seat from the table so he could look at us more fully. He made no pretence about this and I was amazed at his brazenness. I could wish I was so forthright.

Once again, all I could do was try.

"Miss Stornaway and I both have complex family situations that were made yet more complex this autumn by quite unexpected inheritances that, moreover, had—*have*—remarkable conditions attached to them. Mine is detailed in this week's *New Salon*. Miss Stornaway's was noted earlier in the autumn, though I believe her name was not at that point given."

I could see Hal's mind working, and when his suspicion latched onto the correct idea, for his eyes widened with astonishment and (dare I say it) hope. He turned smiling to her, though his expression fell when she turned her face away, biting her lip against welling tears.

"Mr. Coates found out certain a key point regarding Miss Stornaway's inheritance, and endeavoured to extort an agreement with her that would prevent her from marrying as she wished, and, indeed, I believe also interfere with the full inheritance."

"The *cad*," Hal muttered, not very quietly.

"Quite," I agreed, suppressing a smile.

I turned next to Anna. She refused to meet my, or anyone's, gaze.

"Miss Garsom was by her own admission unwillingly wed to Mr. Coates. While it would usually be a fairly simple, if unpleasant, matter to reject an unwelcome suitor, in this case it was made most difficult—perhaps seemingly impossible—by certain information of which Mr. Coates was in possession and held over her."

I didn't know all of what that information was, but I could guess, from that ugly, illuminating conversation the siblings had had outside Henry Coates' door this morning. Anna appeared stiffly mortified, but said nothing.

"We have seen," I said with as much delicacy as I could muster, "that extortion and blackmail were not unknown to

Mr. Coates. A sufficient motive for murder? Perhaps. There are certainly less understandable accounts in the broadsheets. Miss Garsom has admitted to stabbing the corpse through the eye in a fit of pique when she found it in the parlour."

"About that," began Mr. Veitch.

"We will come to it in good time," I told him with more assurance than I felt.

He subsided with a mutter into his handkerchief. I really needed to replace mine.

"We come now to Mr. Garsom." I looked down the table to where he sat twitching in anxiety. It seemed unfathomable that he was only a year or so younger than Hal and Mr. Dart and myself.

"Henry was my *friend*," Ned Garsom exclaimed when our silent regard proved too much for him. "I don't—I couldn't— you can't *think*—"

His words were met with turned heads and disbelieving expressions. I let the jeering silence unwind for a few moments before going on.

"Mr. Garsom had, as we have heard, a close relationship with the deceased. They spent a great deal of time together—at the races. at the gambling dens, at the drinking holes, and at the houses of, ah, other pleasures."

For all that half those activities were illegal in Chare, I had no doubt Garsom had spent more time at them than his books. When I'd visited Mr. Dart I had been astounded how many places of iniquity there were in and around Stoney-bridge. I supposed it was a densely populated region, and there were all those universities. We'd been generally more wholesome in our activities at Morrowlea, if you could dismiss the manipulations of the budding criminal mastermind and the double spy.

"The Garsom siblings attended two of the most prestigious, and concomitantly most expensive, universities in Northwest Oriole. They were not, to my knowledge, the Charese Scholars to either. Certainly Miss Garsom was not, as Miss Stornaway *was*."

I glanced at Hope to see if she had caught my unsaid corollary to this. She met my gaze with a frown, obviously wondering what I meant. I urged her silently to think. If I had the scholarship seat from Rondé, as I had told her, that meant that Hal had to have paid his fee ...

Her eyes opened wide. I couldn't resist a nod. She fought a smile entirely unseemly for the present discussion. Discourse, really. I was after all the only one speaking.

"Mr. Coates was not, I fancy, an inexpensive friend. He was, however, a *useful* one. Full of introductions to the secret clubs, and, as Mr. Garsom's experience increased and he not unnaturally found himself with increasingly expensive tastes, introductions also to those who could assist with the finances. It does not take long, when you play at certain games, to get in deep, does it, Mr. Garsom?"

Ned Garsom was flushed a dull red, and he refused to lift his eyes from his plate. I let the silence sit there, accusing in its very prolongation. We had all heard Mr. Veitch's castigation, and Garsom's own comments and complaints and half-drunken boasts.

"I suspect that Mr. Garsom did not realize quite how deep he was until Mr. Coates insisted on an invitation for the Winterturn holiday to be spent at Mr. Garsom's uncle's country house. We know that Mr. Coates was blackmailing two members of the household, and setting up a scheme of extortion with a third; it is no surprise that what had been concealed warnings would now become open threats. It is not inconceivable that a young man of hot temper might decide to rid himself permanently of the problem."

"Henry Coates was stabbed in the back," Mr. Dart said in a tone scathing in its very lack of judgement.

"Indeed," I said. "Several times."

Mr. Veitch said, "This is all very well, but—damn it all, man, who did it?"

I shifted in my seat to look at him. "We haven't yet come to you and your wife's motives, Mr. Veitch."

"The damnable man was blackmailing us, we already said so," he cried impatiently and intemperately. "We had as much motive and opportunity—and as little—as everyone else. Tell me, you so-clever young lord, *who did it?*"

"Ah," I said, and swept my gaze around the room for any assistance. I was *fairly* sure I knew who did it, but I truly had no proof whatsoever. Just the sense that while any of the four principally being blackmailed had motive and opportunity alike, the one who surely *cared* the most about how his household and family were being sullied was also the only one who I was absolutely certain *could* remove the dagger from the wall.

Dared I state outright, with him looking with that hooded, fierce, gaze at me, that it was Master Boring himself?

I hesitated. Everyone leaned forward eagerly, but for Mr. Dart, who settled back in his chair in an excessively obvious pose of relaxation and calm. I looked around the room, gathering their attention, and looked at the master of the house, our host and the murderer, whom no one else seemed able to see.

Mr. Dart spoke into the silence in a clear, ringing voice: "Why, isn't it obvious? The butler did it, of course."

CHAPTER TWENTY-SIX

If I were surprised, that was nothing to the expression on Master Boring's face.

As I watched, his expression moved from shock to confusion to dawning realization to amusement. I was glad he found it so; I didn't.

Neither did anyone else at the table. Anna, Ned, and Mr. Veitch were frowning at each other. Ned actually said, "You didn't do it, Anna?" out loud.

"Of course not!" Anna replied with an indignation the stronger, I suspected, for her relief.

(Was I wrong? Had there been all those stab wounds as a kind of initiation for the heirs? — That was outlandish, but the requirements of my and Hope's inheritances were equally so. But our titles were of old, pre-Imperial families who had worked their way to Imperial positions.

This house, this family, the Borings of Hillend Towers, were wealthy and eccentric and not entirely morally sane. They no longer guarded a sacred grove where a unicorn might be found; they had a house locked against all without and congested with belongings within, where the unicorn was in a dusty, forgotten, forgettable box, able to be found only by one who heard the inanimate.

Surely Mr. Dart knew that it had to have been the master —he'd been the only one with access to the *implement*.)

"Now look here," Mr. Veitch said crossly. "What do you mean by this? There isn't a butler here! I had to fetch my own wine from the cellar."

Mr. Dart caught my eye, so I rallied myself and went once more into the breach. "I didn't," I said as neutrally as possible.

"What possible cause could the butler have?" Ned Garsom said, frowning as if this made no sense to him whatsoever. "What harm did Henry do to *him*?"

Anna scoffed. "There *isn't* a butler, Ned. He's dead. Remember, Uncle told us that when we saw him, that we would have to manage our … own … behaviour …"

She trailed off there, cheeks flushing, and I could not blame her for being unable to finish that sentence.

"Uncle also told me that I shouldn't have brought Henry with me, as he wasn't invited and wasn't welcome," her brother said grudgingly. "He wasn't the *right sort*, he said."

"You can't think that he was? Really, Ned! Not to speak ill of the dead—"

"It's a bit late for that," Mr. Veitch muttered, unrepentant.

"He blackmailed me into matrimony!"

"Well …" Ned Garsom gave her a foolish, sheepish grin. "He *was* fun, in town. I don't think the country agreed with him, what."

What, indeed.

That seemed about all the eulogy that Henry Coates was going to receive. Ned leaned forward, heedless of the silent, appalled Jullanar Maebh—I wanted to assure her that things weren't *always* like this around us, except that I truly couldn't in any good conscience—and said loudly, "So, what about this butler, then? Do you think that Uncle was bamming us the whole time?"

He'd been bamming *me*, that was for certain. He'd never *said* he was the butler, but he did act every inch the part.

Anna probably got her flair for dramatics from his side of the family.

"The servants must have all been in on it," Anna said, with growing enthusiasm. "Look at how odd they've been behaving! I thought it was just that Uncle was eccentric and didn't have a wife to manage his staff."

Madam Veitch, who had been ruminating silently this whole time, stirred at this. "And do you want to take that position, dear?"

It was such a *normal* question that I confess I felt my jaw drop slightly at it. Anna also appeared flustered. "I do wish to marry, ma'am, but if my Uncle needs a housekeeper ..."

"So no, then," Madam Veitch said summarily. "Now that your suitor is dead you are no doubt hoping for a Season in Highbury?"

"Orio City is the centre of fashion, ma'am, and there will be a new court formed when the prince weds this Winterturn."

"True, true," said Madam Veitch.

I spared a glance over Hope and Hal's inattentive heads — they were holding hands, if I didn't mistake their posture, under the table, and otherwise staring with secret smiles at the bread and cheese still untouched in the middle of the table — to Master Boring. He favoured me with a reiteration of last night's impish smile. It was even more deeply uncomfortable now that I knew he had murdered someone since then.

I wondered if I dared, and decided that yes, yes I did. "You may wish to reconsider Orio City, Anna," I said, "as the prince's new wife is Lark."

That startled Hope out of her pleasant daydreams (I presumed), for she looked up at me in horrified dismay. "Oh, no, Jemis!"

"No wonder she threw you over," was Anna's pronouncement. "You didn't have the title yet, and anyway a prince is better than a viscount any day."

"Thank you, Miss Garsom," I replied dryly.

Master Boring tugged on an embroidered bell pull hanging between the masks on the wall beside him. After a moment the door opened and Walter and Hettie came in. I noticed that Walter glanced quickly at the master before focusing on the table, but Hettie gave no indication of knowing he was there.

"Hettie, dear," Madam Veitch said as they began to clear away the plates of uneaten sausages, rutabaga cakes, and cabbage, "is the butler available?"

Walter stilled momentarily, then resumed his work. Hettie bobbed a curtsey and looked confused. "There's no butler now, ma'am," she said. "He's gone."

"When did he go?"

Hettie looked at Walter for assistance. He turned so he could glance sidelong at Master Boring, who made a flicking gesture with his hand, and then focused squarely on Madam Veitch. "I'm sure I can't say, ma'am."

It was an impressive non-answer, which only worked because Madam Veitch was still emotionally compromised from the wireweed and the other interested parties were deeply uninterested in the activities of servants. Even Anna, who should know better, merely shrugged and turned flirtatiously to me.

"How clever you are, my lord," she said, with a sultry look in her eye.

"Er, your husband was murdered this morning."

She waved her hand with the loose, airy gestures I remembered from Morrowlea. "Eh, you have heard how little I liked him. Now I am free—my whole *family* is free—from his clutches. My uncle is a wealthy man, as you can see from his house, and—"

It was at this that Jullanar Maebh finally erupted. She

threw her napkin down onto the table with as much force as the linen would allow.

"How *can* you!" she cried, her brogue strengthening with every word. "You are the greatest passel of self-centred, self-interested, pusillanimous wretches it has ever been my fortune to spend a meal with! A man was murdered in this house this morning, and all you could do was presume your own relations' guilt. Ha' ye no *heart*?"

Jullanar Maebh was magnificent in a temper, I thought in admiration. Her copper hair shone in the light coming through the windows, and her righteous anger had brought colour to her pale features. Her grey eyes flashed.

I had an inconsequential thought that the Honourable Rag had bit off more than he could chew in disappointing her.

I did have to wonder what he was doing upstairs all this time. Surely Henry Coates was not that interesting?

Well, his blackmail material might be. And the Honourable Rag had stated that he—or rather the Hunter in Green—was here for a rendezvous, if not with the late extortionist.

—With the master, perhaps?

And it felt as if the world turned a quarter-degree, and clunked solidly into place.

Henry Coates, according to everybody, was a dab hand at blackmail and extortion, and particularly interested—so said the Veitches, and there seemed no reason now to disbelieve them—in Master Boring of Hillend Towers. And why would he be *particularly interested*?

For any of the multitude of fortunes and miscellaneous objects stored here, perhaps. Or because of its location, privately set into the woods not far at all from the pass over the mountains from the Coombe and Ragnor Bella, where far too many things of interest had happened this year.

The mysterious letters—the blackmailing ones, presumably —to Madam Veitch, Hope, Mr. Veitch, Anna, *Master Boring*, and Ned Garsom. He had all the opportunity of the rest of us

—more, given the element of surprise—easy access to the weapon, and as for motive? Quite apart from whatever he might be personally shameful of, his entire family was compromised.

Had he not given me all the clues? *Love-in-a-mist* tea, which was named for a flower also known as *devil-in-a-bush*. A pair of common names indicating not just the possible natural consequences of a certain type of love, but also something of—perhaps *demonstrating*—the consequences of a lonely man, cocooned in a house filled to the brim with the past, facing a man hell-bent on destroying his few remaining family members.

"I agree with Miss Dart," Hope said, drawing my attention back to the table.

"Hope," said Anna, with a warning in her voice.

"No, Anna, I've listened to you too often. You were wrong about Jemis, you were wrong about Hal, and you're wrong about this. You may not have struck the fatal blow, but you *would* have. I am so disappointed in you."

Anna presented vast injury. "How can you say that? I have only your best interests in mine—can you really say that Hal is the best possible match for you?"

"Hal likes me for who I am, as I am! And I love him just the same!"

"You have to think about your future," Anna said.

"I," said Hope stoutly, "am the Ironwood heiress. My future is, I dare say, secure."

I could see the interest pique in the others. Mr. Dart and Jullanar Maebh were just being polite about it, it was clear, but as for Anna and Mr. Veitch and Ned Garsom—I could see their calculations beginning. "Now, Miss Stornaway," Ned Garsom began in a wheedling tone.

Hope gave him a cold stare I had never before seen from her. "Please don't embarrass yourself any further, Mr. Garsom. You have said quite enough already today."

He sat back in visible affront. I felt like applauding, but refrained in favour of the still-central question, which Hope asked before I could quite formulate it.

"There has been a murder, and it seems we have determined who did it," she said baldly. (So she had caught the elision performed by Mr. Dart's interjections, too.) "This begs the question of—what are we to do now?"

"We wait for the physician to come and give his account of the death," Hal said, "and then we speak to the constables when they come."

"But what do we say?" Anna asked.

Hal gave her a look of sublime dislike. "What accords with your conscience, Miss Garsom. There has been enough talk of blackmail and extortion in this house. Better for all to come to light."

Master Boring stood forward a step. I looked at him, and he nodded at me with a kind of respect in his bearing, a light in his eyes. He knew what Mr. Dart had just done, I thought; though neither of us knew why.

Bessie came in at that moment and said, ostensibly to the room but with her body angled towards Master Boring, "The physician is come."

Master Boring touched the curious greenstone brooch he wore at his breast. It must have been what generated the semblance of absence, for after a kind of ripple to the air everyone else could see him clearly.

"Uncle!" Anna cried, to the general confusion of everyone except myself.

"Bring him in," Master Boring said Bessie, ignoring all the questions that were frothing forth. He smiled around the table, with a grim humour that softened only when his gaze rested on Hope and Hal. "What a cluster of fools my sisters bore," he proclaimed.

"Uncle," Anna began, visibly rallying protestations.

He held up his hand. "No, no, there will be plenty of

opportunity to discuss your behaviour over the coming days. In the meantime—ah! There you are, Sir Frederick."

Sir Frederick was a portly, well-favoured man with obvious Shaian background in the mid-brown of his skin and the tight curls of his hair. He greeted Master Boring with a professional enthusiasm. "What's happened, then? You are looking well this afternoon, Master Dick! I hope you haven't been too active of late?"

"No, no, I have been behaving myself most carefully," he said, which was a total lie except that presumably he'd had Walter move the body rather than do it himself, as Henry Coates had been a large man and, while tall, Master Boring was nowhere near sufficiently muscled.

"Good, good." Sir Frederick looked around the room with a genial smile much warmer and less smarmy than Mr. Veitch's. "I see you have some guests—good heavens! Your grace, I didn't see you there."

And he bowed to Hal, who shifted position to greet him kindly in return, even as Hope mouthed *your grace?* This, perhaps unfortunately, permitted the physician a direct view to me, at which point we all learned that he'd been the one to declare me dead two nights before.

CHAPTER TWENTY-SEVEN

The death of Henry Coates was almost inconsequential to the two discoveries that I had returned to life by divine miracle and that Hal was actually the Duke Imperial of Fillering Pool. Opinions varied on which was the more remarkable.

It didn't take very long for the orientation of the room to shift from me to Hal. I soon found myself sitting in a widening pool of silence. At one point I looked up and caught Mr. Dart's eye. He smiled wryly at me and shrugged. There was too much noise elsewhere in the room to talk down the table.

Bessie eventually led the physician off to recover his equilibrium and examine the body of Henry Coates. Mr. Veitch and the Garsoms focused on making up to Hal in a frankly grotesque display. Only Hope, sitting next to him, said nothing.

Hal himself was visibly resigned. He straightened his shoulders and let his accent revert from the softened one he'd used at Morrowlea to the one natural to him. The very fact that he responded so easily was all the confirmation anyone needed, had they been inclined to doubt Sir Frederick.

Eventually Madam Veitch said, "Oh, Uncle Dick, may we still Hunt the Unicorn?"

The Veitches and the Garsom siblings turned with eager eyes to our host, who had stayed standing by the door watching over his toad-eating relatives with a jaundiced eye. He smiled at Madam Veitch. "Yes, do run along now, my nieces and nephews. Remember, one item each, and return in an hour! And if you find the golden seed, be sure you keep it close!"

"Thank you!" they each cried, and made haste to dash out of the room, quite as if they were thereby escaping the uncomfortable truths and all consequences.

I could have told them that neither truth nor consequences were so easily evaded, but they would find that out soon enough for themselves.

The room fell very quiet with the four of them gone. Jullanar Maebh was pale and wan, and deeply unhappy. Hope and Hal were visibly trying not to forget about the troubling events in favour of their own burgeoning relationship. And Mr. Dart and I were sitting there, having done nothing but lay out the terms of a mystery that brooked no good solution, and—I, at least—wondered.

Master Boring stepped forward and spoke to Hal and Hope. "You two, I see, have found the golden seed. It is planted: tend it well, and you will find it blossoms widely."

Hal gave him a smile that was both politely gratified and slightly ironic. As a result of the expedition he had sponsored to seek new lands and the plants that grew on them, the Duke of Fillering Pool's botanical interests were fairly well known.

"Thank you," he said, and stood. He inclined his head to Master Boring, then offered his hand to Hope. "Shall we? I think we have some private matters to discuss."

Hope's eyes lit and she smiled prettily. "Yes, let's."

Hal looked at me, one eyebrow quirked. "I'm sure we'll

hear more of what's toward later. We still have to find a means to get home."

Master Boring interjected his words smoothly. "Sir Frederick mentioned that he passed by a black falarode that was unable to pass through the path excavated by the groundsmen. I remember that carriage well from my time at court. Ah, the Marchioness was a firecracker in her young days! I suspect it will be not long before you can continue your journey. With *her* horses you can get well underway before dark."

"We shall see you soon, in that case," Hal said, bowing slightly, and tucking Hope's hand into his elbow he led her out of the room.

Once the door had shut behind him Master Boring sat down in Mr. Veitch's vacated spot at the head of the table, to my left. He regarded the three of us remaining, though Jullanar Maebh seemed disinclined to participating in any conversation.

"I wonder," Mr. Dart said politely, "just how much of this was planned."

Master Boring gave him a sly smirk. "You think it unwise of me?"

"There was a murder done this morning."

"Lord St-Noire's account was admirably clear in demonstrating how little direct evidence there is."

"The stab wounds?"

"The needle through the eye does require some explanation, I grant. The others ... that particular suit of armour, which so ostentatiously fell down the stairs last night, has quite remarkable protuberances at its joints. Ineffective in real combat, of course, perhaps even dangerous, but fearsome in appearance and potentially quite damaging if it, for instance, should happen to tumble down a set of stairs alongside you."

"A fine story," Jullanar Maebh scoffed.

"My dear Miss Dart," said Master Boring, "I commend

your righteousness. But tell me this: is the world a worse place for the death of a conniving extortionist and blackmailer?"

"Justice—" she began.

"I am the master here," he said. "My peers hereabouts will not be surprised to hear that the man I had engaged to replace my late butler proved a disappointment. They all know the difficulty I have faced in finding someone, you see, what with the remoteness of my dwelling and the oddities of my collection. If he found himself in a compromising situation with a known blackmailer, he might in a fit of rage kill the man and then, overcome with remorse, flee into a ferocious blizzard. He could easily have lost his way, and equally easily never be found, not in the mountains when the wind has swept all signs of any passage away."

"I see," she said, bitterly, and was silent.

I entirely agreed with her sentiments, but I also couldn't see what we could do. I did not want to enter into blackmail myself; nor did I have any proof of anything but my own suspicions.

Mr. Dart said, with mild curiosity, "How did you keep yourself from being seen?"

Master Boring lifted his hand to his greenstone brooch. "A gift from an old friend when we were at court together, who knew I sometimes wished for a few moments when no one was looking. I am not surprised that her grandson could see through its screen: the Marchioness would never have wanted to prevent herself from seeing my fun."

What an old reprobate, I thought, not entirely disapprovingly. I could not applaud his recourse to murder, but I did rather appreciate the performance.

"Now," he said, clapping his hands. "You are all much wiser than any of my relations, and know that one does not ever *hunt* a unicorn: that is not how they are found! And though you may not have found the golden seed, you still have won a gift."

"That is really not necessary," I protested. "Your hospitality—"

I did falter there, for it had been a very strange and troubling refuge indeed.

He smiled unrepentantly at me. "I know exactly what I'd like *you* to have, my lord. You wear those clothes as if they were tailored especially for you."

～

The return journey home was amazingly uneventful. After the physician proclaimed the injuries commensurable with those that might occur from falling down a set of stairs under a suit of ornamental armour such as that rather obviously recently dented and damaged one at the top of the west staircase, we were all free of any reason to stay.

I went upstairs with Mr. Dart to collect our few belongings. The Honourable Rag, in his full costume as the Hunter in Green, was lounging in my room with Henry Coates' suspicious belongings strewn about him, Ballory the unicorn watching alertly.

"You've been a while," he commented languidly. "Solve the murder successfully?"

Mr. Dart went over to fondle the unicorn foal's ears, to adoring response. I sat down on the wingback chair with a sigh. "Master Boring committed the deed, but will not admit to it save obliquely, and we have no proof. The physician has given a coroner's verdict of accidental death."

"A nice accident!"

"Quite. In happier news, Mr. Fancy seems to have received our note, or perhaps had another means of following us, and is waiting at the end of the drive for the snow to be cleared or us to come to him."

The Honourable Rag tilted his head at me, bright eyes sparkling behind the mask. "Is that an invitation?"

"Did you need one?"

He laughed, no doubt recalling how he had held up the coach on our outward journey to request conveyance. "My business is done here, I reckon. The finding of the unicorn explains the appearance of the storm, and—well! Perhaps I will yet have cause to go deeper into my other business with you two, but for now I must report in and wait to hear what response I receive. I have a hunting party or two to join over Winterturn, you know."

Mr. Dart said, "And what will you be hunting at this season?"

The Honourable Rag returned with a sly jab about poaching, and they were off bickering as we had so often as youths, before we had fallen out and gone to our varying universities. How strange that the three of us were drawn back to Ragnor Bella, only to find that the wider world insisted on coming with us.

"—And what of it?" cried the Honourable Rag, in mock indignation. "Our local bookseller's apprentice recommended the book, I'll have you know, not three months ago. Megalip— or was it Merganser? —a great expert on hounds, at any rate."

"If you want to go plunging about in freezing-cold rivers, go ahead," Mr. Dart retorted. "I shall be otherwise occupied. Right, Jemis?"

I had no idea what they were talking about, apart from a vague memory of the book in question. "I think it was Melanger, actually. *Art of the Greyhound*, wasn't it?"

"That was what I asked for, but you gave me a tract on otter- and boarhounds. Gave me a right turn, I tell you, I was sure you were in on the secret *then* already."

"Do I even want to know?" I got up and began to tidy together the transcriptions I'd made of the *Etiquette Questions Answered* columns.

"Depends what you find when you get through your decryptions. Unless you've already finished?"

"You give me too much credit, sir! I have had some other thoughts on my mind these past few hours." He laughed riotously. I stopped and stared at him. "Please say you didn't let me spend all morning copying them when they're already *yours*."

He produced a cloth sack from somewhere about his person and began to place Henry Coates' items in it. "Peace, Jemis. Far from it! I am excessively interested in what you find, as a matter of fact. *Our* secret messages are always in the crossword."

~

Mrs. Etaris had told me once that we never learned the whole story, whether of an adventure or a mystery or real life. We came in and out of other people's stories, she'd said, while living our own. And just as no one else knew the precise trajectory of ours, we never knew theirs.

One thing I have learned, she'd said, *is that everyone has a secret life. Some are just much more obvious about it than others*.

She herself, for instance, was a former revolutionary from Galderon.

Hettie showed up with my clothes in a cleaned and neatly ironed stack. When she had gone Mr. Dart departed for his room, the unicorn and the Honourable Rag in tow, with the comment that they would meet me downstairs in the parlour shortly. I changed, relaxing in the familiar garments, though I found I missed the swing of the long coat against my thighs and the fall of lace against the backs of my hands.

It was entirely trivial but it could be fun to shock the aristocracy gathered for Hal's Winterturn Ball by wearing the teal suit. Though—perhaps I should modernize it a little. If I were to combine it with a new hat—

A brisk knock on the door interrupted my thoughts. I

answered it to find Hal and Hope standing there. Their hands were clasped and their faces bright with joy.

"I take it congratulations are in order?" I said, deciding not to enquire too pointedly about the vexed matter of Hope's true name.

"Oh, Jemis," Hope said fondly. "You knew the whole time!"

"You had asked me to keep quiet," I said, sharing a knowing smile between the two of them. "I am truly very happy for you both. And to think, Hal, you didn't believe your Aunt Honoria when she said the Ironwood heiress was a delightful girl and an excellent match for you!"

"Oh, did she really?" Hope said, blush visible in her dark cheeks. "She was such a great comfort to me. I hope your mother likes me half as well."

"How could she not?" Hal said, with a melting glance at her. "She will adore you."

I imagined they could continue this for hours, so after a few moments of them more or less cooing at each other like wood doves I cleared my throat. "Oh, yes," Hal said, shaking himself. "Walter said that our carriage had arrived?"

"Somehow, yes. I don't think it can clear the snow in the drive, but none of us have much in the way of luggage, so once you are prepared to go we can leave."

When Hal hesitated, Hope said, "Jemis, may I travel with you? I find I don't want to stay here any longer, and ..."

And this entirely solved the problem of being seen to have adequately chaperoned Jullanar Maebh on our way home from Orio City. I smiled. "Of course. There's plenty of room in the falarode, and if you don't like to go to Fillering Pool now —"

"It would be somewhat inappropriate," Hal admitted with a pained grimace. "Without anyone to be a chaperone, there would be talk."

"By all means, let us avoid that," I agreed. "Hope, you and

Miss Dart would be company for each other, and I'm sure there will be no difficulty about hosting you once we are home."

She professed her gratitude and went to collect her belongings together. This delayed us by about half an hour after everyone else was ready, but that simply gave us the time to inform Jullanar Maebh of the plan. She was not entirely happy with it—or with anything at the moment, I suspected—but did understand precisely why Hope did not wish to stay a moment longer in the house, and agreed that if she couldn't have one of her own friends with her in Ragnor Bella, at least Hope was pleasant-mannered, interesting to talk to, and didn't appear to have committed any major crimes of late.

The delay also gave the household staff sufficient time to pack a sled with two trunks of costumes for me, an entire crate of tea, and another of quinces, which were (Master Boring said, as we made awkward farewells) something of a specialty of the region. He pressed on Hal a crate of the Inarkios wine, saying that none of his family had anything like the palate to appreciate it.

I appreciated that he did not offer Jullanar Maebh anything beyond a hearty apology for any discomfort she might have felt.

"I am grateful for the refuge from the storm," she said, with a short, precise curtsey and a stony face.

We did not see the Veitches or the Garsom siblings, nor did the Honourable Rag make his appearance at the door or in the courtyard. I told Master Boring to watch out for Madam Veitch's tonic, which I feared—I did not say I *knew*—contained wireweed, and then at last we were on our way. Master Boring's fierce eyes bore into me for a moment before he grunted and said that it was a great improvement over her previous behaviour, but he would take my concern under advisement.

"Good," I said, and then, with what I hoped was meaningful emphasis, added: "Finoury's Inn burned to the ground yesterday. I'm sure they could use some supplies and assistance. I don't think they had a good experience with Ned Garsom or Henry Coates when they came through the other day, and it left an ill respect for this house."

Master Boring smirked. "I won't forget them, I promise you."

And with that I supposed I had to be content.

Walter, with the assistance of young Wally (who was indeed his son), pulled the sled to the end of the drive. We passed several of the grooms and gardeners along the way, digging out the freakish snowfall. The air was crisp rather than cold, the sky blue, and the sun brilliant on the fresh snow.

It was such a relief to be leaving the close confines of the house, and to see waiting for us, as we emerged out of the woods at the gate, the six Ghiandor horses and the great black falarode.

"Goodness me," Hope said faintly.

Mr. Fancy the coachman was enveloped in his great many-caped black coat. He touched the whip to his hat when we approached. "Took a wrong turn or two, did you? Up you get, now! There's room enough for you all."

And despite the quantity of books and other items I'd acquired on behalf of half of Ragnor Bella and the village St-Noire in Orio City, and the crate and the trunks and Hope's own luggage, room enough there was. Mr. Fancy had even procured soft wool blankets from somewhere to keep our feet warm.

I settled in next to the window and pulled out one of my new books from Orio City, a collection of humorous verses in Classical Shaian. There would be time enough and to spare to start deciphering the *New Salon* riddles.

At the corner of the estate wall the Hunter in Green stepped out of the woods and bade the coach halt. Mr. Fancy reined in the horses and gave him a glower. "You again."

"Mr. Greenwing offered me a lift when I needed one," he replied easily.

I opened the door and beckoned him in. "It's a little full but we've room enough even for your long legs and large personality," I said, and he laughed and joined us.

The introductions were vague. Jullanar Maebh and Hope both appeared entirely mystified at our lack of surprise at his appearance, but he set himself to jollying Jullanar Maebh out of her glooms, as he put it, and as a consequence the journey passed much more pleasantly than most of our thoughts would otherwise have allowed.

We passed Finoury's Inn without stopping and made it to a pleasant, clean, and otherwise unremarkable small-town inn an hour or so after nightfall. I didn't look too closely into how the Ghiandor horses were so sure-footed on the soft road; the snow had either melted or turned to rain a couple of miles past the crossroads at Finoury's Inn. I didn't examine their speed, either, though I was fairly certain it did not usually take half a day to reach Grightmire's Cross from that part of Lind.

Hal met his own coach and servants there, for his family had received his letter and sent outriders to meet him. Those farewells were more heartfelt, but not too harsh as we had all promised to come to Fillering Pool for the Winterturn Fair and coming-of-age ball. Only Hope was tearful, but that was understandable.

We cheered her up by letting her discourse on Hal's many virtues for some time, though I fancy we were also all glad when she spied an intriguing rock formation in middle Ettadale and started talking about geology instead. Indeed, Jullanar Maebh responded with a comment about hydrology, and we spent most of the rest of the way learning more about natural philosophy than I, at least, had ever desired to.

We collected Cartwright at his mother's, along with the kittens I had entirely forgotten about. Hope immediately claimed one, and the grey one appeared to have adopted me, so delighted was it to see me again. The Honourable Rag stated gravely that he had given care of his powderpuff kitten to a friend of his, and would be reclaiming her soon.

Even Jullanar Maebh had started to smile by this point.

We turned back onto the old Imperial Highway at Yrchester. Passing the still-smouldering ruin of Finoury's Inn had reminded me of my own responsibilities, and I made sure to stop at the bank and arrange for payment of the various wagon-loads of goods I had ordered for St-Noire. With that done, we set off at a distance-eating pace faster than a trot, and I felt like I was coming home at last.

I confess I was also very much looking forward to seeing everyone's faces when we turned up with two extra people and a unicorn foal in tow. Winterturn was going to be something special this year.

ALSO BY VICTORIA GODDARD

The Hands of the Emperor

The Bride of the Blue Wind

Till Human Voices Wake Us

ABOUT THE AUTHOR

Victoria Goddard is a fantasy novelist, gardener, and occasional academic. She has a PhD in Medieval Studies from the University of Toronto, has walked down the length of England (and across that of Spain), and is currently a writer, cheesemonger, and gardener in the Canadian Maritimes. Along with cheese, books, and flowers she also loves dogs, tea, and languages.

Read more at Victoria Goddard's site.

Made in the USA
Las Vegas, NV
28 February 2024